REMOTE

BRIAN SHEA
STACY LYNN MILLER

SEVERN RIVER PUBLISHING

REMOTE

Severn River Publishing
www.SevernRiverBooks.com

This is a work of fiction. Names, characters, businesses, places, events and incidents are either the products of the author's imagination or used in a fictitious manner. Any resemblance to actual persons, living or dead, or actual events is purely coincidental.

ISBN: 978-1-64875-430-2 (Paperback)

ALSO BY THE AUTHORS

Lexi Mills Thrillers
Fuze
Proximity
Impact
Pressure
Remote
Flashpoint

BY BRIAN SHEA
Boston Crime Thrillers
The Nick Lawrence Series
Sterling Gray FBI Profiler Series

Never miss a new release!
To find out more about the authors and their books, visit

severnriverbooks.com/series/lexi-mills

1

A stubborn sense of gloom hung over Darryl like the dark clouds overhead, threatening to unleash a blinding late-winter snowstorm as he drove deeper into the heavy pines of Tahoe National Forest. The last strings of sunlight had disappeared over the horizon several miles back, and Darryl relied on the bright headlights of his Tesla to guide him along the route the car's navigation system had laid out after plugging in the proper address for his meeting. His phone hadn't picked up a tower signal for twenty minutes, and if the car lost satellite reception, he feared he would never find his way back to the highway.

About two miles ago, before he narrowly missed running over a rabbit, Darryl questioned if the address to Benjamin Foreman's mountain cabin, as his assistant had described it in her email to him yesterday, was correct. Not even all-knowing Google had a satellite or street-level image of the property. He half expected the unusual invitation of a hush-hush, private meeting to be a ruse, a punishment of sorts for his boss's foot-dragging after pledging to muster support on the Senate Armed Services Committee for Foreman's latest high-tech weapons program. And if the address was correct, this far from civilization, Darryl expected the hunting cabin to be off-the-grid rustic, heated by a roaring fire with a dear head wearing a rack of antlers the size of King Kong mounted above the stone mantle.

But making the last turn listed in the navigation instructions proved him wrong. Dead wrong. "A mountain cabin, my ass," he said. It was no coincidence this place didn't show up on Google. A man of Foreman's wealth and connections could scrub all evidence of its existence from the public domain.

When the car straightened on the road and passed through an opening in the stone wall, a cavalcade of warm amber lights popped on in succession, illuminating the compound of a majestic mountain home fit for royalty. Darryl knew Foreman was rich, but this was off the charts. The multi-peaked alpine structure dressed in wood and stone accents was virtually a football field long and concave, forming a crescent moon shape along the ground. Four-car garages flanked both ends of the three-sectioned two-story house. Each window, smaller than expected for a home in such a scenic setting, glowed from the inside, telling of much more than a deer's head awaiting Darryl's visit.

A driveway of pavers lined with accent lights meandering between the lush landscaping and rocky central pond invited Darryl to the dramatic entrance at the center of the building. He parked there. Stepping out of the car, he smoothed his wool winter overcoat for vanity and tightened it to combat the rare frigid mountain temperature this late in the season.

A glint of motion high on the portico covering the steps leading to the sizable double doors caught his attention. A security camera was following his movement, and a scan of the building's lines and edges confirmed several more cameras were as well. They made him uneasy. Working in the Russell Senate Office Building and the Capitol for Senator Jackson over the last decade had numbed Darryl to video and audio surveillance at work, but he loathed the intrusion outside the Beltway, no matter the circumstance, and intentionally kept his lifestyle void of too much tech. If he wanted a documented account of his life twenty-four-seven, he would never leave his office and have Siri and Alexa respond to every curiosity.

"Welcome to Shangri-La, Mr. Yarborough," a disembodied female voice greeted him through a speaker built into the portico ceiling. "Other than your near miss with a rabbit, I take it the drive was uneventful."

What the hell? How did she know about Thumper? Suddenly, Darryl felt trapped in an Orwell novel under the careful watch of Big Brother, and it was unnerving. "Yes, I had no problem finding the place."

"Mr. Foreman is expecting you." The door lock clicked softly. "He'll be with you shortly. Please come in. His man, Harold, will be happy to take your coat and get you something to drink."

"Thank you." Darryl turned the knob and opened the right door, expecting the inside to match the alpine exterior. He was not disappointed. The massive scale of the two-story entry room was impressive, more so than the elite Washington mansions along the Potomac he frequented over the years as Senator Jackson's chief of staff. Darryl let a furtive grin grow on one corner of his lips. All the trust fund babies at Harvard who turned their noses up at this former scholarship kid from Bakersfield would have chewed off their right arm to be in the fabled home of Benjamin Foreman, the third wealthiest CEO in the country.

A short, trim man dressed crisply in a black tux stepped from behind the wooden log bar that took up more real estate than Darryl's kitchen. As Darryl unbuttoned and removed his coat, the man crossed the room, carrying a silver tray with a single cocktail glass in the center. "Good evening, Mr. Yarborough. A Manhattan with Canadian Whiskey, not Rye."

This was becoming a little scary. Harold had prepared his go-to drink to a *T*. If a little man popped out, offering a basket of his favorite brand of toothpaste and body wash, Darryl would hightail it out of Shangri-La. "Wow. Thank you, Harold."

"I'll also take your coat, sir."

After the exchange, the man retreated behind the bar, and Darryl explored the room, sipping his perfectly crafted cocktail. He wasn't far off with the deer head fantasy, finding two elk heads mounted above the fireplace, each angled in opposite directions, protecting their flanks. Leather couches and chairs and tables made from polished knotty pine adorned the rest of the room.

Dark brown and red fabric accents nicely complimented the Charles Russell original canvas paintings on the walls. One caught his eye. The muted aged oils depicted three Old West cowboys subduing a grizzly bear twice their size while on horseback, using only lassos for weapons. The horses strained against the animal's thrashing to escape its bindings, and the men were the picture of calm and determination under extreme stress. If one rope broke, any of them could have died.

"It's titled *Capturing the Grizzly Bear*," a distinctive man's voice said from over Darryl's shoulder. He had studied dozens of videos to prepare for today's meeting and didn't have to turn to know it was Benjamin Foreman, founder and CEO of Falcon Industries, the premier developer of high-tech military weapons. The man's intentionally slow cadence and confidence behind every word were recognizable and had butterflies swarming in Darryl's stomach.

"It's violent but oddly awe-inspiring." Darryl kept his gaze on the painting, trying to appear more cultured and collected than the little fanboy melting inside. He took another sip of his drink to calm his nerves.

"You have a good eye. The painting is my favorite piece for that very reason. It depicts the power of synergy, showing nothing is insurmountable when you have the right people with the right tools and enough fortitude."

Darryl finally turned. In his job as chief of staff to the second-highest-ranking senator in the Republican Party, he'd met presidents, prime ministers, movie stars, and musical performers of all genres. He even shook Bono's hand once. But they all paled compared to Benjamin Foreman. He was the Howard Hughes of their time—a rich, powerful, and creative mover and shaker who had become a recluse last year. Darryl sympathized with Foreman's solitary lifestyle and his closing ranks from a relentless media. Politics was a dirty business, and he often found himself on the receiving end of a rabid press attacking his boss for any of a thousand reasons. The hit pieces on the military-industrial complex last year were no better, driving Foreman behind these walls.

"It's a pleasure to meet you, Mr. Foreman." Darryl extended his hand, which Foreman shook. *Eat your hearts out, Buffy and Chaz*, he thought. This scholarship kid had made it to the top while his tormentors were still hustling to get their names in *Page Six* of the *Times*. "Senator Jackson sends his apologies. His presence was needed in Washington for several critical votes tonight, but he should be in the area tomorrow for the fundraising gala at his estate in Incline Village."

"It's criminal how Congress has abdicated its responsibilities through continuing resolutions. They should budget based on the present and future, not the past. Sometimes I think we should rid ourselves of all five hundred thirty-five and start from scratch." Foreman's matter-of-fact tone was disturbing, bordering on having put in considerable forethought and planning. If some drunk at the corner bar had said such a thing, his friends would have waved off the statement as merely blowing off steam. But Foreman had the means and the money to make such a cataclysmic event happen, making him dangerous and potentially a formidable enemy.

"If we did, I would be out of a job, but yes, our system of government needs a gradual overhaul." Darryl laced his reply with a positive tone, hoping to steer it in a less creepy direction.

Foreman harrumphed, cocking up one corner of his lips—a quirk they had in common but for entirely different emotions. "Gradually takes too much time, Mr. Yarborough. Time we don't have with the Russians, Chinese, and radical Islamists breathing down our necks."

"I can't disagree. Time is short, but there's still time for diplomacy." Darryl sensed the man's patience running thin, requiring a deft pivot. "Your home is impressive, Mr. Foreman. How long did it take to build?"

"Four years from groundbreaking to the champagne party."

Darryl issued a whistle of amazement. "Why so long?"

"Materials mostly." Foreman checked his watch. "We have some time before my team will be ready for a demonstration." He extended an arm to his side. "Care for a tour of the slicker features?"

What sane person wouldn't want to see the inner recesses of Benjamin Foreman's Shangri-La? Buffy and Chaz would give up their firstborn to be in Darryl's shoes. "I'm intrigued, yes."

Foreman winked and shifted his head slightly toward the room's center. "Computer, red alert. Shields up." At his command, metal plates slid into place with sharp, echoing thuds, covering each window and glass slider simultaneously. A similar sound came from the entry foyer.

Darryl followed the sounds, spinning his head like a swivel. If he guessed correctly, Foreman had sealed them inside. "That was intense." And the real-life Star Trek command was beyond cool.

"An Air Force A-10 Thunderbolt pilot sits in a titanium bathtub up to one and a half inches thick. It can withstand anything up to 57mm explosive rounds. I doubled it, creating a high-grade titanium shell for the main part of the house. In theory, it can withstand everything short of a bunker buster bomb."

"You're set for an invasion and a zombie attack."

"Computer, shields down." The titanium plates retracted, and Foreman glanced over his shoulder at Darryl after stepping toward a hallway past the bar. "Aren't you?" He gestured his head in his direction of travel. "Now for the really cool stuff."

Darryl swigged the last of his Manhattan and placed the crystal glass on the bar on his way by, issuing Harold a grateful nod. "The drink was perfect, Harold. Thank you."

The long corridor led past several rooms—a butler's pantry off the bar, an office, and a game room with a billiards table—and ended at an elevator door. The door swooshed open automatically when Foreman approached it, revealing a long car six feet wide, like the ones in hospitals used to transport gurneys between floors. There were two buttons, up and down, hinting this thing made only two stops, here and wherever the really cool stuff was.

Once settled inside, Foreman pressed the down button. Darryl expected a quick ride to the basement, but it continued much longer than expected. "How deep is this place?"

"About four stories down. The capsule is deep enough to withstand a nuclear blast."

"The capsule?"

"My control room. I based the blueprints on the Minuteman III launch capsule but scaled it to my needs. You can't be too careful. North Korea already has long-range missiles capable of reaching the California coast. It's not as sophisticated as NORAD, but it will do in a pinch."

The door slid open to a deep, underground seven-foot-tall concrete tunnel leading to an open blast door. The door dimensions were incredible. Over three feet thick of solid steel, it had six retractable five-inch round steel pins to lock the door in place. The thought of needing that much stopping power was mind-bending.

Once past the threshold, Foreman stepped aside, revealing a two-level communications center in low lighting equipped with every high-tech gadget imaginable. Seamless, integrated LED screens adorned an entire wall and showed several scenes from a test lab to a city intersection to remote rocky terrain to several feeds of security cameras of the interior and exterior of Shangri-La. Operators with headsets dressed in black utility uniforms occupied a half-dozen workstations along the lower level watching the screens, while one man in a suit sat behind a desk at the top level, surveilling the action below.

As he and Foreman stepped toward the room's center, Darryl marveled at the operation center, wondering what activities Foreman would need to track as they happened. "This is impressive. It's like the situation room at the White House."

"It's much better without the bureaucracy. My team manages the security of my mountain cabin from here and oversees every test of every weapon in development at Falcon Industries. They can communicate with every department and team in real time. I haven't needed to visit our Virginia headquarters in over a year. I see everything firsthand without layers of management to dilute my observation. This way, I make decisions based on accurate data."

"I'm curious. How far does your surveillance around your cabin reach?" Darryl asked.

"The cameras are close in, but the early warning radar system provides three-hundred-sixty-degree coverage two hundred miles out." When Darryl furrowed his brow, Foreman continued. "You're wondering how we knew about your near miss with the rabbit."

"It was a little disturbing."

"It is all part of tonight's demonstration." Foreman extended his arm, inviting Darryl toward the exit. "Shall we?"

Once they returned above ground, Foreman led Darryl to the dining room, where three men were seated around the polished dark oak table with seating for ten. The room was smaller than expected, considering the scale of the entry room, but the closer walls, floor-to-ceiling sheer green curtains, amber soffit accent lighting, and a stone wall with a floating fireplace created a warm, intimate atmosphere.

The men at the table stopped their conversation and stood when Foreman entered.

"Gentlemen," Foreman stepped toward the men gathering near the fireplace, "I'd like to introduce Darryl Yarborough, Senator Keith Jackson's chief of staff." He pivoted, and one by one, he introduced the men, and Darryl shook their hands. "Mr. Yarborough, I'd like you to meet Andrew Bohm, my legal counsel, Kyle Sands, project manager, and Robert Segura, chief engineer." Each was dressed impeccably and had the appearance of being in their thirties or forties, but Segura didn't carry himself with poise like the others. He appeared shy, making only brief eye contact.

The kitchen staff served a delicious three-course meal, and the conversation around the table centered on politics and the country's direction with the first female president at the helm. Opinions differed only slightly, but they all agreed the United States needed to return to its constitutional roots and project more decisive leadership on the international stage. Segura, however, had remained mostly silent, offering only brief comments, making his political leaning hard to discern.

While Darryl savored the last bite of the apple crumble, Foreman wiped the corners of his lips with a cloth napkin after receiving a message on his phone, and then he reached to the edge of the table's underbelly. A moment later, the framed picture above the fireplace rose mechanically to the ceiling, revealing a sixty-inch monitor. A video filled the screen.

It took several seconds and him seeing a rabbit dart across the road for Darryl to make out what he was watching. It was a recording of his car as it had traveled toward Shangri-La an hour earlier, but the feed wasn't from a fixed position. It paralleled Darryl's vehicle and kept pace. The drone he was there to scout for his boss must have shadowed Darryl along the route without him seeing it.

"Mr. Yarborough, you asked how we knew about your run-in with our local wildlife," Foreman said. "This is how."

A fly circled Darryl's head, and he swatted at it when a buzzing noise near his right ear got loud. Foreman, Sands, and Bohm laughed while Segura fiddled with his cell phone in both hands. The fly landed on the table between the five men. Darryl glanced at the screen above the fireplace, discovering the video feed had changed. It showed him at the table, sitting next to Bohm, at an angle that could have only come from the tabletop.

Darryl squinted at the fly. Bigger than a common housefly, it rivaled the size of a horsefly, maybe slightly larger. It rose and lowered an inch several times, bouncing as if saying hello.

"That's enough playtime, Mr. Segura," Foreman said with a fading smile. He returned his attention to Darryl. "Now imagine a special forces unit controlling this little fella from miles away. It can relay live video and audio feeds to its handler who can transmit it via satellite with only a two-second delay. It can carry a two-ounce payload and has a battery life of twelve hours."

"Payload? The executive summary you sent said nothing of payload capabilities. What can it carry?"

"Anything. Munitions, explosives, poison, electronics, electrical current. You're only limited by weight and imagination." Foreman redirected Darryl's attention to the monitor. "You asked for a realistic demonstration of its capabilities. What better test than from an operative in the field?"

The video feed changed. It was daytime, and the drone video showed it skirting across rocky terrain, similar to the one Darryl had seen earlier in the underground control center. A building came into view when the drone reached the top of a cliff. It was rudimentary, made of clay and planks. Four older men dressed in long tunics and colorful keffiyeh were in front of it, sitting in rickety metal chairs.

The drone focused on one man near the center. Foreman asked, "Do you recognize his face?"

Darryl strained to distinguish the man's features and soon realized the man on the screen was the number two al-Qaeda man in Afghanistan. "Aziz Sarbaz."

The drone floated closer to Aziz, circling once.

"A conventional drone strike would entail a rocket launch with enough explosive power to take out all four men and the building, but the locust is cutting-edge technology in military-offensive precision. It is a force multiplier, particularly when swarmed. Its firepower is limitless." Foreman brought his cell phone to his ear. "Identity confirmed. You have a green light."

A wave of nausea swept through Darryl. He'd confirmed Aziz's identity, but for what purpose?

The drone circled again, this time stopping to hover at the back of Aziz's head. The feed switched to a second drone hovering nearby, showing a frontal view of the four men.

A bang. A puff of smoke.

Debris sprayed from Aziz's head, pelting the two men on either side of him. Aziz slumped in his chair before tumbling to the ground. The camera focused on the body, showing half of the man's head was missing.

Darryl flicked his stare to Foreman, looking for confirmation of what had unfolded on the screen. The muted grin on his lips confirmed Darryl had witnessed an assassination in real time. The other men in the room appeared unaffected.

Darryl stood dumbfounded, requiring a Herculean effort to open his mouth to speak. "Who authorized this?"

"This was an off-book CIA op. You must know it wasn't sanctioned, but I can tell you the DNI could have shut it down but chose not to."

Darryl remained still and silent, weighing the implications of a virtually undetectable weapon explicitly designed for assassination. If their enemies got hold of this technology, the commonly accepted agreement of placing heads of state off limits to assassination would be void. The locust was a game changer. The world stage would become a Wild West show, reminiscent of the days before diplomacy.

"Senator Jackson's instincts about this weapons system were right, and so were those of the other Republicans on the Emerging Threats and Capabilities Subcommittee," Darryl said. "The concept could revolutionize warfare, but so did nuclear weapons. In the wrong hands, they threaten all humankind, as the new president has warned. There is no way Senator Jackson will support funding this, especially when I tell him about your demonstration and its true intended use."

Foreman's face flushed; his eyes narrowed. His stiff posture left no doubt. He was angry. "The locust will save countless lives of the men and women in our special forces and intelligence community. We will no longer have to send operators into the lion's den to gather intel or exact justice." Foreman rose from his chair and leaned forward, placing his fists on the polished wood tabletop. "I can't believe Senator Jackson would turn his back on our brave service members."

Darryl flinched, reading a veiled threat behind those words. And when

Benjamin Foreman made a threat, people typically fell like dominoes. But Darryl wasn't about to back down. He was the chief of staff to the second-ranking Republican in the Senate, a position of much power in government circles.

After pushing back his chair, Darryl rose to his feet. "I think I've seen enough. If Harold would be so kind, I'd like my coat."

Foreman stood straight and snapped his left thumb and middle finger together. "Very well."

Seconds later, Harold entered, carrying Darryl's coat. It was freshly pressed and cleaned. He held it out for Darryl to slip on.

"Thank you for dinner and excellent hospitality, Mr. Foreman."

"Harold will see you out," Foreman said, his tone flat without emotion.

The moment Yarborough stepped out of the room, Benjamin snapped his fingers at Robert Segura. "I'm ahead of you, Mr. Foreman," Robert said while thumbing his phone screen at a feverish pace.

A new video feed appeared on the monitor above the fireplace, showing Shangri-La's exterior front portico. The door opened, and Yarborough walked through. Harold followed steps behind. When the Tesla's parking lights flashed, signaling Yarborough had unlocked the car using the key fob, Harold rushed ahead and opened the driver's door for him.

"Drive safely, Mr. Yarborough. The roads can be tricky at night."

Yarborough settled in behind the wheel, and Harold retreated up the stairs when the car door shut. The engine started, waking the bright head-lights. After Yarborough's car departed and the compound's main gate closed, the on-screen video feed above the fireplace switched to a locust clinging to a backseat headrest.

"Signal jammer, please, Mr. Segura. Just in case," Benjamin said. Cell service was spotty in the forest, but there were a few areas outside the tree canopies where roaming service came in. He couldn't take a chance.

"Of course, sir." Robert fiddled again with his phone. "I've narrowed the band to only the tower used by his service provider."

After Yarborough drove down the access road and turned onto the two-lane public road, he said, "Siri, call Ballbuster." He waited a moment before throwing his phone in the front passenger seat. "That's right, no signal."

"Have you picked a spot?" Benjamin asked. The grin on Robert's face said he had.

After several twists and turns, Yarborough approached the section of road where he'd narrowly escaped hitting the rabbit. Robert flicked some virtual toggles on his phone screen, sending the locust into a slow, controlled flight. It flew to the front dash, landed there, and bounced up and down several times.

"You have a cruel sense of humor, Robert," Foreman said.

"My benefactor has trained me well," Robert said with a measured smile.

"I'll have to thank him for loaning you out the last three months. Your work improving my design has been impeccable."

"Thank you. Once I acquired what I needed in Mexico City, the fix was simple. I'll pass along your message."

"What have you loaded this unit with?" Foreman asked.

"Sodium azide in a plastic casing and in sufficient quantity to cause instant death." Mr. Segura smiled, proud of his invention. "An electrical pulse will trigger a reaction, turning the powder into nitrogen gas. The gas will explode instantly. It's the same compound found in airbags, so investigators will think it malfunctioned, causing his head injury."

"Brilliant."

Seconds later.

"Shit!" Yarborough swatted frantically at the locust, but Robert kept it out of his reach. The drone circled to the rear of the cabin. "Shit. Shit. Shit." The car swerved.

The feed went dead.

2

The warmth Lexi discovered waking in her wife's arms was as comforting as the first spring breeze, but the peaceful feeling vanished once the silence took over. Two years of building a life together, a safe place to seek refuge in, wasn't enough to hold her demons at bay. Every recent failure haunted her, starting with Kris Faust's death and ending with her mother's.

The familiar sting of guilt punctuated the memory of how she'd become careless, unable to see the dangers that had stared her in the face. She'd almost lost Nita and her father and thought her mother had escaped Tony Belcher's rage, but her nemesis had exacted his revenge from the grave when her mother succumbed to her head injury weeks later. Common sense told her there was no accounting for a madman, and no precaution could have prevented Belcher from striking at her heart.

The logic terrified her when the Raven, every bit as evil as Belcher, sent her a message three months ago. He was coming for her, so she could never leave her family vulnerable. So when it was time to replan their honeymoon, what better place to go than a resort swarming with Secret Service agents in advance of the president's coming visit this weekend? There were more badges and SIG-Sauers per square foot at the Silverado Resort than at a police convention. She felt safer here than at home, which reminded her of the security improvements she still wanted to make at the Ponder house

—more cameras, more exterior lights, a security door on the back porch, and a fence around the property perimeter. There was so much to do.

Nita stirred, shivering and squeezing her arms tighter around Lexi's torso. "It's cold."

Their room had become humid last night after making love—or was it earlier this morning?—so Lexi had slid their patio door open halfway hours ago to draw in the crisp air from outside. The room had cooled too much in the dewy Napa morning, so Lexi raised the blanket covering them. "I'll close the slider."

Nita pulled her in much tighter. "Don't you dare leave this bed. I'm not done with you, Mrs. Mills." She drifted a hand down Lexi's abdomen, skimming the skin ever so slightly, waking Lexi's core with the first twinges of desire. She whispered, "Spread your legs."

A loud clang rang outside their hotel room sliding door, sounding like someone had kicked over a chair around the gas firepit on their private patio or the small table between them.

"Damn it," a familiar voice uttered in a failed whisper from the other side of the screen door, breaking the mood completely.

Lexi raised the covers over her exposed chest and shifted to a less embarrassing position for her next words. "Dad? Are you okay?"

"I'm fine, Peanut. Go back to sleep."

Lexi had thought Nita would have balked at the unorthodox idea of insisting her father go with them on their honeymoon. They had delayed it by three months until both were emotionally stable after the death of Lexi's mother, and both needed the time alone together. But Lexi couldn't bring herself to travel while her father was home alone. Who would be there to keep him company? And more importantly, who would protect him?

"I called the hotel. They can set us up with a suite with two bedrooms and bathrooms separated by a living area and kitchen. We won't even know he's there," Lexi had said. Thankfully, her wife knew the meaning of unconditional love and encouraged him to say yes. Little did she know their private patios were connected, and her father would get up early each morning and go to her and Nita's side to watch the golfers tee off from the fourth hole.

"We're awake. Give us a few minutes." Lexi flopped back, her head hitting the pillow with a quiet thud against the goose feathers. She came to terms with a sad fact. Her honeymoon wasn't turning out as she'd hoped.

"Not so fast," Nita whispered before cocking her head toward the door. "We need to take showers, Dad. Give us an hour."

"Just like your mother in her younger days," her father said through the screen door. "So much time primping."

Nita returned her attention to Lexi, a naughty grin forming on her lips. "I'm not letting that shower bench go to waste even for one day."

"You *are* bad." Lexi mirrored her playful expression, thinking certain things were back on the morning menu.

An hour later, sated and dressed for a walk along the resort trail, Lexi drew back the drapes and fully opened the glass and screen doors. Her father was seated near the gas firepit, facing the lush fourth hole and nibbling on the complimentary continental breakfast the hotel delivered daily to their suite.

Lexi walked out, holding Nita's hand. Eight months ago, she wouldn't have dared to display such affection in front of her father, unwilling to upset him further and put more distance into their already fractured relationship. But his miraculous transformation, thanks to his friend Gavin and her mother, had changed him from narrow-minded and unforgiving to sharing a suite with Lexi and her new wife on their honeymoon.

Low flames warmed their cozy covered patio, removing the bite of the cool mid-morning air. "Good morning, Dad." Lexi kissed him on the forehead.

His eyes still held the sadness of losing a life partner of forty years, but the sign of being lost in the world had finally left them. "Good morning, you two. The cold snap finally passed through, so I thought you might enjoy sitting out here today." He gestured toward the glass door, where a serving cart with covered food trays, juice, and a coffee carafe sat. "I hope you don't mind, but I had your breakfast delivered out here today."

"It's perfect, Dad," Nita said, kissing him on the forehead before selecting some pastries, a hard-boiled egg, and a yogurt container.

Nita had started calling him dad at his insistence on their wedding day, but saying it took on special meaning after Nita had brought her mother back to life following a devastating brain bleed, if only for a few hours.

Whenever Nita said dad or he referred to Nita as her daughter, Lexi's heart melted around the meaning behind those words. She doubted he understood how profoundly his gesture had affected both women. Nita had lost her father as a teenager and hadn't had a fatherly figure in her life since. The joy in her wife's eyes after realizing she finally had a dad again meant more to Lexi than all the accolades and riches in the world.

Lexi retrieved her food and sat in an end chair next to Nita. Two golf carts had pulled up to the farthest tee box, and four men lined up, preparing to hit their drives. It had been decades since Lexi had accompanied her father in a golf cart, but after the first man hit and the ball had barely trickled past the forward tees, it became abundantly clear they had no business playing from the tips.

Lexi and her dad chuckled.

Memories flooded back of Lexi as a little girl, joining her father on weekdays during the summer when his crew was home for a rare week off. Her feet had barely reached the pedals, but he let her drive the cart between shots once they cleared the first hole and the watchful eye of the starter near the clubhouse. Those daredevil days had fueled her desire to test drive her father's racing car for the first time.

"Hey, Dad. Now that you have more use of your leg, do you think you'll ever take up golf again?"

He reached across his chair arm and patted Nita's hand. "Thanks to this one, it's a possibility again."

"I've helped several golfers rehab injuries and get their swing back. With a little more work, I'm sure we can get you playing," Nita said with certainty in her eyes.

"Maybe. With Gavin," he cleared his throat and visibly swallowed, "and your mother gone, I might need another hobby."

Lexi forced back the emotions swelling her throat and welling her eyes with moisture. Gavin was his best friend, mechanic, and crew chief, dating back to when they were young men. His death at Belcher's hands had delivered her father a crushing blow, and losing his wife weeks later came close to destroying him. All he knew was tinkering with cars with Gavin and doting on his wife, and with them gone, he would need something to occupy his time.

"Maybe I should learn," Lexi said.

Nita squeezed Lexi's hand. "We can all take lessons together."

Her father's silent nod meant taking up golf again was more than a possibility.

Lexi's phone buzzed in her hoodie pocket. She'd turned off notifications for all her apps, including the news, and had turned on "Do Not Disturb," allowing messages and calls from a select few on her contacts list. Everyone on the list knew she was on her honeymoon and had strict orders not to contact her unless it was important. So the humming in her pocket meant something needed her attention, according to whoever was calling.

Lexi pulled out her phone, receiving a side-eye from Nita. She had promised Nita and herself not to let anything interfere with their honeymoon, but curiosity had gotten the best of her. She had to know who was trying to reach her, so she turned the phone over. Nita likely picked up on Lexi's deep, breathy sigh after she glanced at the screen. Her boss was calling.

Lexi thought the call might have had something to do with the Raven, but she'd given her partner explicit instructions to text first and label his message with "SOS." This had to be something different since Willie Lange was calling. When Lexi left the office last Friday, she'd made it clear to her boss that she was unreachable until her return the following Sunday night unless the country was under attack or something time-critical involving the Raven came up.

Despite her continued curiosity, Lexi rolled her neck and chose her family. She pressed the power button, sending the call to voicemail, and squeezed Nita's hand while letting a self-satisfied grin sprout. "It can wait."

Before Lexi returned her phone to her pocket, it whirred with an incoming text. She closed her eyes, expecting the message to blow up her honeymoon, and took in three calming breaths, her custom before disarming every bomb. Lange's text read *Urgent. Call ASAP.*

Lexi squeezed Nita's hand again and forced herself not to frown. "Lange says it's urgent."

Nita hid her frustration well, but her eyes couldn't lie. She was upset. "I understand."

Lexi brought Nita's hand to her lips and kissed it. "I'm not happy about this either. Let me see what it's about, and I'll be right back." She pushed herself up from the chair, grabbed a pastry and the glass of juice she'd poured, and went inside their suite bedroom, closing the slider behind her. Whatever Lange was calling about, Lexi wanted Nita to hear it from her, not from a one-sided conversation.

She dialed. The call connected on the first ring.

"Mills, great. Thanks for calling me back." Lange sounded harried.

"My wife wasn't happy I took your call."

"She'll understand when she hears nine lives are at stake," Lange said.

Lives hanging in the balance were Lexi's kryptonite. No matter how much resolve she had to put her family first, she had to act when innocents were at risk. "What's happening?"

"Two hours away from your location, a bank manager equipped with a bomb vest took four employees and five customers hostage. A teller tripped the silent alarm. When police arrived, he claimed a man had held him at gunpoint this morning, put the vest on him, and ordered him to rob the bank and drop the money off in a remote location. Now he just wants the damn thing off. The regional bomb squad is out of their depths and asked for ATF assistance."

Lexi recalled reading the ops bulletin before leaving for her overdue honeymoon. "If I remember correctly, the San Francisco Field Division Special Response Team is in Denver, augmenting for an international summit. That's why you're calling me."

"Right," Lange said. "I realize this is a big ask, but because of its location, we can't get a team there for at least four hours. You could cut that time in half."

"Why the urgency?"

"The vest has a timer with three hours remaining." The scenario Lange laid out hit each of Lexi's buttons—innocent lives and time sensitive.

"Fine." Lexi ran her free hand down her face, wondering how to explain this to Nita. Whatever she said, it had to start and end with a kiss. "Text me the info. I'll leave in ten minutes."

After sliding the phone into her hoodie pocket, Lexi considered changing from her joggers but couldn't find her preferred cargo pants with extra pockets in the dresser drawers. She remembered packing only one pair, not expecting to work on her honeymoon, and recalled she'd worn them on the plane and spilled a drink on them. They must have been in the laundry bag.

Without time to waste, she returned to the patio door. Leaving weighed heavy on her shoulders while she watched the action before her. Her father had explained to Nita the flaws in the golfer's swing and instructed her how to maintain a smooth, fluid motion from the backswing to follow-through. He smiled, demonstrating the ideal golf swing, the first outward display of happiness Lexi had seen grace his lips since before he found his wife unresponsive in bed. Three months was a long time to go without feeling joy, and leaving him now felt like punishment for being good at her job.

Both turned to face Lexi when the screen door she slid skidded loudly across the rail. Her father had a broad smile, and Nita matched it inch for inch. Nita approached, circled her arms around Lexi's neck, and kissed her. "Your expression tells me you're torn. Don't be. I trust your judgment."

Lexi swallowed the emotion growing thick in her throat. "If I leave now, I can save nine lives."

"Text me where you'll be." Nita lowered her arms.

"Only if you promise not to come."

"I learned my lesson in Gladding." The sincerity in Nita's eyes said she meant those words. Witnessing the danger of Lexi's role in a bomb disposal scene firsthand last spring was more than Nita could handle. If she did it again, Nita would stumble harder in her battle with addiction, a consequence Lexi couldn't live with.

"Thank you." Lexi turned to her father. "Dad, I'm sorry, but I have to go."

"I know, Peanut." The corners of his lips dropped, and sympathy filled his eyes. Thankfully, the cloud of grief hanging over his shoulder was less prominent this morning. "Nita gave me a heads-up. They wouldn't have asked for you unless you could help. We'll be fine here. Those people need you more than we do."

3

To get a feel of the accident scene, Detective Jan Hopkins bent near the starting point of the skid marks, assuming the catcher's crouch he'd perfected while on the high school varsity team. Surprisingly, the knees still worked like they did when he was a teenager, making roadside investigations a snap well into his forties.

While his partner imaged the scene, Jan focused on the road in the direction the car had come from, staring into the bright morning light. The location and skid marks perplexed him. Ninety percent of mountain accidents happened on the curves due to speed, conditions, or critters. The other ten percent occurring on the straightaways, like this one, related to poor weather conditions, but last night's snow hadn't reached this far down the mountain. With five hundred investigations on these roads under his belt, Jan suspected something else was at play.

Once Jan pushed himself upright, he set his sights on the wrecker lowering the winch below the shoulder drop-off to the vehicle's rocky, brush-covered grave. The Tesla had come to rest at a steep enough angle to prevent him from inspecting it before the equipment arrived, but the photographs the firefighters had taken before removing the body were enough to convince him the extensive head injuries might make a quick determination of death impossible without a full autopsy. Now, the real investigation was about to begin.

Jan shifted his attention to the coroner's technician kneeling over the body firefighters had brought up moments ago on a gurney. He walked toward the scene when the tech inserted a thermometer into the victim's torso.

The tech popped his head up when Jan stopped three feet away. "Taking into account the overnight temperature, I'd place the time of death between eight and midnight last night."

Jan acknowledged with a nod. "What can you tell me about his injuries?"

"Trauma to the head and chest is severe and consistent with a rollover accident." The tech pointed to the right side of the victim's head. "He has more damage on the right side than the left." He stood, removing his latex gloves. "We'll have to wait until we get him on the table to learn the cause of death, but I found no signs of gunshot or knife wounds."

"I figured as much. Can you tell Doctor Moore to give this one a critical eye? Something isn't right here."

"Sure thing, Detective Hopkins."

Once the coroners loaded the body into the rig, Jan set his focus on the vehicle being brought roadside. The Tesla remained surprisingly intact for a rollover crash, a good sign he might find a clue to what happened here last night.

The wreckage landed on the soft shoulder with a dull thud. Lines and cracks covered the shattered windshield, making it completely opaque. A collection of wires extending from the door dangled the crushed driver's side mirror. The body had dents and scrapes, but not as much as Jan expected if the car had rolled over completely, making him rethink the rollover theory. The nitrogen gas had escaped the deployed side airbags, leaving them floppy and looking like the durable shower curtains in his high school locker room.

"Thanks, fellas," Jan said to the tow crew resetting the winch to load the vehicle onto the wrecker. "I'll need a few minutes."

"You got it, Jan," one said. "Let us know when you're ready." He returned to his partner at the back of their truck and accepted a steaming Thermos cup from him.

First responders had pried open the driver's door to extract the victim, and it was ajar. Jan opened it with a loud creak after putting on latex gloves. Shards of glass littered the seats and floor, and blood covered the deflated driver's airbag. The tablet-sized touchscreen mounted on the dashboard had several cracks but still had power, a testament to Tesla's sturdy construction.

A glance at the rearview mirror disappointed Jan. This Tesla model didn't have an interior camera installed. However, pressing on the touchscreen made him smile. It was still responsive, so Jan navigated to the footage from the exterior front camera and played the last file stored when the car was in motion. It showed the headlights illuminating the path ahead as the car twisted through a turn on the highway. The road straightened, but the driver suddenly swerved for no reason. No deer or other animals. No oncoming cars or motorcycles. No cyclists. Nothing. The road ahead was clear. He thought the driver might have experienced a medical emergency like a heart attack or stroke.

An inspection of the front area yielded a cracked cell phone but no other clues, so Jan moved to the backseat. The door popped open easily, lending credence to his theory. The car didn't roll over but had only been beaten up by going through the shrubs and glancing off a tree. One question popped into his head if his hypothesis were true: Why did the victim have such severe head trauma? He concluded this was no ordinary accident.

Jan combed through the back with a flashlight, looking for anything out of the ordinary, but the Tesla was well kept. The only things on the seat and floor were glass shards and bits of plastic from the airbag covers. Jan shined the light underneath the leather driver's seat. Several wires and mechanisms blocked most of the view, but the light glistened off something shiny —one, no, two small pieces of metal. He retrieved them with a pair of tweezers from his coat pocket and placed them into separate clear plastic evidence bags. A more thorough inspection of the interior cabin did not reveal the source of the remnants he'd collected.

Once Jan searched the trunk, he inspected the metal pieces in the evidence bags more closely. One appeared thin like a sewing needle but a quarter of the length. The larger one had some type of electronics attached to it. While Jan was by no means an expert on this make of car, and the only times he'd stepped foot into a Tesla was to investigate a crash, these items didn't appear to be native to the vehicle. They weren't much, but beyond the pending autopsy, they were the only evidence he had to go on.

Jan returned to the wrecker team. They were still standing near the back of their rig, sipping on the contents of their Thermos. "All done?" the older one asked.

"For now. I'd like this one dropped off in our evidence bay, not the yard."

"Sure thing, Jan. Can you tell them to expect us?"

"I can do better. Would you mind if I catch a ride to the department with you?"

"Not at all, but you get the middle. My legs are too long and don't work so well these days." The older one grimaced, patting his left leg.

"No problem." Jan noted the clouds overhead. Some were dark, and he remembered there was rain in the forecast. "And could you toss a tarp over this one? I don't want the rain washing away evidence."

"You got it."

While the crew readied the Tesla for transport, Jan walked to his partner documenting the scene with a 360-degree camera. "How's it coming, Chet?"

"Just finishing up."

"Would you mind wrapping up here?" Jan held up the bags with the evidence he'd collected at the crash site. "I want to run these ASAP."

"What's the rush?" Chet asked. His partner was a competent investigator with the tools of the trade, but he lacked instinct when reading a scene. That was Jan's strong suit. His gut rarely led him astray.

"Things aren't adding up," Jan said.

An hour later, after the tow truck crew stowed the wreckage safely in the county sheriff's evidence bay, Jan arrived at the open door of their on-site lab. Only one person was working this morning. He knocked on the frosted glass window.

"Morning, Micha." Jan hoped the early departure from her bed this morning without saying goodbye hadn't put her in a sour mood. He'd never met a man or woman more capable of holding a grudge.

She glanced up. The glint in her eye suggested all was forgiven, but the twinkle turned quickly into a scowl. "A goodbye might have been nice."

Jan stepped closer. "You looked like you were having a pleasant dream. I didn't want to wake you." The corners of her lips drew slowly upward, saying he was on the right track. Now to hit it out of the park. "Maybe I can do it right the next time."

"You're assuming there *will* be a next time."

"Just hopeful, Micha."

"We'll see." She smirked.

Jan held up two evidence bags. "Is there a chance you can run these today?" He offered an impish smile. "Before lunch?"

"You're assuming benefits outside the office equates to benefits inside."

"Would dinner at Joe's help?" A meal at their favorite steak place might be enough to tip the scale in his direction.

"Not really," she shrugged with an unreadable expression.

Jan had struck out. The only card left to him was to appeal to Micha's political junkie side. "Would it help if the victim worked for Senator Jackson from Nevada? And that I think the crash might not be an accident?"

Micha snatched the bags from his hand. "Why didn't you say so in the first place?"

4

While driving up to the bank hostage scene in Penn Valley, Lexi realized bottom-hugging, tight athleisure pants designed to turn her bride's head on their honeymoon, might not have been her wisest choice of wardrobe for a disposal operation. They were well-equipped with pockets and specially altered with an inner seam zipper to access her prosthetic easily, but she didn't consider the media circus clogging the street. This was not the audience she intended to impress.

Lexi recalled the images of the vest bomb Willie Lange had texted and parked a safe distance away, an entire block short of the media armada. She exited the rental car and zipped her tight hoodie higher, taking care to cover more of her tank top. Not wearing her typical work attire made her feel out of uniform, like an MLB ballplayer walking onto the field for the first pitch still in warm-up gear. At least she had her service weapon secured to a belly band holster under her joggers and her handcuffs stuffed inside it.

Lexi pushed her uneasiness aside and walked through the throng of onlookers and reporters, keeping the credentials hanging from her neck on a chain hidden inside her light jacket. She received several dirty looks for acting like a crowd bully but didn't stop until reaching the long run of crime scene tape.

She assessed the mountain city shopping center, scrutinizing the area around the bank. The dated, two-story building was home to an eclectic mix of businesses, including real estate, law, and medical offices, a shipping store, and Twin-Counties Bank, the location of today's bomb threat. Cars filled most of the two-row parking lot, and airy California foothill pine trees formed a loose barrier between the parking lot and the street, where the media had swarmed with their mobile satellite vans. Lexi estimated a hundred-foot cordon separated them from the bank entrance, which was way too close. Lange was right. This sheriff's department was in over their head.

Lexi nudged past several bystanders and news station cameras and located the nearest officer guarding the outer cordon line. She pulled out her credentials and displayed them to the officer. "Special Agent Mills. Your on-scene commander is expecting me." She intentionally left out her agency and first name, hoping to remain off the radar and not alert the news crews that her special skills were needed at today's scene.

His eyes beamed with recognition as he lowered the stanchion. "Of course, Agent Mills. It's an honor. Lieutenant Schmidt is in the van."

As Lexi stepped past the lowered tape, a reporter shouted. "Lexi Mills, right? If you've been called in, an explosive must be involved. What can you tell us about the hostage situation?"

Lexi cringed. The local sheriff had kept the bomb vest out of the media to avoid public panic and unnecessary speculation. Unfortunately, Lexi's recent celebrity now made the closely held detail common knowledge. She paused her stride and put on her media smile before turning. "Yes, I'm Lexi Mills. The Nevada County Sheriff's Department requested federal assistance. I was nearby. Sorry to cut this short, but I need to receive a situational briefing and get to work."

Lexi turned on her heel to the sound of clicking cameras and shouts of more questions, but she took long strides to escape the frenzy. She intentionally walked flatfooted without swaying her hips to avoid drawing attention to the clothes making her self-conscious. The line of official cruisers, SUVs, and the response team van was twenty-five feet away. Lexi scanned the officers' collars, located the one with the lieutenant's bars, and walked up to him.

He turned. The grin on his lips suggested no need for Lexi to introduce herself. "Agent Mills, thank you for coming so quickly." He extended his right hand. "I'm Kevin Schmidt."

Lexi shook his hand. "Happy to help, Lieutenant. We can start by expanding the outer cordon to the next shopping center and increasing the inner standoff distance to two hundred feet."

He cocked his head back. "We're following protocol for standoff distances when a vest bomber is inside a building." His curt tone suggested Lexi had offended him. So, her response required more tact.

"And the distance would be correct for fragmentation injuries from the explosion. However, Lieutenant, looking at the amount of glass at the front of the bank, I'm concerned about flying shards, which could cause severe wounds up to one-hundred-fifty feet." She gestured toward the dozen officers standing watch. "Every one of your deputies could lose an eye."

Schmidt's eyes widened with realization. He turned to a deputy with sergeant's stripes. "Kendry, reset the inner and outer lines according to Agent Mills' instructions."

Kendry took off with a sense of urgency in his step and voice. "Listen up," he shouted.

While the officers set up safe standoff distances, Lexi accompanied Schmidt to a quiet location between the cordons beneath a tree. The response team commander, including SWAT and the bomb squad, joined them. This man appeared too young to have much experience with hostage scenarios involving bombs, but he also came across as professional and eager to learn.

"Thank you for coming, Agent Mills." The tactical commander shook Lexi's hand. He sounded calm, but the beads of sweat collecting on his brow said he was nervous or worried. "My regular tech is out with COVID, which meant I was next in line. Once I saw the configuration, I knew I wasn't skilled enough." He brought up video footage on his tablet, showing the bank's interior from several angles. "Here's the situation. The bank's national office sent us a link to the live security feed." He explained the manager's statement about being forced at gunpoint to put on the vest and rob the bank.

"Wait. The robber didn't have the manager spray-paint the camera lenses?" This robbery resembled the work of amateurs with its poor planning. Something wasn't right. "What about the hostages? Why hasn't he released them?"

"The manager said the robber would blow up the vest if anyone but him left the bank before he had the money." The commander directed an interior security camera toward the manager sitting in a chair in front of the bulletproof teller's booth. The man's face was flushed and sweat coated his forehead and cheeks. His right leg bounced up and down fast enough to put him in danger of having a stroke. The camera focus shifted, zooming more tightly on the vest bomb. "You can see it's padlocked in place using a metal waistband, as is the timer."

Lexi studied the six pipe bombs and wires, paying close attention to the timer and a metal box all the cables fed in and out of. Her breath hitched, not at the forty-nine minutes remaining but at their shape and configuration. They were hauntingly familiar, surfacing memories of disarming the Raven's massive dirty bomb. The boxes didn't match those used in the Las Vegas casino ballroom, but the wiring, down to the color and gauge of the wires, was identical. If her instincts were right, and this was the Raven's work, the vest had a redundant trigger.

"Do you still have communications with the manager? Can you have him stand and turn around? I want to see the back of the vest." Lexi asked.

"Yes. I can activate the microphone and speaker on the security camera." The tactical commander pressed a series of buttons on the tablet screen. "Mr. Drake, this is Sergeant Davis again. The explosives expert has arrived. We need you to stand with your back to the camera so we can inspect the vest."

"It's about damn time." Drake gained control of his piston-like knee and rose to his feet. "When are you going to get me out of this thing?"

"Soon, Mr. Drake. Now stand still," Davis said, pressing a button to mute the microphone.

Lexi zeroed in on the back of the vest, trailing a wire snaking below the arm opening. It ended at a small plastic or metal box attached to the collar at the center. She couldn't be sure because the man's hair blocked a part of it, but its size resembled an RFID receiver for a drone. A remote trigger augmenting the timer, like the one used in the Raven's dirty bomb, made sense.

"Do you have a tactical jammer with a decent range in your van?" Lexi asked.

"Yes, ma'am. It can block signals for forty meters. But if the trigger is a timer, how would a jammer help?"

"Call it a gut instinct. Drake said if the others left, the vest would blow up. That tells me there's a remote detonator. If I'm right, the trigger person is here watching. Do you know what Drake's tormentor looks like?"

Davis nodded. "According to Drake, he's a white male on the small side in his forties. What do you recommend?"

"Before I enter the kill zone, I want to find the triggerman. If this bomb is the work of who I think it is, there's a chance the trigger might work on a frequency your jammer doesn't block, so this will be tricky. First, we set up the jammer at the front of the bank but don't turn it on until we're ready so as not to alert him. When we think we have him, we hit the jammer and take him down. Afterward, I'll put on a bomb suit and disarm the vest."

"I'm on the jammer, Agent Mills." Davis jogged to the tactical van and barked out several orders.

While his team set up the equipment, Lexi pulled out her phone from her hoodie pocket and dialed her boss. The call picked up on the first ring.

"Mills, is everything okay there?" Lange asked. Her tone was more measured than during her earlier call this morning.

"I'm not sure yet. Parts of the explosive resemble the dirty bomb in Vegas."

"Do you think the Raven is involved?"

"My gut tells me yes, so I'm proceeding with extra caution. Things on the ground are moving fast here, so can you notify Croft? I'd like him out here ASAP." Lexi watched two officers in tactical uniforms carrying a large suitcase by its handles on both sides dash across the parking lot, deep into the inner cordon. They reached the building and were now in the kill zone, minimally protected by ballistic vests and Kevlar helmets.

"Will do, Mills," Lange said. "And Lexi..." her voice dropped off.

"Yes, Agent Lange?"

After both officers placed the suitcase on the ground at the base of the bank's front door, one opened it and extended the antennae.

"Steady hands, Lexi."

"Thank you, Agent Lange."

Both men dashed across the parking lot again to safety. She hoped the jammer had a broad enough range and was sophisticated enough to block whatever frequency the remote trigger had. Lexi closed her eyes, willing her hand to steady when the time came so she could complete her work and return to her bride.

5

With a final adjustment of his necktie in front of the bedroom mirror, Benjamin Foreman was ready for the impromptu meeting with his trusted senior advisors. He had much to sort through after last night's debacle. His company's future and perhaps his life depended on what he decided next.

While walking down the stairs of his mountain cabin, Benjamin realized regrouping was never his strong suit. The ability to adjust on the fly was more in his wheelhouse, but the blow Darryl Yarborough delivered last night wasn't merely a glitch. It was a eulogy for the Locust Program unless Benjamin developed a new game plan. He'd already sunk a billion dollars into the project and was indebted to the Raven, who had a reputation for disposing of those who crossed him. The Raven's chief engineer, Robert Segura, had saved his bacon by solving a critical payload deficiency, and now Benjamin owed the Raven more than money. He owed him silence and a future favor, an uncomfortable position.

After pushing open the thick pine door to his private office, Benjamin discovered his team had already assembled around the small, polished conference table made from the same wood as the door. The empty plates near the table's center said Benjamin had arrived later than expected.

Kyle Sands appeared the most disappointed. As the project manager, he'd lived locust production night and day for two years, and Yarborough had said the program was dead before he could get it off the ground. Andrew Bohm, his legal counsel, and Salvador Cabrera, his financial advisor, tied for the busiest. Both flipped through documents atop their folios, studying each one for several moments before moving on to the next. Their furrowed brows suggested neither was seeing a workable path that was profitable and legal.

"Good morning, gentlemen."

The three scooted their chairs back on the Persian area rug and rose, showing their respect but coming short of bouncing to attention like lower-ranking soldiers. Each acknowledged with single-word greetings and returned to their seats while Benjamin poured a cup of coffee from the carafe on the serving table against the wall. The pastries were a nice touch for his visitors but not for his A1C level, so he limited his selection to fruit, eggs, and toast, all kept at the appropriate serving temperature in their trays.

Benjamin assumed his seat at the head of the table closest to the desk and the roaring fireplace to the right. He already suspected the direction this meeting would take and was sure it would not disappoint one man around the table with the outcome he envisioned. Though, one or two might disagree with the method he was about to suggest.

"What are our options, Mr. Sands?" Benjamin asked, but he already knew the answer. Other channels were available to them, government and civilian, but none could infuse the money he needed within the next four quarters to meet his obligations like a United States military contract could. His company had suckled at the government teat for over a decade, and if Benjamin didn't get creative, it would all end abruptly.

"In terms of American allies, British MI6 has shown interest in the technology, but the process will take six months to work it through official channels to get the type of production commitment we're looking for."

Mr. Cabrera removed his eyeglasses and held them between his fingertips. "With a lengthy buildup, we wouldn't see funds for another twelve months, and the British government contract would be a tenth the size of the one we'd hoped for with the United States."

"And their adversaries?" Benjamin asked Sands.

"The Chinese are already experimenting with the technology, but like we had until Mr. Segura came on board, they can't solve the payload problem. While carrying any extra weight, the battery life reduces to minutes, which defeats the locust's primary purpose of sustained, long-range operations."

"But as a current military contractor," Mr. Bohm said, shifting uncomfortably in his chair to direct his ire at Sands as if he'd suggested they rob a bank, "We are legally barred from doing business with their government."

"I didn't suggest getting permission," Sands said.

"And how do you propose we hide the income from the IRS?" Cabrera shook his head at the absurdity of laundering billions. He put on his glasses again as if he was the only one in the conversation seeing clearly.

"That's your department," Sands said, throwing up a hand dismissively. "Not mine."

Unfortunately, his advisors presented nothing Benjamin didn't already know. Legal options were few and wouldn't meet his needs, considering the timeline involved. "Gentlemen, the solution is to give the Senate subcommittee a reason to approve funding immediately."

Sands turned his attention to Benjamin, his eyes round with desperation. "How do we do that?" If Benjamin read him correctly, Sands would offer his firstborn to keep this project afloat. He had ten million reasons to —the dollar equivalent to his bonus when the Department of Defense contract came through.

"By creating a need."

"Benjamin," Bohm said. "I think we need to clear the room." Andrew's use of Benjamin's first name was an attention-getter. He only said it in front of business associates to stress the importance of something.

Benjamin acknowledged his old friend with a polite nod. "Mr. Sands. Mr. Cabrera. Thank you for outlining your ideas and concerns. Let's table our discussion until next week during our video conference. Harold will see you out."

Sands and Cabrera gathered their things without objection and bid their goodbyes. Once the door shut after them, Benjamin grabbed his coffee and moved to the overstuffed leather chair close to the fireplace. Warmer weather had made a few appearances recently, but the mornings were still brisk, and sitting at the fire always cleared his head.

"Join me, Andrew."

His friend of a quarter century since their West Point days sat in the matching chair, with only a narrow end table separating them. He'd brought his coffee too. "Creating a need for weapons is a topic best kept between us. As loyal as Mr. Sands and Mr. Cabrera are, conversations with them in the room nullifies lawyer-client confidentiality."

"You always watch out for my best interest, my friend. Thank you."

"Now, tell me." Andrew sipped his mug. "What do you have in mind?"

"War." Three gentle knocks on the door told Benjamin his trusty manservant was on the other side. "Come in, Harold," he called out.

The door opened, and Harold strode inside, dressed in his daytime uniform of a tailored black business suit. "My apologies for the interruption, Mr. Foreman, but the control center is monitoring something they think might interest you."

"Thank you, Harold. Tell them I'll be right down." Once Harold left, Benjamin turned to Andrew. "Can you reach out to our friend? His contacts from his mercenary days should prove helpful in finding the right man for the job."

"Of course, Benjamin. I'll take care of it today."

Benjamin finished his coffee, took the elevator to the subterranean capsule, and entered the control center. He noticed the large center section of the giant wall of monitors was streaming two live feeds. The text in the lower left corner of the screen listed GPS coordinates, and he noted the videos were from a locust prototype.

"Who authorized a flight, Matthew? Mr. Sands mentioned nothing of a test today."

The shift supervisor clomped down the metal stairs from the mezzanine level above. His legs moved quickly like a hamster on a training wheel. "No one, sir. The unique identifier returns to a prototype assigned to Mr. Segura."

Benjamin refocused on the center collection of monitors, trying to decipher the events unfolding on screen. A crowd had formed near a police-cordoned-off area near a shopping center. "Where is this coming from?"

"Penn Valley, a town fifty-two miles west of here. We listened to the police frequencies and confirmed a bank robbery in progress involving the branch manager wearing a suicide bomb vest and nine hostages. Should I shut it down, sir?"

"Not yet." Benjamin sat in his command chair and continued to observe, wondering if this was the job for the Raven that Robert had mentioned last night.

One locust was stationary inside the bank while another hovered twenty feet over the secure area for several minutes, scanning the police officers from one end of the scene to the other. The stream's focus changed, zeroing in on a woman emerging from the crowd and walking toward the command van. The camera zoomed in on her face. It looked familiar, but Benjamin couldn't place the name.

"Can you run facial recognition on the woman?"

"No need to, sir. I'd recognize her face anywhere. She's ATF Special Agent Lexi Mills, the hero of Spicewood and Las Vegas."

The video feed focus didn't change, staying on Lexi Mills wherever she went. The country had been enamored with this woman for a year since her heroics in Texas. This one-legged darling of the nation would make an attractive target and could save Benjamin much time and planning. However, he dismissed the idea, doubting her death would be enough to send the country to war.

Benjamin watched, unable to peel his eyes away. He lifted a handset from a nearby desk and dialed. The call connected.

"Benjamin, I wasn't expecting your call for another few weeks. I trust Robert's services have been satisfactory," the Raven said.

"Yes, he's been an invaluable asset, but I'm troubled by his use of the product in public without my approval."

"I see." The Raven's slight pause and vague response suggested he was equally surprised by Robert's actions. "I'll have a word with him."

"Thank you. I can't afford this technology getting into a competitor's hands before I secure my DoD contract." Benjamin detailed the events unfolding on the screen before disconnecting the call and returning the handset to its cradle.

The video streams hadn't changed their orientation. One still shadowed Lexi Mills from a distance, and the other kept watch on a man wearing a suicide bomber's vest, piquing Benjamin's curiosity. "What are you up to, Robert?"

6

Everything about this robbery is off, Lexi thought. What bank robber in his right mind would hold up this specific bank if the intent was to have the branch manager get away with the money? The bank likely had minimal cash on hand on a Tuesday morning, and the sheriff's department was two blocks away. It was as if the robber meant for the job to fail.

Lexi threw off her uneasy feeling and studied the live feed of bystanders on the commander's tactical tablet as the camera slowly scanned the people. She disregarded women, elderly men, and men of color and concentrated on locating anyone in the crowd who fit the description of the robber Drake had provided. She and the commander had identified three possibilities. All three were white males in their forties with cell phones in their hands, possibly the trigger device.

"What's your game plan?" Lieutenant Schmidt asked.

"We've narrowed it down to three suspects in the crowd who might control a remote trigger to the bomb vest," Lexi said. "We'll need three officers in plain clothes to filter through the crowd and take each down simultaneously to not give any suspect a chance of getting away."

"We don't have anyone in plain clothes, but I might have civilian jackets in the tactical van," the commander said. He left to search for them and returned a minute later with two. "This is all I have."

"It will do," Lexi said. "I can go into the crowd. Give me an earpiece, so we're all in communication."

Once Lexi, the tactical commander, and another officer had dressed appropriately and geared up with radios and earpieces, they fanned out in intervals to not draw attention, reaching the crowd of onlookers from different directions. Each targeted a different suspect.

Lexi chose the one on the left, thinking he was likelier to be the trigger-man. Smaller and thinner than the others, he didn't fit the profile of a tough bank robber, but he looked like someone who could devise a clever ruse. His unassuming presence, marked by thick, dark-rimmed eyeglasses, plain attire, and a clean-cut appearance, made him the perfect Raven point man. The Raven would choose someone who could blend into a crowd easily.

Lexi pressed the mic on the radio clipped to the waistband of her joggers and spoke in a quiet voice. "Lieutenant Schmidt, update us on their locations."

"Copy," Schmidt said. "Mills, your man is near the tape, twenty feet right of the light pole. Davis, center of the crowd, five rows back. Maclure, far right at the front next to a woman with a stroller."

"All right, people," Lexi said. "Sound off when you're in place. Wait to take down on my mark." Timing was essential. If the jammer had a range broader than Davis had claimed, the triggerman might notice the signal drop. And if they didn't take down the three suspects at precisely the same time, one might get away. And what if the jammer didn't work? The triggerman might still detonate the bomb.

Lexi had circled the crowd's edge, entered from the side near the light pole, and eased her way through the lookie-loos. The closer she got toward the front, the tighter the people had packed themselves in the crowd. She closed in on her target by dipping a shoulder here and sliding sideways there. As she passed through the crowd, the conversations varied from conjecture about the lazy police sitting on their hands doing nothing to one woman worrying about how she would mail her package with the UPS store evacuated.

"Davis in place."

"Maclure in place."

"Almost there," Lexi said. Two stubborn watchers refused to give way, forcing Lexi to go around to the other side of her target. She settled behind his left shoulder, drawing her service Glock from her belly band and holding it against her thigh. "In place. Schmidt, hit the jammer in one. All teams, go, go."

While stepping forward, Lexi raised her weapon two inches above her waist, poking it into the small of the back of her target. She whispered to not panic the crowd, hoping the others did too. "Police. Don't move. Drop the phone." Most people tightened their shoulders when someone shoved a gun into their back, but the man didn't flinch, making Lexi suspicious.

"What if I hand you the phone? I don't want it to break." The man's calm voice didn't sound as if he was surprised. It was another clue he expected Lexi. Her gut told her he was the triggerman.

"Slowly. Over your left shoulder." Lexi pressed the muzzle of her gun harder, stressing she would shoot if forced.

The man offered the phone, sliding it against the fabric of his light jacket at the shoulder. "What is this about?"

Lexi snagged the phone, examining the lit screen. A game of solitaire was visible on the display.

"He's running," Davis said over the radio.

Lexi's pulse picked up. She'd guessed wrong. After returning the phone to the man, she said, "Sorry, sir. I made a mistake."

Screams came from the middle of the crowd, and people pushed against Lexi, forcing her back. Other armed officers had taken a post behind the group to stop a possible runaway suspect. "Containment! Containment!" Lexi shouted into the mic.

Lexi pushed against the tsunami of terrified onlookers and weaved her way to where she thought Davis and his target should have been. The sea parted. In the clearing, the target Davis shadowed was clasping a woman against the front of his body with his left arm while pressing the muzzle of a semi-automatic handgun against her temple with his right hand. He held a cell phone in his left with his thumb raised a half inch off the screen. If the phone was the trigger and the jammer wasn't effective, he could detonate before anyone could get a shot off.

Davis had his gun trained on him and barked, "Drop your weapon."

The suspect continued backing up, dragging his hostage in a stuttered step. The woman was tall, posing an effective shield against a headshot from the front. Terror was in her eyes. The rage of a trapped animal filled the suspect's. Lexi had seen the same look twice before when she chased the stragglers from the Red Spades and Gatekeepers, and both times, the suspect gave the members of her task force no choice, forcing them to take the shot. This would not end well unless cooler heads prevailed.

The screams quieted, but the sound of shoes pounding against the pavement continued.

The smell of fear hung in the air.

Lexi stepped forward, raising her weapon toward the sky to show she didn't pose an immediate threat. "I know you're scared, but there's no escaping. You're surrounded." She placed her gun in her waistband at the small of her back and raised her head high with her hands splayed open to show she couldn't shoot him. "Whoever put you up to this set you up. They designed this robbery to fail. Think about it. The bank is two blocks from a police station. You're being used." Lexi paused when the man furrowed his brow, scanning left and right. Sweat formed on his forehead and stuck to the horizontal creases. The pressure was getting to him.

The man's thumb, the one hovering over the screen, rose straight up. The motion told Lexi the phone was the trigger, and she'd gotten through to him. That he wasn't as willing to go through with a crime in which he was the patsy. A little more pressure might give him the push she needed.

"There's no escape, but there is a way to get out of this alive. It starts by putting your gun down, dropping the phone, and letting the woman go."

"I want a deal." He pressed the gun harder against the woman's head. Her body quaked to breathy whimpers.

"If you give us the person pulling the strings, I guarantee you a deal." Lexi saw the man's chest heave. He was undoubtedly weighing his crappy options. "Can you disarm the timer on the vest? If you stop it now, I'll have these officers stand down."

"I don't know how." The man's jaw muscles rippled. His anger was verging on outrage. "It will go off no matter what I do."

"I can take care of that," Lexi said. "I disarm bombs for a living. No one has died, and if you give up, you won't either."

"All right." The man let out a deep breath and relaxed his hold on the woman enough for her to wiggle from his grasp and move toward Lexi. Before she took a single stride, a shot rang out, and blood spatter covered her cheek. The man's face turned blank, and he tumbled limply to the ground.

Shouts and screams filled the air again.

Panic filled the woman's eyes.

Lexi collected the man's phone, swung an arm around the woman's back and ushered her toward the closest police vehicle. Shoving her inside the driver's seat, she shut the door and ordered, "Stay here."

Lexi secured the trigger in her belly band, spun on her heel, and pressed her mic. "Who took the shot?"

"Unknown," Davis said. "All units, sound off and report on firing."

"Romeo three-six, negative."

"Lincoln two-eight, negative."

One unit after another chirped over the air, each reporting that they had not taken the shot. Lexi concluded the robber wasn't working alone or whoever was pulling the strings had sent someone as cleanup. But the mess outside was the least of Lexi's worries. A ticking bomb was still inside the bank, along with the manager and nine other innocent people.

7

Jan Hopkins entered the restricted area of the department's parking lot and pulled into his designated spot. The radio squawked more about the Penn Valley bank robbery in progress. Every unit in the western part of the county had deployed there to handle the hostage standoff and bomber. Activity at the scene had been at a standstill for hours until an ATF explosives expert arrived. He had listened to the chatter and griping about expanding the cordon while in the drive-thru, and now, he heard something about shots fired. It was the most action their county had seen since last summer's wildfires, but Jan had to arrange for a Florida deputy to notify a father that his son had died in a traffic accident. His only solace was in a gut feeling—this "accident" was really a homicide.

He exited the car while balancing the drink tray in his left hand and closed the cruiser door with a healthy knee shove. After reaching the door, Jan stuffed the top of the bag of street tacos, chips, and salsa between his teeth like a dog with a chew toy, entered the code into the access panel, and pushed open the back door. Before he turned to go down the corridor, someone snorted.

Jan came eye to eye with the person he liked the least in the entire department. Hell, the whole county. Mark Reyno walked around this place like his crap didn't stink after rescuing a toddler from a rollover accident six months ago. The God complex he'd developed was tiresome and had moved on to loathsome when Micha showed up at the department Christmas party on his arm. Thankfully, it took her three dates to realize her gross lapse in judgment and kick him to the curb.

"Most people don't eat the bag, Hopkins," Reyno said with an annoying smirk.

Jan opened his mouth, dropping the bag into his right hand. "Micha tells me I'm unlike anyone she's met. Thanks for the affirmation, buddy." Jan strutted past without looking back, not bothering to hide his Cheshire cat-like smile.

He pushed open the lab door with his butt and backed in. Locking eyes with the cutest thing in a lab coat and latex gloves, he held up the bag. "I brought your favorite."

"You seem happy. Win the lottery?"

"The day you agreed to have drinks with me was like winning Powerball." Jan distributed the drinks and laid out the tacos and chips on her desk, waiting for Micha to bring up the test results. He'd seen her feisty side when another detective impatiently hovered outside her door for the results of a ballistics test. It was a lesson learned without being in the line of fire.

"Thank you on both counts. I'm starved." Micha removed her gloves and joined Jan at the desk. "Have you heard anything new about the bank scene in Penn Valley?"

"Just what was over the radio. It sounded like things were heating up."

They ate in silence for several minutes until Micha snickered.

"What's so funny?" Jan asked.

"Your patience is impressive."

"You're worth the wait." He winked, letting the compliments linger between them.

"Most people would have asked by now."

"I'm not like most people." He let his stare smolder, or at least he hoped it was, and not fizzling.

"No, you're not." A beep sounded on Micha's workstation, but she kept her stare fixed on him for a few beats before pushing her chair back to stand. "That sound means your results are in."

"That's nice."

"No need to play coy now. You've already earned your callback." Micha said with a dampened smile, but the effort failed to mask her glowing approval. She went to her lab table and jiggled the computer mouse, bringing the screen to life.

Jan walked up behind her, unable to make sense of the graphs and words on the display. He knew how to calculate slope, drag factor, the radius of a curve, velocity, and the critical speed of a curve for his investigations, but whatever was written on Micha's screen was as unreadable as Sanskrit.

"What did you find out?" he asked.

"Both pieces are made of magnesium alloy, but the larger one has traces of graphene."

"What is that?"

"It's the lightest, strongest material on earth," she said. "When used in batteries, it greatly improves performance and lifespan."

"Is it commonly used?"

"Not at all," she said. "It's new technology and is insanely expensive to implement. You'll see it in experimental designs."

"Like what?"

"High-end medical and military applications, mostly."

"Interesting." Jan's theory of something nefarious at play suddenly got legs. The victim was a senior aid to Nevada Senator Keith Jackson, head of the Senate Armed Services Committee, another military connection. "Anything else?"

"The larger piece had some traces of organic material."

"Human?"

"Avian." Micha focused more intently on her screen. "The DNA matches the common raven."

"Even more interesting. Why would a raven be inside a car? It's not like people keep them as pets."

"That's a question for an investigator, so go investigate." She playfully shooed him back.

"Yes, ma'am." Jan saluted smartly before exiting the lab, confident this thing brewing between him and Micha might have a chance of turning into something tangible.

With the autopsy still a few days away, Jan returned to his office, curious about the tidbits Micha had discovered. Details swirled in his head while he flipped through pictures of the vehicle and crash site—politically connected, military technology, and raven's DNA. He switched to the Tesla's footage one minute before the crash, reviewing the files from all eight cameras, and neither angle offered a clue as to what caused Darryl Yarborough to swerve.

"What did you see, Darryl?" Jan fixated on the raven DNA, wondering if a bird had flown into the car and created enough havoc to make the driver panic. But he ruled out the option, remembering all the vehicle windows were up when he and Chet had arrived on the scene.

Without an obvious explanation, Jan began his search for answers by logging into the FBI's National Data Exchange. During Jan's five-year stint in property crimes, this database was his bread-and-butter source of information in solving a string of burglaries spanning four counties in two states. Maybe N-DEx could be the game changer again.

Toggling to the search panel, he entered the term raven and filtered by lab results, hoping to find other investigations where detectives or agents might have stumbled across the particular DNA. Eighteen results populated the screen, and the words raven, raven DNA, and raven feather were highlighted throughout the page.

He clicked on the first line for raven DNA, brought up the associated case file, and focused on the summary line—Terrorist Attack in Las Vegas. Checking the date, he was sure the event was the attempted dirty bomb at the Bellagio. The Vegas incident was the closest the country had come to experiencing another 9/11-style attack and had captured the nation's interest for weeks.

Jan clicked on the other cases from the search results. Some were weapons cases, and others had to do with explosives, but they all had one thing in common—they all belonged to the ATF. Most listed the contact number of Special Agent Nathan Croft as the investigating officer, but all noted an ATF intelligence officer as the person to contact for more information. He jotted down the intel officer's phone number and dialed. His gut told him this person could provide him with answers.

The call connected. "Intelligence. This is Agent Shaw."

"Agent Shaw, this is Detective Jan Hopkins of the Nevada County Sheriff's Department in California. You're listed as a point of contact on several N-DEx cases involving raven DNA."

"Yes, I am." Her voice sounded guarded.

"I was investigating a fatal traffic accident and stumbled across the same DNA on some metal fragments inside the vehicle. I hoped you could shed a little light on the topic."

"Where and when was the accident?" she asked.

"Last night in the Tahoe National Forest."

"What can you tell me about the accident?"

"It was a one-car accident with no apparent cause, so I started digging. The metal fragments I found under the driver's seat didn't appear native to the car, so I had our lab run them. Funny thing. Our scientist said the metal is some new high-tech alloy not available commercially. She said it's only found in advanced medical and military applications."

"Tell me about the victim," Shaw said.

Jan provided Yarborough's name and his connection to Senator Jackson and asked, "How is this connected to the Las Vegas terror attack?"

"We're tracking the bomb builder," Shaw said. "You may have stumbled across a piece of his work. I'll need you to preserve the evidence until I can get ATF Agent Lexi Mills out there."

"Lexi Mills? Then this *is* tied to the dirty bomber." Jan had heard only the last name of the ATF agent who had been called out to the bank robbery scene at the other end of the county but had been too distracted with his own case to make the Vegas connection until now.

"It's a distinct possibility," Shaw said.

Jan finished the call and leaned back in his chair with his hands behind his head, fingers laced together, thinking his instinct was spot on. Darryl Yarborough was murdered. And the prospect of unearthing a case Lexi Mills might be interested in had him dancing inside. It wasn't every day he got to work with a law enforcement legend. "Eat your heart out, Mark Reyno."

8

Who the hell was their regular bomb tech? The Jolly Green Giant? Lexi thought after Sergeant Davis helped her with the borrowed blast suit trousers. The small suits issued through the ATF were a tad long on her, and she'd become accustomed to the pants bunching between the knees and ankles, but this pair was ridiculously long. They would cause a tripping hazard if she didn't jury-rig them.

"Do you have a roll of duct tape?" Lexi had no doubt the tape would hold. She remembered Crew Chief Gavin's advice on fixing a car quickly to get it back in the race. *"If something is moving that's supposed to be still, duct tape the bugger. It won't come off until we rip her off."* Her primary concern was the suit's bulkiness. The extra six inches of Nomex and Kevlar in the pant legs and sleeves would slow her down, but given the urgency, this was her only available solution. The clock timer was still ticking on the bomb inside the bank.

"Coming right up." Davis opened a metal tool chest and rummaged through one of the four drawers at breakneck speed.

Lexi drifted her stare to the parking lot at the outer cordon. The EMTs who waited nearby during the standoff had rushed to the triggerman's side minutes earlier as he lay on the ground, but their lifesaving measures proved fruitless. Whoever took the headshot was an excellent sharpshooter and had hit the man in the left temple.

"Got it." Davis popped his head up, holding a partially used roll.

With no time to waste, Lexi instructed, "Tape the bottom of each pant leg to bunch them above my ankles so I won't trip. Do the same with the jacket sleeves after I put it on."

"Got it," Davis repeated, rushing his words.

They quickly worked together to help Lexi don the rest of the suit, taped up the protective material around her arms and legs, and slipped the tools Lexi would need into the sleeve and chest pockets. She switched her helmet comms to Tac 2, knowing she wouldn't be in radio contact with Davis until she turned off the signal jammer once she was done. If she were lucky, the surveillance cameras inside the bank were hardwired, and Davis could see what she was doing. In turn, she could talk to him through the microphone.

"Is there anything else you need, Agent Mills?" Davis sounded professional, but his eyes didn't lie. Their extra-roundness and the deep crease between them said he was worried for her.

"I have everything I need, Sergeant Davis," Lexi said, holding up a battery-powered angle grinder in her left hand. "After sending out the hostages, I'll work on the explosive." Lexi patted him on the upper arm and offered him a confident smile before flipping down her protective helmet visor. But she was anything but self-assured. Her suit was two-sizes too big and fifteen pounds heavier than what she was used to, she didn't have her regular tools, and Davis was the only one spotting for her.

The odds were against Lexi, but she remembered the last time she had visited Northern California. Tony Belcher had ensnarled her in an elaborate trap of revenge to extract his brother from prison, and he'd led her from one bomb site to another without her having the benefit of protective gear. She'd come close to death, escaping Belcher's clutches only because her partner, Noah Black, had her back. Lexi had to trust Davis would do the same.

Lexi turned heavily on her prosthetic foot and flipped on the switch to the internal helmet demister. The low mechanical hum would keep her company during the long walk to the explosive. After seeing the deputies deposit the signal jammer at the front door, she was confident a straight path was safe but pivoted her eyes left and right to scan for tripwires and proximity devices. She took long strides to build momentum in the bulky suit and to not appear like a waddling duck to the onlookers.

Before passing two cars parked near the entrance, she glanced inside them, checking for wires and flashing lights but saw nothing that might tell her whether a device was inside either vehicle. She continued to the double glass doors where the jammer was sitting. The three green lights on the front panel showed the machine was working and blocking an array of radio frequencies, hopefully including the correct one if a second trigger person was nearby.

Lexi fixed her stare at the doors, inspecting them for similar signs of a trigger or explosive device. Once satisfied they were safe, she opened the right door and stepped over the threshold. Her surroundings dimmed a fraction as the sunlight filtered through the glass and partially drawn window blinds.

From the video feeds earlier, Lexi had seen the hostages huddled in a corner near a desk. She glanced there. Their hands were bound with zip ties, but their feet were not—an excellent starting point. Before clearing the building, Lexi needed to reassure the manager that the conditions outside were under control. The man was still in his chair at the front of the teller's counter, bouncing his knee wildly up and down and producing enough energy to power the entire town. The glistening sheen on his face suggested he'd been sweating for hours and was dehydrated.

She flipped up her face shield so he could hear her clearly. "Hi, Mr. Drake. I'm Lexi Mills of the ATF. I'm here to get everyone out of here. We found and neutralized the man with the remote trigger, so I'm only concerned about the timer on the device right now. There is no threat if the hostages leave. Do you understand?"

"Yes. Please get them out. I never wanted to hurt them." Drake's voice was brittle and rushed, a sign he was on edge and in danger of panicking.

Lexi turned toward the hostages. She spotted an elderly woman who appeared frail. A man in his twenties was sitting next to her. "Young man, I'll need you to help the woman next to you out the front door. The rest of you wait until I tell you it's safe." The last thing she wanted was a stampede.

When the man and woman were past the glass doors and officers in tactical uniforms had ushered them away, Lexi pointed to one person at a time and said, "Go" in intervals to avoid the hostages getting hurt clogging the exit.

Only two were left, Lexi and the nervous manager. She went to him, plodding in her oversized blast suit with the pant legs rubbing together and creating a rhythmic swoosh. "Let's see about this crazy vest of yours." She placed the grinder on the floor and lowered her face shield, noting twenty-four minutes remained on the timer. She visually traced a wire from the timer attached to the shoulder strap at his left pectoral muscle. It led to a metal box attached to the other strap on the right. Both were directly above three pipe bombs slipped into utility pouches of each vest flap. Wires from each pipe ran to the black box on the right breast strap.

"Not to be pushy, but would you mind hurrying up?" His harried tone punctuated his impatience.

"We have plenty of time, Mr. Drake. I've done this a hundred times." Lexi locked eyes with him, giving him a playful wink before continuing her inspection. She deduced the box was the power source and retrieved a screwdriver from a sleeve pocket.

"This is no time to flirt, young lady," Drake said, forcing a laugh.

"If you won't tell my wife, I won't either." Lexi's fingertips didn't reach the end of the fingers in the oversized fragmentation gloves paired with Lexi's borrowed suit, making her grip on the screwdriver too clumsy. She stepped back, removed the gloves, and stuffed them into a cargo pocket on her right trouser leg.

Returning to her task of getting the cover off the power source box, she gripped the tool much tighter. She easily slipped the screwdriver tip into the slot of the first screw. After she'd removed the fourth and stowed it in the jacket's loose belly pouch with the other screws, Lexi carefully lifted the lid, exposing a collection of meticulously placed wires. The designer had painstakingly straightened and pulled them taut without a millimeter of slack, tacking them down to the circuit board. This was, without a doubt, the work of a professional bomb maker, not a basement amateur.

Two nine-volt batteries and a circuit board were inside. At first blush, the configuration suggested a simple series circuit with the second battery acting as a backup power supply to extend the life of the device. But she asked herself why the bomber set the timer for only a few hours. The type of battery used had a much longer lifespan.

Lexi examined the wires and circuit board more closely and discovered an alarming addition. A well-camouflaged wire leading from the secondary battery to the circuit board she didn't expect to find suggested it wasn't a backup but a second primary power source. Its presence explained the use of resistors to control power flow to the bombs. She couldn't be sure without tracing each connection with a magnifying glass, but her gut told her if she cut one power source, the other would send a charge and detonate the device. Consequently, she had to cut all three wires to both batteries simultaneously.

Most explosives she'd come across in the field were the mark of an amateur, essentially pieced together with wires and duct tape. The bomb makers employed by the Gatekeepers were a step up in sophistication with the material and triggers, but this was as intricate, if not more so, as the dirty bomb she'd defused in Las Vegas. Any doubt about this being the Raven's handiwork flew out the window.

Lexi pulled out two pairs of wire snips from her left sleeve pouch and used one to snap off the cinches mounting the camouflaged wire to the circuit board to give it some play. She moved on to the primary wires leading to both batteries, removing the mounting brackets until all three wires had enough give to wrap the snips around them.

"Okay, Mr. Drake. I have to cut a few wires, so I need you to remain very still. Can you do that for me?"

He clutched the sides of the chair seat with both hands, holding on for dear life. His spine went stiff, but his breathing became labored, moving the circuit box attached to the vest strap on his chest up and down substantially.

Lexi held a pair of snips in each hand. "I'll need you to hold your breath on the count of three and not release it until I tell you it's safe." Lexi left out the part that if she'd guessed wrong about the power supply, neither of them would be alive for him to take another breath.

She positioned the tool in her left hand around the wire to the primary battery before scooping up both wires from the secondary battery with the other snips in her right. To steady herself, she closed her eyes and took three calming breaths. When she opened them on the third exhale, she discovered her hands hadn't moved.

"Ready, Mr. Drake?"

He nodded like a nervous child, heaving his chest harder.

"On three, hold your breath and be absolutely still." Her heart increased its pace. Lexi knew the blast suit wouldn't protect her this close to the explosion if she'd guessed wrong about the wires.

He nodded again.

"One." She thought of her mother, wondering if she would see her in the afterlife or if all those Sunday school lessons were a big lie.

"Two." Lexi imagined her mom in the Ponder house kitchen, pulling out a freshly baked pie from the oven and turning on a heel to greet her with a smile. For a split second, she swore she smelled apples inside her helmet and thought, *I love you, Mom.*

"Three." She waited for the power box to settle on Drake's chest, confirmed both snips were still in the proper position, and mouthed, *I love you, Nita*, before squeezing both hands firmly and rapidly with one audible snap.

As Lexi released a breathy exhale, she focused on the timer box attached to the other flap of Drake's vest. The glowing red numbers were gone, and the display screen was blank. She'd neutralized the immediate threat, but they weren't out of danger yet. "Breathe but stay still, Mr. Drake. We're doing good so far."

"So far? Jesus. I thought we were done." He slouched.

"Be still." Lexi's order came out sharp. If the two ends of the cut wires touched, the spark could be enough to blow them to bits. "I have to do a little more cleanup before I can cut the padlock off the metal waistband."

After taping off the six ends of the wires, Lexi rested a little easier while snipping the cables leading to the timer and device at the back of Drake's collar. Her initial assessment was correct. It was an RF receiver, and she estimated it had about a five-hundred-yard range. Lexi then carefully removed the blasting caps from the six pipe bombs, placing each in a canvas satchel she'd brought inside. After stowing the bag between two desks to not block their path of egress, she marked it with a red flag for the disposal team and returned to the bank manager.

"All right, Mr. Drake. Let's get this thing off." Lexi scanned the room, looking for a jacket, spotting one slung over the back of a desk chair. She grabbed it and draped it over Drake's head, covering his neck and much of his arms, while explaining, "Sparks will fly when I cut off this padlock."

"Burn scars might be an improvement on this mug," he said, his voice muffled.

Lexi put on her oversized gloves and retrieved vise grips from a cargo pocket and the angle grinder from the floor. Next, she extended the padlock as far as possible using the grips and placed the grinder's blade close to the lock's shank. "I'd appreciate you being still again. Otherwise, this thing might slip and give you a messy appendectomy."

Drake moved his head up and down. "Let's not do that."

"Easy peasy," Lexi said before pressing the power button. The grinder whirred. Once she eased the spinning blade against the metal, glowing orange sparks flew like fireworks. The buzzing grew louder. The grinder jerked when she'd cut through to the other side of the shank. Lexi released the power button, pulled back, and shimmied the lock through the guide holes holding the waistband in place.

After placing her tools down, she removed the coat from Drake's head. "Ready to take this thing off?"

"Hours ago." He forced a chuckle and wiped a ton of sweat from his forehead.

"This is still dangerous, so I need you to do exactly as I say." After his affirming nod, Lexi had him stand and extend his right arm slightly to his side. Next, she clutched the right side of the vest, eased his arm out of it, and repeated the process for the left side until she held it in her hands. After placing the vest gently on the floor, she stared into the security camera mounted near the ceiling on a nearby wall, gave a thumbs up, and shouted, "Schmidt. Davis. I'm sending out the manager."

"Good work, Agent Mills," a male voice said through a speaker. She couldn't tell who had replied.

Turning to Drake, she said, "I need you to exit the bank but walk, don't run, and hold your hands up when you walk outside. The deputies will arrest you until they sort this out."

His shoulders slumped in palpable relief. "Thank you, Lexi Mills. You saved my life." He jogged to the door, pushed it open, and raised his hands above his head before walking outside. "Don't shoot." His voice muffled when the door closed behind him. Two officers in tactical uniforms took him by the arms and ushered him away.

Lexi returned to the vest and snipped the dangling wires from each pipe bomb. The device was now ready for the disposal team to secure it into a containment vessel for a controlled detonation, but she wanted to preserve one for lab analysis. She pulled one pipe out, hoping to find the Raven's calling card embedded inside, and placed it several yards from the vest, noting a large horse fly lying motionless on the floor. If that was an example of the size of the insects in the Sierra foothills, she'd have to cross this area off her bucket list of places she and Nita should visit.

Lexi gave the camera another thumbs up and exited the bank. She propped the door open to make access easier for the disposal team and turned off the signal jammer on her way toward the parking lot. A large fly buzzed her head from behind. She swatted at it, and it flew away.

Once clear of the standoff perimeter, Lexi removed her gloves and helmet. Several yards from Schmidt and Davis, she dropped a glove and stopped mid-stride to pick it up. A shot rang out, and a bullet whizzed above her head. She flinched, but her instincts kicked in, and she quickly returned the Kevlar helmet to her head and jogged toward the SWAT van for protection. Police officers scrambled, taking cover and pointing their weapons in every direction. The tactical radio she'd tuned to the operational channel before going into the bank squawked.

"Shooter on the grocery store roof."

"I lost him."

"The tree line behind the store."

"All perimeter units converge behind the store."

No, Lexi thought, reaching the safety of the reinforced steel van. Pulling everyone off the perimeter will expose the crime scene with an active bomb still inside. She yelled for Davis, seeing he was crouched near the van's rear, holding his service weapon at the ready. "Help me with this damn thing."

Davis sprang into action and helped Lexi remove the blast suit. While removing the heavy jacket, she asked, "Do we still have someone with eyes on the bank? The pipe bombs still pose a danger."

"Just the security feeds." He pressed his mic. "Fisher, return to position. You have a green light on anyone who penetrates the cordon." Seconds passed, and when no one responded, he said to Lexi, "It looks like we're on our own."

Unsure whether the sniper shot was a diversion, Lexi removed the trousers and drew her Glock from the back of her belly band, ready for a fight. One way or another, she would make sure no one entered the bank.

9

A thirty-minute fruitless search for the sniper made it clear. Lexi wouldn't learn who took the shot from the grocery store rooftop any time soon. The deputies returned empty-handed and took over security, saying they'd lost him in a nearby ravine. The containment vessel arrived minutes later, and the tactical team geared up to dispose of the explosives.

Lexi leaned closer to Sergeant Davis, reminding him, "Be sure your team transports one of the pipe bombs to the lab for analysis. This could be linked to a case I'm working on."

"Sure thing, Agent Mills. We've got it from here. I appreciate your help today."

"It's a good thing you asked for us. It was a tricky device to disarm."

Once Davis left to tend to the disposal, Lexi finally had a moment to process the unfolding events. Her mind shifted from who had fired at her to why. It couldn't have been to stop her from disarming the bomb, so what was the end goal?

The glaring flaws in the bank robber's plan steered Lexi to an obvious conclusion. The bomb vest was bait, and she was the target. But the shooter had plenty of opportunities to take the shot while she was outside. Why didn't they shoot when Schmidt and Davis were briefing her? Or when she was talking down the triggerman? It made little sense unless having her die in the vest explosion was the desired outcome, and the sniper shot was the emergency plan in case the bomb failed. If her supposition was correct, the Raven had her in his crosshairs and would strike again.

A sense of dread hit her. She'd learned her lesson with Tony Belcher. Striking at her could also mean targeting her family. Lexi stabbed a hand into her hoodie pocket and retrieved her cell phone. Several missed call notifications from Kaplan were at the top of the display screen. A text message from her was below. *Raven bomb link close to your location. Call ASAP.* Kaplan would have to wait. Lexi dialed, the call connecting on the second ring.

"How's it going there, Lexi?" Nita had stripped her voice of emotion, but Lexi read relief into it.

"Everyone is safe, but someone took a potshot at me after I came out of the bank. Something doesn't feel right, Nita. Kaplan left a message, saying a link to the Raven popped up nearby, and my gut tells me he might be behind this robbery attempt. I want you and Dad to stay inside the hotel suite until I figure out what's going on."

"We're on the winery tour we'd scheduled when we arrived on Sunday. The resort van won't take us back until after lunch."

"I'd forgotten about the tour." Lexi rubbed her brow, worrying how vulnerable Nita and her father were at a public venue. "Get to the manager's office and stay there. I'm at least two hours away, but I'm not sure how long I'll be. It all depends on what Kaplan says."

"Do you really think I can convince your father to stay in some stuffy office for hours? It's only a few miles back to the resort. I can arrange for a Lyft."

"No." Lexi's reply came out sharper than it should have, but she was done taking chances with the people she loved.

"There's no need to bite my head off," Nita said with an edge. "I was merely trying to help."

Lexi softened her tone. "I'm sorry, Nita. I don't want a repeat of Tony Belcher."

"None of us do." Nita sighed. "Somehow, I'll convince your dad to stay put."

"In the meantime, I'll reach out to Maxwell Keene. Maybe he can arrange for one of the Secret Service agents roaming the resort to pick you up."

"That might make Dad less grumpy."

After exchanging an "I love you," Lexi concluded the call and dialed Maxwell's number. If anyone could get an agent to the winery to safeguard her family, her friend could. The Deputy Director of the FBI had considerable pull across agencies.

"Lexi?" he answered. "I thought you were finally on your honeymoon."

"I was until my boss tracked me down to help with a bomb vest in a nearby bank robbery. Now I need your help." Lexi detailed the specifics about the sniper shot and her suspicion of who might be behind the events. "I'm hours away from the hotel and am worried the Raven will go after Nita and my father. The Secret Service advance team is at the resort, preparing for the president's arrival this Saturday."

"Say no more," Maxwell said. "I'll have the ASAC send an agent. They'll be in good hands, Lexi."

She released a long breath full of relief. "Thank you, my friend. I'll text you the addresses." Once she finished the call and forwarded the information, she sent a text to Nita, saying an agent would be there soon to pick them up. After another deep sigh, Lexi called Kaplan.

"You're a hard one to get hold of," Kaplan said. "I heard about the bank robbery. Did everything turn out okay?"

Lexi explained about the sniper and her gut feeling. "When I got your text about a possible Raven lead close by, I knew my suspicions were right. What did you find out?"

"I received a call from a California detective about raven DNA he found in some metal fragments he recovered from a deadly car crash involving Senator Keith Jackson's chief of staff. The accident site is less than fifty miles from your location. The detective mentioned the metal he found was high-tech, military-grade stuff. This sounds precisely like the work of the Raven."

"I need to tell Croft and Lange about this."

"Already covered. After I couldn't reach you, I called both. I knew you'd want to jump on this quickly. Croft is on a plane to Sacramento and should land in a few hours."

"Thanks, Kaplan. Things are developing fast here. I even have Secret Service agents picking up Nita and my father in case the Raven tries to pull a Belcher."

"Goodness, Lexi. I didn't consider your family. I'm glad they're safe."

Or soon will be, Lexi thought. Armed with the name and location of the detective, she ended the call with, "I'm heading there now," and she was more anxious than when she first feared for Nita and her father. Lexi never liked coincidences involving her job. It was no twist of fate that the county SWAT team was out of its depths to handle the bomb. Nor was it accidental that Lexi was the only ATF explosives expert in the area qualified to help. The Raven must have been pulling the strings.

Lexi sat in the Nevada County Sheriff's Department waiting room, returning her cell phone to her hoodie pocket after reading Nita's text. A Secret Service agent had picked up Nita and Lexi's father, and they were back in their hotel suite. Nita also said another agent was standing watch outside their patio and would check on them regularly. Her breathing came easier, knowing her family was safe.

She adjusted her position on the hard plastic chair, similar to the ones she remembered using in grade school. Despite their adult size, they were still as uncomfortable as the ones from her childhood and sparked the instinct to swing her feet incessantly while waiting for the recess bell to sound. They also surfaced a memory of her crush on the athlete in her sixth-grade class, unable to take her eyes off Della Duran. Lexi didn't recognize the signs of a girl crush back then and remembered attributing her infatuation to a desire to be friends. On closer reflection, it was an incredible foretelling of her magical first kiss with a girl years later and the path her life would take.

When the door to the restricted area finally opened, Lexi craned her head toward it, discovering a dark-haired man in his forties of average height and build. Most would overlook him in a crowd as appearing ordinary if not for his Hollywood dimples and square jaw. He locked his stare on Lexi, his eyes dancing with recognition and excitement. She'd seen similar reactions hundreds of times in the last year. Some, like the officer at the access control point earlier today, treated her like a celebrity, while most merely expressed their respect. Drained of patience since the reemergence of the Raven today, she hoped this man aligned with the latter crowd.

He stepped toward her, and Lexi rose to her feet. "Detective Hopkins, I presume."

He extended his hand, which she accepted. "Please call me Jan. It's a pleasure, Agent Mills. When Agent Shaw said she would be sending you, I had no idea you would arrive so quickly. I understand defusing the explosive at the bank robbery scene in Penn Valley had some unexpected excitement."

"That's an understatement." Lexi liked this man. He showed his respect and moved on to business without skipping a beat. "I'm here about the evidence you discovered with raven DNA."

"I've encountered some strange things in my career, and this one ranks right up there." Jan extended an arm toward the restricted area door. "I've asked our lab tech to brief you on her findings. Shall we?"

"Thank you," Lexi said. She followed Jan through a labyrinth of corridors, stopping at the door with a square frosted windowpane set in the upper half. The lettering on the glass read "Forensic Lab."

Jan pushed the door open, revealing a small facility the size of her living room. The equipment and space were dated but reflected the care of a meticulous scientist with its spotless and well-organized appearance.

"Special Agent Mills, I'd like you to meet our very special forensic scientist, Micha Rodriguez." The two women shook hands. "She discovered some fascinating aspects of the metal remnants I recovered from inside Yarborough's vehicle."

Both relayed their pleasure at their meeting, and Micha brought up two photos of the evidence on her workstation monitor. "The smaller piece is made of a simple magnesium alloy. The big guy, though, was full of surprises. To start, I discovered trace elements of raven DNA on the skin. If you look more closely at the piece, you can see its concave shape." Micha's hand floated delicately in an arc over the image, and her head cocked to one side as she explained. Her slow cadence and use of drawn-out words at specific points left no doubt this woman loved her job and knew her stuff.

Kaplan Shaw did the same while explaining some intricate method she'd used to find a critical piece of intel.

Micha continued, "I discovered the traces on the underbelly, suggesting whatever had contained raven DNA was inside an object made of this unique alloy."

"That makes sense," Lexi said. "The bomb maker I've been tracking uses raven feathers as his calling card. He embeds it in every device he creates." She angled her head to inspect the piece on the screen. "You said it's unique. How?"

"The larger piece is lined with graphene, the lightest and strongest material on earth," Micha said with a faint self-satisfied grin of awe.

"My intel agent said something about it being rare. What can you tell me about it?"

"Currently, it's available only in experimental medical and military devices." Micha's expression turned more serious, her eyes narrowing in concentration. "Whatever this was part of, the person who constructed it had access to some exclusive, cutting-edge technology."

"This also sounds like the bomb maker I'm tracking. You could save me hours of research by sending information on graphene. The less technical, the better? If you could toss in a little translation, I'd be grateful. Beyond chemistry related to explosives, I tend to get lost."

"Sure. I'll do my best, but I'm not sure I completely understand some of the applications under development."

"And that's saying something," Jan said with a hint of admiration mixed with pride, "because she's the smartest person I know."

"I have no doubt," Lexi said, turning to Jan. "Micha mentioned the graphene is found in some experimental military devices. I recall seeing in your case notes that the victim is Senator Jackson's chief of staff."

"I was curious, too, Agent Mills. Jackson is the ranking member of the Senate Armed Services Committee, so there's a military connection."

"When I was in your waiting room, I Googled him. He also leads the Emerging Threats and Capabilities Subcommittee, which oversees developmental weapons systems to counter future threats."

Jan appeared impressed. "I didn't dig deep into his senate assignments, but the Nevada State Police were kind enough to give me his address."

"I'll need that."

He pulled out his phone. "Can I AirDrop it to you?"

"Sure." Lexi checked her phone, confirming her Bluetooth was on.

"It's not far from here, actually."

"You did a great job uncovering this evidence, Detective, and I appreciate your skill and hard work, but I'm taking over your case." A satisfied grin formed on Jan's lips as he sent the senator's home address, a puzzling reaction. "You're taking this a lot better than I expected."

Jan shrugged. "How could I be disappointed? My fatal traffic accident investigation has turned into a murder case, and Lexi Mills is heading up the probe. The pool of available resources to tap into and the chances of solving it have increased tenfold. It doesn't get any better."

Lexi's appreciation of Jan jumped exponentially. He cared more about the case getting solved than getting credit for it.

She thought about the bank robbery scene, comparing it to the traffic accident, but couldn't see a link. Her gut, though, told her they were connected. She needed to follow up on the traffic accident if she had any hope of staying on the Raven's trail, but Nathan was still hours away. She could talk to the senator alone, but if she'd learned one thing during her time on the task force that took down the Gatekeepers and the Red Spades, it was to never go off on a case alone. Fortunately, a solution was standing in front of her.

"Maybe it could get a little better. How would you like to interview the senator with me?"

Another broad smile delivered his answer.

10

Keith Jackson closed the file on Falcon Industries' latest proposal guaranteed to revolutionize war fighting and placed it inside his wall safe. He couldn't disagree with Benjamin Foreman's assessment. His new weapons system was genius, but in the wrong hands, it could be insidious. There would be no guarding against it. As a result, no one would be safe. These locust devices could break into Fort Knox. Keith had sent his chief of staff to Foreman's mountain home last night for a private demonstration, but he had yet to report his findings.

"Where the hell are you, Darryl?"

Keith pulled out his daily pill case from his desk drawer and swallowed the concoction of heart and blood pressure medication with water, the final preparation before heading out to his guests. He fully expected a tiresome evening. Twenty-two years in politics, and he still hadn't developed a liking for fundraisers. He'd rather be hung by his fingernails than shake more hands, kiss more asses, and make more deals with devils to fill the election coffers. But his point man and best friend since his first campaign had better ideas. If not for Darryl Yarborough's ability to fan the proper flames and herd unwieldy cats, Keith would still be a congressman on the administration and ethics committees and considered the pariah of the House.

His office door swung open, and the woman who stepped inside brought a smile to his lips. She walked up to him and adjusted his tie for no reason other than doing so had been her job for the last thirty years. "Our guests are getting impatient, my love."

Their heights were complimentary, with her lips coming even with his following a gentle raise of her chin by his hand. "They can wait a moment longer." He eased her head closer, pulling her in for a tender kiss. Since the day he saw Peggy walking across UCLA's campus, he'd wanted no other lips but hers. They had magical powers, giving him strength when he felt weak and comfort when he felt lost. Despite Darryl's expert wrangling, none of his accomplishments would have come to be without this woman's love and steadfastness.

When she pulled back, her eyes narrowed in concern. "Any word on Darryl?"

"No, and I'm starting to worry. It's not like him to be out of contact for this long. I've asked Judy to check his home in Carson City."

She patted his chest like she did the time their son ran away when he was fourteen, healing his aching heart. "I'm sure it's nothing," she said. "You know how Darryl gets when he's in town. He meets a handsome young man at a casino and loses all track of time."

"He's picked one hell of a time for another fling. I wish he'd remarry and finally settle down again."

"Darryl is the type who loves deeply. It will take him some time to get over losing Timothy."

"I know," Keith sighed, recalling the agony in his friend's voice over the phone after his husband had passed from COVID. It was a pain he hoped to never experience. Wanting to die before his wife was a coward's wish, but Peggy was better equipped to move on. She hadn't alienated their children by being absent for most of their adolescence and would have them to lean on to get through her grief. Keith would have no one, only his dear friend.

"Then let's mingle and get you on track for reelection."

Keith stepped into the hallway with his wife on his arm, and for the next hour, he shook hands and kissed the asses of every deep pocket in the great room. He even made a deal to introduce a man to the leader of the Senate in exchange for a sizeable contribution. Keith had learned an important lesson a long time ago. Politics revolved around two things—money and alliances. Darryl had made him better at building both.

While half-listening to the latest pitch for congressional support, he spied Peggy from across the room. His assistant, Judy, had arrived moments earlier and had asked for his attention, but he'd asked her to wait until he'd finished his conversation. In other words, wait until he'd reeled in another sizeable donation. She'd stepped away, presumably to find his wife. Judy clutched Peggy by both upper arms and said something, causing Peggy to throw a hand over her mouth and wobble at the knees.

"Excuse me, Michael." Keith couldn't rip his stare from his wife and rushed toward her when Judy reached out to steady her. He braced her by the elbow, noting her face had turned pale. "Peggy? What's wrong?" Her only response was an audible sob. He turned to Judy. "What happened?"

"Let's go into your study, Senator," Judy said, sadness filling her voice.

Keith led Peggy down the hallway with Judy supporting her by the other arm. Her sobs had quieted some at the door but hadn't relented. He ushered her inside, sat her in his leather easy chair, and poured her a glass of water from the wet bar. "This should help."

Peggy gripped the glass with both hands and took two sips but still looked thrown for a giant loop. Whatever news Judy had passed along, his wife's visceral reaction to it had Keith on edge. He sat on the edge of the coffee table in front of the chair and leaned closer to her. "What's happened, dear?"

Judy stood nearby but remained quiet.

Peggy met his gaze, tears rolling down her cheeks. "It's Darryl," she croaked. "He's been killed."

Every muscle fell limp. Keith went numb, processing what Peggy had said. His best friend was dead. But she'd said killed, meaning he didn't die from some medical issue. Something awful must have happened.

His mind stopped spinning long enough to ask. "How? When?"

Judy placed a hand on his back. "It was a car accident last night in California about sixty miles from here. He swerved and went off the road. The police are calling it suspicious."

"Suspicious?" Keith struggled to wrap his head around the idea that someone wanted to kill his dear friend. "What do they think happened?"

"The deputy I spoke to wouldn't say," Judy said, "but he gave me the name and number of the detective investigating the accident."

"Thank you. Can you give my apologies to our guests and tell them I won't return to the night's festivities?"

"Of course, Senator."

"Have the staff escort them out and send everyone home. Ask the caterer to return tomorrow for cleanup."

"Yes, sir." Judy quietly exited, closing the door behind her.

The crushing silence in the room made him feel empty. Darryl should have been there, sharing a celebratory scotch over the number of campaign donations he'd secured. Should have been there to laugh over a man's toupee that had gone askew when he'd bent to pick up a dropped napkin. To give Keith a stern private lecture about not placing sentiment over political reality. It finally sunk in. His friend was gone.

Peggy rose from the chair, wrapped her arms around his neck, and whimpered, "He was too young."

"Yes, he was." Keith squeezed her tighter. "I'm sure his father has been notified as next of kin, but I need to call him."

"It's late in Florida." She pulled back. "No one wants to have this sort of conversation late at night."

"You're right." Keith imagined how Darryl's father had taken the news of his youngest child's death. He thought of how he might react if faced with his own son's death and was sure it would destroy him. Reopening the wound should wait until the light of day.

"I can't believe he's gone." Peggy sniffled, wiping the tears from her eyes with a fingertip.

"This will take some time to fully sink in."

"You look pale." Peggy placed a hand on his chest over his heart. "Did you take your A-Fib medicine? I'm worried about your pacemaker acting up again."

"Yes, I took it right before you dragged me out to greet our guests."

A knock sounded, feeling like an intrusion in his vulnerable state. The door slowly opened, and Judy stuck her head inside. "I'm sorry to interrupt, Senator. The guests and staff have all left, but an ATF agent and the detective investigating Mr. Yarborough's accident are here to see you. They said they had some questions."

"ATF? Why in the world would they be involved?" he asked. Judy fidgeted at his rhetorical question. She was new to his staff and wasn't accustomed to his thinking out loud. Before she opened her mouth, he said. "I guess they'll tell me. Please send them in."

The long stream of well-dressed men and women gathering their coats and exiting Senator Jackson's mountain estate had finally ended. Half-filled cocktail glasses and plates partially filled with finger food littered every tabletop in the rustic great room. Whatever party had been going on had stopped abruptly.

Lexi waited with Detective Jan Hopkins at the room's wall of glass leading to the deck and took in the magnificent view. The moon was out and extra bright tonight. Its reflection glistened off the gentle surface ripples of Lake Tahoe, and its beams backlit majestic ponderosa pine trees ringing the rocky shoreline. She wasn't familiar with Nevada real estate but knew enough to realize this was an exclusive lakefront property valued in the eight figures. Typically, much power accompanied that amount of money.

Lexi whispered to Jan, "What can you tell me about the senator?"

"He's a military hawk and well-liked by the voters."

"Good to know." If Jackson's senate seat was safe, he was a mover and shaker in DC who could have ties to the Raven. Lexi would have to construct her questions carefully to not reveal her suspicions.

The woman who had greeted her and Jan at the door returned, her image reflecting on the glass door. "The senator is anxious to see you. Please follow me." She led them down a hallway decorated with canvas paintings. If Lexi had to guess, they were originals and worth quite a bit.

The woman opened a door and invited Lexi and Jan to enter. Lexi recognized the man as Senator Jackson from the pictures she'd seen of him during her internet search. He was comforting a woman in a leather chair but stood when she and Jan stepped farther into the room, revealing his tall height. She expected a confident presence, but he met her gaze with an element of sadness while extending his hand.

"Thank you for coming. I'm Keith Jackson. This is my wife, Peggy. We just learned of Darryl's death."

Lexi acknowledged the woman with a polite nod. Her eyes were puffy, and their rims were red, signs she'd been crying. Jackson's pale complexion suggested he was shaken as well. "It's a pleasure, Senator. I'm Lexi Mills of the ATF. This is Detective Jan Hopkins of the Nevada County Sheriff's Department in California. I apologize for the interruption, but we have questions about Mr. Yarborough's accident."

"Mills?" Jackson raised his brows in faint recognition while releasing his grip on Lexi's hand. "From Spicewood and Task Force Zero Impact? If you're interested in this case, it must be serious."

"Yes, sir. It is. Detective Hopkins discovered some trace evidence that piqued my curiosity. Can you tell us why Mr. Yarborough was on that road last night?"

"I'd sent him to meet with Benjamin Foreman, the president of Falcon Industries, at his mountain home."

"What was the meeting about?"

"The topic is classified, but I can tell you it had to do with a project Foreman is trying to get Congressional approval for."

"What kind of project?"

"The specifics are also classified, but it's no secret that Falcon Industries researches and develops new technology with military applications."

Like graphene, Lexi thought. She was on the right track.

"The car Mr. Yarborough was driving is registered to your nonprofit campaign organization," Jan said. "Was it a fleet vehicle or assigned to him personally?"

"The Tesla was his whenever we were home."

"Do you know where he kept it?"

"When he wasn't here, I presume he stored it at his home in Carson City," the senator said.

"Did he live alone?" Jan asked.

"Yes, since his husband died early last year."

"I'm sorry to hear that. When did you last see Mr. Yarborough? How did he seem?"

"Sunday evening in DC. He flew to Reno the next morning for his meeting with Mr. Foreman. He was fine. Nothing flustered that man. I swear he could juggle china plates in a windstorm blindfolded. The only time I saw him agitated was when he accidentally ate an appetizer with shellfish. He had a mild allergy and had to pop a Benadryl."

"Thank you, Senator. You've been a big help," Lexi said. "Can you tell us where last night's meeting took place and how to contact Mr. Foreman?"

Jackson went to his desk, retrieved a tablet from the tabletop, and thumbed the screen alive. He showed it to Lexi with the calendar app open to yesterday's date. The seven p.m. appointment was labeled "Private Demo." *Demo of what?* she thought. An address was listed in the details section. She jotted it down in a memo on her phone.

"I've been there," the senator said. "His compound is more secure than the White House. And Foreman is a bit of a recluse. There's no way in hell you're getting in to see him without an appointment. Let me see if I can line up something for tomorrow."

He returned to his desk, fished a cell phone from the top drawer, and dialed. "This is Senator Keith Jackson. I need you to get a message to Benjamin. My chief of staff was killed in a car accident after leaving his compound last night, and the police have some questions...Yes, I'll wait... Thank you. Tomorrow at nine will be fine. They'll be there."

Once Jackson finished the call, he turned to Lexi and Jan. "I want you to get to the bottom of this, Agent Mills. Darryl was a very dear friend. If someone else is to blame for his death, they need to pay." He jotted down something on a pad of paper and handed it to Lexi. "Call me on my personal number if I can be of more help."

Lexi left with more questions swirling in her head than when she'd arrived. The senator seemed close—too close—to Benjamin Foreman to not think he was hiding behind the cloak of classified material to avoid being forthright.

She hopped into her rental. Jan slipped into the passenger seat, shutting the door with extra zest. "He was holding back," he said.

Lexi twisted the leather wrap on the steering wheel. "The important question is why."

11

Today's events at the bank didn't turn out as Robert Segura had planned, but he didn't regret defending his mentor. After stepping off the elevator and dragging his suitcase down the hotel corridor, he whispered, "You're so stubborn, Starshiy." His brother, as he liked to think of his old friend, had been the cautious one since their orphanage days, always waiting for the right moment to present itself before exacting his revenge. Starshiy would call it being patient, but Robert lacked his brother's most refined attribute when family was involved.

He stepped to his room door and held his keycard over the electronic reader until the lock clicked. After a twist of the handle, he pushed through, leading with a shoulder. He stopped, sensing danger. The hairs on the back of his neck tingled. The hallway light was on, but he remembered turning it off when he'd left that morning. He'd declined maid service at check-in, so something else had to be at play.

There were noises, so he listened, discerning Chopin playing from somewhere in the suite. Every tense muscle relaxed simultaneously while a grin formed on his lips. No intruder would play Nocturne Opus 9 Number 2 during a break-in. But his grin dropped quickly, considering who must have been waiting for him. His unannounced arrival could not have been good.

Robert left his suitcase near the door and went farther inside, discovering his mentor sitting on the couch with a cocktail glass in his hand while staring into the flames dancing in the gas fireplace.

"Interesting choice of hotel, Robert. Napa is quite beautiful in the winter."

"Starshiy, this is a pleasant surprise. Do you have more work for me?"

"We've known each other too long for you to play innocent with me, Robert." His voice was lighthearted, but Starshiy kept his stare on the swaying orange flames, which was troubling. He always greeted Robert eye to eye. "Benjamin told me what you've been up to." The glass he was holding suddenly shattered in his hand.

Robert rushed closer, seeing blood dripping from his mentor's hand. He dashed to the bathroom, retrieved two small towels, and hurried back. "Let me see." After laying one towel on the couch arm, he dabbed away the blood on Starshiy's hand until he discovered two cuts. They appeared small enough to close with proper pressure for several minutes, so Robert wrapped the clean towel around the hand and tied it tightly. "Your temper will get the best of you one day, Starshiy."

"You've been saying the same thing since I was twelve. It hasn't bested me in the last thirty-three years, and I doubt it ever will."

Robert raised the injured hand and rested it on Starshiy's chest so it was above his heart. "You need to keep it here for twenty minutes."

"How many times did you nurse my wounds growing up?" Starshiy asked. "I think I remember how to tend to a cut."

"Too many times, but I appreciated every time you defended me. You saved me from countless beatings at the hands of the other boys."

Robert recalled the first time they'd passed in the corridor on his first day in the orphanage. Starshiy had rubbed his stringy mop and said, "*Don't worry, little man. I have your back.*" Robert was only seven years old then, but his pretty face was like a magnet to the delinquent clique. He'd thought those ruffians had intended a beating when they'd cornered him in the bathroom, but the oldest boy in the orphanage knew better. They'd wanted to initiate him in the worst possible way. Thankfully, Starshiy intervened, sending two of them to the infirmary but not before cutting his knuckles on a mirror over a sink. Blood had covered Starshiy's hand, but Robert remained calm and tended his wounds with a towel much like the one he'd used tonight. And from that day, Starshiy was Robert's protector, rescuing him from several beating attempts. Many new arrivals had tried to knock Starshiy from the top of the pecking order until he aged out, but none succeeded.

"What were you thinking today, brother?" Starshiy's voice was tight with tension. "I told you Lexi Mills could wait until the time was right."

Robert looked sheepishly into Starshiy's eyes. Without his Raven persona red contact lenses in them, he expected to see anger behind those soft blue pools but saw something far more devastating. He saw disappointment.

Since the day Starshiy returned to the orphanage a week after his transition out and scurried him through a dormitory window in the middle of the night, Robert had sworn to never disappoint him. He'd housed, clothed, and fed him by stealing. He'd entered the criminal underworld for a bigger payout to put Robert through MIT. "*Every bad thing I've done, I did to see you walk across that stage,*" Starshiy had said the day Robert graduated with honors.

"I was thinking it was time to repay you for all the times you protected me." The back of Robert's throat thickened with love and respect, not fear. He could never fear the man who had raised him. Only five years separated them in age, but he had become a father to him.

"We are family, Robert. We don't keep score. Besides, you have repaid me many times over with your expertise."

"It's not the same, and you know it," Robert said. "Lexi Mills is responsible for killing two of your best men. One was an orphanage brother. She must die."

"And she will, but your shenanigans today have upset a very dangerous client. If he takes out his anger on you, I'm not sure I can protect you."

The characterization of Robert's act of devotion took him aback. "My plan wasn't child's play, Starshiy." His reply was sharp, possibly too much, so he softened his tone. "I lured Lexi Mills into the perfect trap. I chose a location with an underqualified bomb squad and ensured the local ATF explosives team was already deployed. It was genius how I got her there."

"That piece of the plan was solid, and I'm sure you designed a superb product, but Mills is a formidable opponent, which is why I told you to wait. Now, she'll be more alert and harder to snare."

"But she was so close."

"She'll be even closer once she returns. Less than a hundred yards if my intel is correct. This is too close, Robert. She saw your face today. You need to be more careful."

"I will, but I won't have access to Foreman's surveillance web for much longer. We should leverage the tools while we still can."

"I've taken care of it. We've tapped into your backdoor. Patience, Robert. Will Foreman still need you for demonstrations?"

"Perhaps. He's asked me to remain available if he encounters trouble with congressional approval."

"Good. Lexi Mills can wait. When she lets her guard down, we'll strike. In the meantime, let me take you to dinner at the hotel restaurant before she gets back."

12

What kind of fancy hotel doesn't have a single racing channel? Jerry thought, mashing the up button for the zillionth time, searching for something worth watching. He found it mindboggling how mining for gold in Alaska, remodeling a hurricane-damaged Florida bungalow, and waiting to see which suitor received the last rose passed for entertainment.

But maybe this would, Jerry thought. He recognized the movie by a single image. Steve McQueen started the engine of a beautiful 1970 Porsche 917 with a distinctive light blue and orange finish. The scene bounced from one cockpit to another while the drivers sweated the next tick of the Dutray clock at the Le Mans starting line.

Jerry rested his feet on the coffee table, ready to settle in for a half-hour of top-notch cinematic racing. A slick track, revving engines, and glory-hungry drivers should be a decent distraction until Nita finished her shower, and they could decide on dinner.

The starting flag dropped on the screen, and one of the most dramatic race scenes in movie history started. Jerry should have been on the edge of his seat, engaged by the heart-pumping passes and lead changes, but his mind bounced between Nita and Lexi like he was at center court at Wimbledon. He could think of little else since Nita told him Lexi feared another criminal she was chasing might come after them. But he wasn't worried about himself. He was concerned for his daughters. Tony Belcher had shown him how dangerous the criminals Lexi chased were. His henchmen had shot him, kidnapped Nita, and hurt his dear wife badly enough that she died a month later. Lexi hunted killers, and now they were hunting her.

A bedroom door opened, and Nita stepped into the living room. She'd pulled her wet hair tightly into a bun and had changed into a set of loose-fitting sweatpants and a T-shirt. The deep creases on her face that had set in after Lexi's call had lifted some, but her stiff body movements were still filled with worry.

Jerry patted the couch cushion next to him. "Sit with me."

Nita sat, crisscrossing her legs like she was thirteen, not thirty-one. He envied her flexibility. "I'm worried about her, Dad."

"I've been worried since the day I took the training wheels off her bike. You should have seen me the first time I let her test drive a racecar. When she took it over a hundred-seventy, I thought I might have a heart attack." Jerry remembered the day like it was yesterday. She'd been driving since she was tall enough to reach the pedals and had tested cars on the track, but never at racing speed. She'd opened the engine up a bit on the straight-away and stayed center on the track for the first and second turns. She'd gunned it coming out of turn two and took the high line, riding inches from the wall. His heart had pounded so hard his chest hurt until she came out of turn four at optimum speed. She'd completed the turn as well as he'd ever done in his sixteen years behind the wheel. Her squeal over the radio was ten times more intense than the day her training wheels came off.

"I went off the deep end in Gladding last year when I had a front-row seat for Belcher's version of parlor games," Nita said. "That madman had rigged one bomb after another trying to get Lexi."

Jerry knew what Nita had meant by the deep end. Neither Lexi nor Nita had told him about her past addiction, but he'd seen the scars on her arms beneath the tattoos during their physical therapy sessions at home. There was no hiding her past, but he could see she was stronger for it. She was more patient and giving than most people her age, accepting Lexi's job without complaint was one small measure. A little reassurance was all she needed.

"She survived each evil attempt. That's how good she is at her job. Whoever this Raven character is, he's no match for our girl."

"I hope so, Dad."

"I know so. You should have seen her under the hood during her NASCAR days. She could diagnose a problem in seconds and have the car back on the track in no time. Gavin said she was a natural with a sixth sense about what made things tick. If I know my daughter, she has the same instinct with her ATF job. She can sense trouble from a mile away and think her way out of it in seconds. Now, how about some dinner? I'm starving."

"Me too," Nita said, snatching the room service menu from the corner desk. "I'm thinking it's a pasta night."

"Good choice. Lasagna it is."

"Let's make it two. I'll call it in." Nita picked up the room phone and dialed. Following a brief conversation, she hung up. "We need a Plan B. They shut down room service early tonight because of a staffing shortage. But the hotel restaurant in the lobby area is still open for another hour, or we could find a place that delivers."

"At this time of night? The restaurant is our best bet," Jerry said.

"I'll bring up the menu." Nita brought up the hotel restaurant website on her phone. "It appears they offer the same things as room service. Still want lasagna?"

"Absolutely." Jerry wagged a thumb over his shoulder toward the patio door. "We better tell our new bodyguard." He slid open the glass door, finding Agent Humphries seated on a patio chair, the site of his morning heckling of the golfers. "Hey, Scott. Room service is a bust, but the restaurant on site is serving for another hour. How about you spring us from this joint so we can get a bite to eat?"

"I think we can arrange that. Two other teams are there right now." He entered the suite and activated the microphone attached to his wrist. "Team Six on the move to the lobby with two packages. Sparrows are hungry." He listened to something coming from his earpiece. "The corridor is clear. Let's get you two fed." Humphries led them down the hallway, slowing where it opened to the lobby.

Jerry recognized a man and woman standing near the indoor water fountain as two Secret Service agents who had escorted him and Nita to the resort earlier. On their way by, he paused at the man who had the same fanboy expression plastered when they met earlier today. "If you drop off the Sunoco cap you mentioned, I'd be happy to add my John Hancock to it."

"Thank you, Mr. Mills. That would be great. My dad will get a kick hearing I met *the* Jerry Mills."

"My pleasure, young man."

Agent Humphries ushered them to the restaurant entrance, where a host guided them to a booth against the back wall and distributed the menus. Secret Service teams in the two adjoining booths flanked them, making Jerry feel safer than the president.

A handful of patrons populated the dining room. Besides the agents, only three other tables were occupied. Two male-female couples, one in their sixties and the other in their forties, were at separate tables near the fireplace. One set studied the menus, and the other concentrated on their meals. Two men were seated near the bar. The smaller one wore thick, dark-rimmed glasses, and the taller one dressed in all black was thin and had his dark hair pulled back into a bun like Nita's. The tall one threw cash onto the table, and both got up to leave when Jerry and Nita sat.

Agent Humphries joined them in the booth. "The lasagna here is pretty good."

"It seems to be a consensus." Nita closed her menu, and when the server arrived with their glasses of water, she said, "We'll make it easy on you. Three orders of lasagna."

"Lasagna all the way around." The server gathered the menus, scurried toward the kitchen, and returned with their meals minutes later.

While eating, their conversation centered on the upcoming golf charity tournament at the resort in four days and the president's visit. "I didn't realize the president was a golfer," Nita said.

"I read she's a twelve handicap," Jerry said, looking over his plate with a sly grin. He didn't expect a straightforward answer, but he had to ask. "Is that true, Scott? Or was it campaign hype?"

"She's better, actually. That woman has incredible focus. She plays once a week by herself for quiet time and breaks eighty regularly now."

"What woman is that?"

Jerry didn't have to glance up to know whose voice it was, and the smile on Nita's lips confirmed it.

Lexi sidled up to Nita at the edge of the booth, eased her chin up gently with a hand, and pulled her head closer for a soft kiss. They didn't let the kiss linger beyond social graces, but during the brief display, each melted in palpable relief when their lips met softly, casting a wave of shame through Jerry. How could he have once objected to such a natural, beautiful expression of devotion? How could he have shunned his daughter for merely loving a woman? Accepting her now in no way made up for fifteen years of closed-mindedness, but Lexi made him feel it was enough. And so did Nita, though he didn't deserve their unconditional forgiveness.

Jerry wiped a tear from the corner of an eye when Lexi focused on him. "I'm glad you're safe, Peanut."

She reached across the table and squeezed his hand. "I am too, Dad." Lexi turned her attention to the Secret Service agent across the booth from Nita and offered her hand. "I'm Lexi Mills. Thank you for taking good care of my family today."

"Scott Humphries. It was a pleasure, Agent Mills." He released her hand. "Your father and wife have been very kind. I was in the room when the previous president awarded you the Medal of Honor. It was a great moment."

"Thank you. There were lots of heroes that day." Lexi's humility made her father proud. She was the best at her job and knew it, but she never let it go to her head. Her modesty came from her mother, not him. The bravado of his youth had left him with a lifelong reminder that no one was as good as they thought they were. If he'd learned the lesson earlier, he would not have had a limp to this day.

"Where are my manners?" Lexi gestured toward her partner standing beside her. "Agent Humphries, this is my partner, Nathan Croft." The two men shook hands.

"Pleasure. It's Scott."

"Please call me Lexi. This might be asking too much, but Nathan and I have to interview a witness tomorrow who could lead us to the man we fear might come after my family. Is there any chance you can watch over them?"

Humphries waved her off. "No worries, Lexi. We still have four days until the president's visit. We're more than happy to lend a hand."

"Thank you. This suspect is a dangerous man without boundaries. He's already killed two federal agents and has a history of leaving no loose ends. I have no doubt he would use my family to get to me."

"Have you two eaten?" Nita asked. "We were about to head back to the suite, but we could wait."

"Thanks, but I ate during my layover," Nathan said.

"I'm starving." Lexi eyed boxed leftovers in front of Nita. She tapped a fingertip against it. "Yours?"

Nita nodded, sliding it closer to Lexi. "Lasagna and garlic bread. There's half. It's all yours."

"Perfect." Lexi yawned. "We need to get some sleep and head east first thing in the morning. The hotel was booked up for the night, so Nathan is going to crash on the couch in our suite."

"Don't be silly," Jerry said, turning to Nathan. "My room has two queen beds. You're welcome to use the extra one."

Jerry had met Nathan Croft once before when Lexi and Nita moved from their old place. He had an apartment there, and he and his teenage son had helped haul some boxes down to Lexi's SUV. Jerry didn't know the entire story between them, but he'd caught enough snippets over the last few months to understand Lexi had been put in charge of the Raven case, an investigation Nathan had started years ago. The day with moving boxes, he'd gotten the vibe that Nathan respected her but still felt slighted. Maybe this was an opportunity for Jerry to pave the way for fence mending.

"That would be nice," Nathan said. "I'm a little too old for couch surfing."

"Hope you brought earplugs," Lexi chuckled. "My dad snores like a foghorn."

13

The bags under Nathan's eyes were a sure sign bunking with Lexi's father wasn't the wisest choice last night. She positioned another paper coffee cup and inserted a second pod into the Keurig machine on the mini kitchen countertop in their suite.

"Where are we meeting this Hopkins guy?" Nathan said, putting on his light jacket and slipping it over the holstered Glock on the waistband of his utility slacks. Since working with Lexi, he'd ditched his preferred suit while working cases, opting to mirror her choice of civilian tactical-styled clothing. Once she'd told Nathan the loose fit better accommodated her prosthetic and was easier to work in when dealing with explosives, the only time he'd worn a suit was to brief the Dallas Special Agent in Charge on another case they'd been working on. His consistently relaxed posture suggested he enjoyed his new casual attire.

"In the parking lot of his office." Lexi handed him the freshly brewed cup of coffee, adding a travel lid from the wire basket of supplies on the counter.

"Are you sure we need him?" Nathan asked. "Too many cooks spoil the broth."

"I'm not sure of anything, but I always find it better to work with the locals than against them. Besides, he discovered the fragment with raven

DNA. He deserves to see where this case goes." His subtle eye roll suggested he disagreed, but the deep yawn following next confirmed Lexi's earlier suspicion. He was cranky and sleep-deprived. She let a grin form slowly. "How did you sleep?"

"Not much."

"I warned you."

"He gets a rhythm going, then—" Nathan grimaced.

"The snort. It's jarring, isn't it?"

"That's an understatement."

The sliding glass door rolled open on its track, and Lexi's father stepped through, carrying two coffee mugs. "Good morning, Peanut. You heading out?"

"Yeah," Lexi said. "I'm not sure how long we'll be, so I'll need you and Nita to sit tight in the suite."

"I won't be a prisoner here all day, Lexi," her father said. His tone was firm.

Agent Humphries appeared at the open door. "We'll take good care of them, Lexi. We can clear or overload an area like last night if they want to go to the restaurant or the pool."

"I guess it will have to do," her father's expression drooped.

Lexi walked up to him and rubbed his upper arm. For decades, his day revolved around his wife and best friend, but now they were gone. His cars back in Ponder and Lexi and Nita were the only things giving him purpose. She could not blame him for feeling cooped up in a hotel room seventeen hundred miles from home.

"I know this wasn't what you had in mind when I asked you to join us on this trip, but I need you to help keep Nita safe. Can you do that for me, Dad?" Lexi thought of the day Belcher sent his heavies to their home, targeting Nita but also hurting her parents. The sadness in her father's eyes said he recalled it too.

He stiffened his spine and puffed his chest suddenly in unmovable determination. "I will, Peanut. I'll protect her with my life."

"Thank you, Dad." Lexi kissed him on the cheek and left with Nathan, knowing they would be safe. They picked up Detective Jan Hopkins two hours later and headed to the address in the Tahoe National Forest Senator

Jackson had given them. The location matched the GPS coordinates last entered in Darryl Yarborough's onboard navigation system before the deadly crash.

Lexi rolled her rental car up to the decorative ten-foot-tall double-panel metal gate with the image of a falcon highlighted in gold on each side. It appeared impenetrable to anything but a Mack truck, like a top-secret military installation, as did the equally tall stonewalls extending beyond what the eye could see on both flanks. Cameras were mounted atop the gate pillars, providing three-hundred-sixty-degree coverage.

She stopped at a pole-mounted box the size of an electrical outlet four feet off the ground at the edge of the paved road. The box had a speaker, a single silver button, and a printed label saying, "Press for Assistance." Lexi lowered the driver's window and pushed the button. Nothing sounded, so she couldn't be sure if it was operational.

A voice came from the speaker a moment later. "Good morning, Agent Mills. Welcome to Shangri-La. Please follow the access road to the main house and park near the front door."

A loud clank. The gate opened from the middle, each panel rolling behind the solid stone wall, one to the left and the other to the right. Once the panels cleared the roadway, Lexi pulled forward, following the tree-lined road. After a quarter mile, the trees gave way to a sprawling structure resembling three connected mountain chalets with an oversized garage on either side of the building. The asphalt changed into pavers and split into a circular driveway. A lushly landscaped rocky waterfall and pond were in the center.

"I've patrolled this county for sixteen years and never knew this was here," Jan said from the backseat, leaning forward over the center console to get a better view.

"Shangri-La?" Nathan said, peering out the front window. "What is this place? Fantasy Island?"

"It does have that vibe." Lexi stopped at the central structure at the foot of a portico-covered walkway leading to a large double door. She opened the car door. "Let's go find Mr. Roarke."

Once at the front door, Lexi raised her hand to knock, but a voice came from a speaker mounted high on the underbelly of the portico. "Harold will be right with you, Agent Mills." Lexi scanned the area, noting several surveillance cameras on the buildings and architectural features. The "big brother" aura was strong.

The door opened to a short, trim man a little taller than Lexi dressed in a dark suit and bow tie, adding to the Fantasy Island vibe. He stepped aside, gesturing for them to enter. "Welcome. May I take your coats?"

"No, thank you. We're fine," Lexi said, walking inside the entry hall. Two tall, muscular men dressed in suits blocked the other end. Lexi stopped short of them and a large, airy room, waiting for Nathan and Jan to enter. One held a detector wand, and the other had a plastic tray. "What's this?" she asked the one with the wand.

"We'll need you to place your cell phones, tablets, smartwatches, and other communication devices in the tray."

"Why?" Nathan asked.

"Mr. Foreman's work touches on classified projects. This is the price of admission. Otherwise, you're welcome to leave."

As long as they didn't demand to take their badges and weapons, Lexi was okay with the requirement. "It's fine." She placed her phone and watch in the tray before letting the man scan her with a wand. He paused at her left leg.

"What do you have in your left cargo pocket? I'm getting a strange reading."

"I thought you were checking for electronics, not metal." Lexi wasn't fooled by their story. They were assessing what kind of firepower they were up against.

"We check for both. Again, you're welcome to leave."

She tapped the polymer shell of her socket. "Prosthetic leg."

"I'll have to inspect it."

"There's no way I'm taking it off. Now, either Mr. Foreman sees us today, or we'll get a warrant for his arrest as a material witness."

The man pressed his index and middle fingers against his left ear as if listening to someone over an earpiece. "That's fine, ma'am. Next."

Once Nathan and Jan turned over their electronics and the guards swept for whatever they were actually looking for, Harold ushered them into the next room. "May I get you anything to drink? Coffee with one cream and one sugar, Agent Mills?" He turned toward Nathan. "I stocked the mint tea you're fond of, Agent Croft. Would you care for some?"

This was creepy, Lexi thought. She and Nathan glanced at each other, both giving a quizzical shrug. The big brother vibe wasn't only alive and well here, it was like the Blob, growing exponentially by the minute. "No, thank you. We're fine."

The rustic décor gave the room an authentic mountain feel. The museum-quality canvas artwork appeared to be worth as much as the house. An internet search of Benjamin Foreman last night revealed he was a retired general who had built his career in the black ops world. During his rise, he'd overseen many top-secret projects with his last stint in an Army future war development program. After retiring from the military, he founded Falcon Industries, the premier developer of innovative war-fighting capabilities and advanced weapons systems. It all told Lexi he'd made a fortune since leaving the military, more than his contracts with the United States would account for. He had to have other dealings.

Harold disappeared down a hallway past the corner bar. Moments later, two men walked from the same hallway. One was in a tailored, double-breasted suit and had lawyer written all over him. Lexi recognized the man walking next to him from the pictures she'd found during her internet search. The military-style high and tight haircut, square jaw, and muscular runner's body were unmistakable. Lexi wasn't sure what she expected Benjamin Foreman to be wearing, but well-worn jeans and a dark charcoal six-string flannel shirt weren't it.

"Agent Mills, I'm Benjamin Foreman. I'm so glad you reached out." Foreman extended his hand, which Lexi accepted. "This is my legal counsel, Andrew Bohm. I apologize for the added security, but I raised our defensive posture once I heard of Mr. Yarborough's accident."

Lexi acknowledged Bohm with a polite nod. "Thank you for meeting with us, Mr. Foreman. This is my partner, Nathan Croft, and Detective Jan Hopkins. Hopkins was the initial traffic investigator looking into Mr. Yarborough's death."

Foreman gestured toward a seating area near a roaring wood-burning fireplace and a wall of windows looking out to a beautiful mountain setting. In the distance, a thick grove of coniferous pine trees served as a backdrop for an ample seating area with a stone fireplace beneath a split-log covered patio.

Once seated, Lexi jumped in with an open-ended query to see what information Foreman might volunteer. "I understand Mr. Yarborough was here to see you two nights ago. Tell me about that evening."

"He'd arrived around seven for dinner to discuss a contract proposal before Senator Jackson's committee. The briefing went well, and he left before nine."

The carefully crafted bare minimum, Lexi thought. According to Nathan, who had spent four years in the army before joining the ATF, there were two types of leaders—the politicians and the warriors. General Bill "Fifty" Calhoun, the former charismatic leader of the Red Spades who Lexi had escaped from during the Spicewood insurrection, was a warrior leader. Benjamin Foreman was nothing like him. This man was reserved and carried himself more like an academic than a warfighter. He was definitely a political general, and like every politician, he was naturally vague. Lexi would have to draw it out of him.

"What was the contract proposal about?"

"The specifics are classified. I'll tell you anything you want to know about the program once the Secretary of Defense issues you a Top-Secret/SCI security clearance and reads you into the special program."

"So, in other words, never," Nathan said.

Foreman shifted his stare to say, "It's out of my hands." His response and tone came across as evasive but diplomatic, convincing Lexi he wouldn't volunteer any information. She'd have to trip him up but doubted he would fall for it.

"My client," Bohm said, "is bound by the terms of his security clearance to not release information regarding his military contracts, including those under development and consideration by Congress."

This was the same nebulous runaround the senator had given her and Jan last night. "If you can't tell us what it was about, can you tell us who else was in the meeting?" Lexi asked.

"Their names are classified, but I can tell you Mr. Bohm was present as my legal counsel, as well as two other company representatives."

"What did you serve for dinner?"

"We started with a smoked salmon appetizer, followed by a filet for the main course augmented with asparagus tips, roasted garlic mashed potatoes, and dinner rolls. We finished with an apple crumble dessert a la mode." Foreman didn't flinch, didn't question her reasoning.

"Was there shellfish in either dish?"

"No. We were careful to avoid Mr. Yarborough's food allergy."

"I'd still like the ingredients list your cook used that night." Lexi and Jan would still review Yarborough's stomach contents in the autopsy report when the coroner released it.

"Of course." Foreman raised a hand over his shoulder and waved it. A moment later, Harold appeared from the hallway, stopping several feet behind Foreman. "See to it that Agent Mills gets what she needs."

"Yes, Mr. Foreman. I've already alerted the cook." Harold turned toward Lexi. "Shall I send it to your official ATF email address?" Lexi reached for her back pocket to retrieve a business card, but he waved her off. "I have it, Agent Mills," he added and scurried off.

More big brother creepiness, Lexi thought.

Jan shifted on his heel and asked, "What did Mr. Yarborough have to drink that night?"

"Harold served him one Manhattan cocktail when he first arrived, and I believe he had one glass of wine during dinner. Do you suspect drunk driving? I can assure you he appeared perfectly fine when he left."

"Thank you. This helps," Jan said. "How was he acting when he left? Was he agitated or upset?"

"It's hard to say. I'd only met the man that night and had no baseline to judge." Another ambiguous answer, signifying their strategy was getting nowhere. Perhaps a little bait dangling might elicit a response.

"Detective Hopkins discovered something interesting in the wreckage. It caught my interest," Lexi said, noting no changes in Foreman's facial expression or posture.

"What's that?" Foreman asked.

"A piece of metal was lined with a rare polymer used in some of your company's experimental designs." The linkage was an assumption, but Lexi wanted to see how he would react. And there it was. Foreman cocked his head slightly to one side and raised his eyebrows.

"What kind of polymer?"

"Graphene."

"Interesting. Not many companies use the material because of the cost of transforming it into a three-dimensional structure."

Some might consider pointing the finger at a narrow pool of suspects a nice dodge, but Lexi wasn't buying his innocent routine for one minute. "Can you provide us with the names of those companies? I understand graphene is primarily used in experimental medical and military applications."

"Of course. I see you've done your homework, Agent Mills. Battery companies have also experimented with graphene skin to dramatically improve their product's performance and lifespan. It's still not cost-effective for mass production, but it's a viable solution for rechargeable energy storage. Imagine a Tesla with a 500-mile range and a battery that can charge to full capacity in 10 minutes and won't need replacing for 750,000 miles. Since most Americans replace their vehicles after 50,000 to 100,000 miles, the resale market will be incredible."

"Speaking of a Tesla, did you notice anything about Mr. Yarborough's vehicle?" Jan asked. "Tires? Headlights?"

"I didn't go outside, so I wouldn't know firsthand."

Firsthand? Lexi thought. He used an odd choice of words. Did he know secondhand from an employee or from the exterior surveillance cameras? "We'd like to review the security system recordings from that night."

"You'll need a warrant, Agent Mills," Bohm said. "Since this structure is a registered Falcon Industries facility, those recordings fall under the purview of national security. The search warrant would require a DC Circuit Court judge signature."

"All right," Lexi said, returning her attention to Foreman. "Tell me why you felt it necessary to raise your security posture at Shangri-La."

"I've made enemies over the years in my line of work and have had a few attempts on my life. Someone possibly mistook Mr. Yarborough for me, so I'm not taking chances."

A little more push to gauge his reaction, Lexi thought. "Could one of those enemies be the Raven?"

"I'm not familiar with that name. If the ATF is following him, I assume he has dealings with illegal firearms or explosives."

"Both, actually," Nathan said. "He deals in them and builds them for exclusive clients with hefty bank accounts."

"Is that what you suspect happened with the accident?" Foreman asked.

"Possibly. We're investigating all angles," Lexi said.

Odd, she thought. They had kept the Raven out of the media since the Las Vegas dirty bomb incident, but his name had become well known in federal law enforcement circles. A man with Foreman's connections and dealings with high-tech military weapons certainly would have heard of him by now. "If I had my phone, I could show you a sample of what Detective Hopkins had pulled from the wreckage."

Foreman waved a hand toward the entry hallway, and the goon who had taken their devices earlier walked in with the plastic tray. Lexi retrieved her phone, brought up the photo of the larger piece of evidence, and showed it to Foreman.

"Does this look like anything Falcon Industries has designed? This is the piece where we found traces of rare graphene. The element sounds like something the Raven would use."

"I don't like where this is going," Bohm said. "Unless you have more questions about Mr. Yarborough's accident, we're done here. Harold will see you out."

Lexi had struck a nerve, which meant Foreman knew more than he'd let on. She stowed her phone, grabbed her watch from the tray, and retrieved a business card from her back pocket. "You probably have my number, but please call if you can think of anything more."

Harold reappeared on cue and extended his arm toward the entryway. "The chef should have the ingredients list to you within the hour, Agent Mills. If you care to follow me, I'll see you to your car."

The others gathered their devices and slipped down the hallway to the front door with Lexi. Once outside, she said, "You're very efficient, Harold. It sounded like you had your hands full Monday night entertaining Mr. Foreman's guests. Was it a large crowd?"

"Oh no, ma'am. Five is a small number around here." Harold held the driver's door open for Lexi.

"Thank you, Harold. We appreciate your hospitality."

Once she pulled through the gate, Jan Hopkins leaned forward from the backseat. "Foreman knows a lot more than what he let on. Did you see how his eyebrows went up when you showed him the photo of the evidence?"

"I did, and I agree," Nathan said. "I don't buy his bit about enemies mistaking Yarborough for him."

"Neither do I," Lexi said. "At least we confirmed there were five people at the meeting. We know Foreman, Yarborough, and the mouthpiece were there, leaving two unaccounted for. Maybe Senator Jackson might be a little more forthcoming with the names. Let's see if he's up for another chat."

14

When the door closed behind Mills and her minions, Benjamin removed his earpiece, slipped it into his front hip pocket, and turned to his security team near the seating area. "I was distracted during their grilling. Please tell me you got it done."

"Yes, sir," the team leader said. "The control center has a live audio and GPS feed from Agent Mills' phone. They're streaming it on your executive app and will update you on any developments."

"Well done. Please conduct a perimeter check of the blind spots. I want to make sure they didn't leave any surprises." Benjamin turned toward the hallway past the corner bar. "Come with me, Andrew."

Andrew sat in the guest chair after entering his office, while Benjamin sat behind his desk, opened the top drawer, and pulled out the burner phone given to him for emergencies. He dialed the only stored number. The call connected on the third ring. "We have a problem."

"Explain," the Raven said.

"We used the locust in an op, and the police discovered a graphene-lined fragment, linking it back to Falcon Industries. Explain to me why it wasn't destroyed in the explosion."

"You needed a solution to the weight and payload problem in less than three months. The criteria you gave Robert had only strength and weight requirements. You said nothing about survivability. Graphene solved your dilemma, but as an allotrope of carbon, it has an extremely high melting point. Would you rather the locusts be nothing but a flying camera?"

"Your decision has implications for both of us. The fragment also contained something the ATF is looking into. They mentioned your name."

"If the ATF is involved, Agent Lexi Mills must have paid you a visit today."

"So you know her."

"We have crossed paths." The tension in the Raven's voice suggested his experience with Mills was not pleasant.

"Her snooping could prove problematic."

"Leave her to me," the Raven said. "I have special plans for her."

"It had better be soon. I can't afford this getting out of hand before my contract passes through committee."

"Have patience, Benjamin."

"We shall see." Benjamin disconnected the call and returned the phone to the drawer. Waiting was never his strong suit, and neither was relying on someone else to resolve his problems. He was willing to wait and watch for only so long before taking matters into his own hands.

"You're not thinking of terminating Lexi Mills," Andrew said, shaking his head in clear disappointment. "She's a national treasure."

"She's backing me into a corner. Once the contract is in place, no one in Congress, the Department of Defense, or the alphabet soup of intelligence committees will want information about the locust getting into the public domain. But if Jackson continues to block it, I'll have no other choice."

"Doing so will attract too much scrutiny. You need to explore every avenue to avoid it. There's more to Falcon Industries than the Locust Project. Killing Mills will destroy the company you built."

"Some things can't be helped," Benjamin said.

"If Senator Jackson doesn't come through, why not give the rest of the committee a reason to approve it?"

"What do you have in mind, Andrew?"

"Me? I don't have a clue. Ideas are my lane. Solutions are your department."

Benjamin's mind marinated on what would persuade stubborn

committee members who follow the political winds in lockstep with their parties. What would entice them to cross the aisle and unite in approving the project? The answer was straightforward. The last time national unity came before partisanship was after the twin towers came down. He simply needed to give the committee members a reason to use the locust technology, but Lexi Mills' death wouldn't provide it.

"All right, my friend. I see your point about Mills. I'll give Jackson one more chance tonight."

"And if he doesn't?"

"He'll give me no choice. With Robert's help, I'll take matters into my own hands. Go big or go home, I always say." Benjamin's personal phone rang. He read the incoming alert from his control center four stories below ground. *Mills phoning Senator Jackson.* He clicked on the app to listen in.

Lexi's call to Senator Jackson's personal cell phone connected. She put it on speaker. "Agent Mills, how was your meeting with Benjamin Foreman? Any break in the case?"

"Nothing yet, Senator. He hid behind the cloak of national security. I know you can't tell us about the project before your committee, but we learned five people were at Monday night's meeting. We know Yarborough, Foreman, and the lawyer who did most of his talking today were there. Who else might have been at the meeting?"

"I would assume those best suited to demonstrate the product. At past meetings, Foreman had sent the manager in charge of the project and the chief engineer to answer technical questions."

"Do you know their names?"

"I suppose personnel names aren't classified, only sensitive, but I don't have the information here. Darryl's father has flown out to view the body. My wife and I are meeting him this afternoon to plan for a service. It should be an emotional day, so I'll call my assistant first thing in the morning and have her go through my records in the DC office. She'll send you the names before lunch tomorrow."

"Thank you, Senator. That would be helpful."

"I know you have no reason to trust me, but I'd appreciate a call when you figure out who killed my dear friend."

"I'll do my best, Senator."

"You're very diplomatic, Agent Mills. I understand the previous president sent your name to his successor as his choice to replace the retiring ATF director. I can see he made a wise choice."

Lexi cringed. Her partnership with Nathan was already shaky after she stole the Raven case he'd spent two years building. His knowing she was on the president's shortlist for the directorship would only make it worse. "I'm happy where I'm at, sir, but I appreciate the confidence in my abilities."

"You'd make an excellent politician, Mills. Don't sell yourself short."

When Lexi concluded the call, the cabin inside her rental car went awkwardly silent. Without a doubt, the giant elephant crowding their space needed addressing before her relationship with Nathan deteriorated beyond repair. "Pretend you didn't hear that, Nathan. I'm not interested in the job."

"Maybe not, but it explains why the director handed you the Raven case. He's throwing his support behind you."

"I'm a field agent and an explosives expert. Despite what the senator said, I'm no politician."

"Come now. You led a national task force, took down those behind the Spicewood insurrection, and prevented a dirty bomb from making Las Vegas a ghost town. Those experiences were quite the proving ground."

"It still didn't make me a politician."

"Oh, please. You had to deal with senior government executives and political appointees from day one. They know your face and capabilities. And you check almost every box. You're a president's dream."

"Well, that's not me." Lexi harrumphed. She wanted no part of a job that required box-checking. Yes, she was a handicapped, biracial, gay woman, but those qualities should have no bearing on her qualifications, nor should they overshadow them. Twelve years in the agency in no way qualified her to run it. But Nathan was onto something. If she were appointed and accepted the position, many in the agency might only see her for her visual attributes, not who she was on the inside. They would never respect her unless she first worked her way up the ranks.

"I know. Your father drilled it into me before falling asleep last night. He filled me in on some things not in the official reports, explaining why your hunts for Belcher, the Gatekeepers, and the Red Spades were so personal. You were just protecting the people you love."

"He told you that, huh?"

"He's a very straightforward man, and he's in awe of what you do. He even told me about his difficulty with your sexuality and how proud he is of your ability to forgive. From everything I've seen and heard about you, you deserved your choice of assignment. Do I resent being bumped as the lead investigator? Yes, but I respect how you've carried yourself. You're the real deal, Mills."

"Thanks, Nathan. I appreciate your understanding." Lexi sensed they'd finally made a turn, and all the uneasiness of how they'd started as partners was now behind them. "We better call Lange and give her an update." After reaching a pocket of reliable cell service, Lexi issued a voice command to call Agent Lange while weaving her way down the mountain road.

Lange answered. "Hi, Mills. Any luck with Foreman?"

Lexi filled her in on the details of her meeting at Shangri-La and her call with Senator Jackson. "So we're heading back to Napa to wait for the senator to provide us with the names of the other people at the meeting. Maybe we can get one of them to talk."

"Until then, take the rest of the day off, turn off your cell, and treat your bride to a nice romantic dinner."

"I think I might."

15

"I wish you'd come home with me, my love," Peggy said over the phone. "Seeing Darryl's father took a lot out of you. Holding meetings at a time like this can't be good for you."

"I'll be fine, dear. We're just discussing a few issues over drinks on the California side of the lake. I should be home before bedtime."

"I'm afraid it might be too stressful. After leaving the funeral home today, you were exhausted and sensed a few flutters in your chest."

"I think it was more heartbreak than the pacemaker. At my last appointment with the DC cardiologist, he said the pacemaker still had three months of battery life and would replace it at the one-month point. It's still a month away. I see him next week, and I'm sure he'll give me a full workup."

"It's still too far away. I'm texting Cameron to have you home by nine. If she doesn't, I'm sending the cavalry to search for you."

"I have no doubt you would. I'll see you by nine." Keith slid the phone into his suit's interior breast pocket while walking into the Emerald Club, flanked by his Capitol Police security team. The exclusive lounge overlooking the rocky shoreline of Lake Tahoe's north shore had been the site of many deal-making and deal-breaking meetings. He sensed this discussion would fall into the latter category, ending his long track record of supporting every new technology the DoD said was critical to giving them an edge in intelligence-gathering and war-fighting capabilities. But the implication that traditional security measures would be ineffective against Falcon Industries' newest proposal would put the United States at risk if it fell into the hands of an adversary.

Keith waited at the entrance to the lounge with one guard while the other checked the few other guests for weapons with a wand, paying particular attention to Benjamin Foreman. Once the guard issued a thumbs up, Keith whispered to Cameron. "Come get me by eight-thirty. Otherwise, I'll be sleeping on the couch tonight."

"I have my alarm set, sir. Your wife's orders."

"At least we both agree on who is the real boss of this arrangement." Keith patted Cameron on the shoulder before walking toward Foreman's couch near the window, his favorite seating area in the lounge for its view and proximity to the stone fireplace. Now in his seventies, Keith found the warmth of the fire extra comforting.

The other security guard joined Cameron, passing Keith on the way by. "All clear, sir."

"Thank you, Marcus." Keith reached the couch. "Evening, Benjamin. What couldn't wait until tomorrow?"

Foreman sipped his cocktail and placed the glass on the coffee table in front of the couch. He stood and shook hands with Keith. "First, my condolences on your loss. I know Mr. Yarborough wasn't only your chief of staff. He was a dear friend."

"Thank you, Benjamin. It came as a shock and will take some time to get over."

"Please sit." Benjamin gestured toward the couch. A server came by and dropped off Keith's traditional drink whenever he visited. Once seated, Benjamin continued. "Thank you for coming tonight, Keith. I thought we should talk about the accident investigation. The ATF came to see me today."

"Yes, I sent them your way since Darryl's accident happened while driving back from his meeting with you." Keith took a sip of his cocktail. *Ahh, the perfect Manhattan*, he thought. He savored it, thinking it was also

Darryl's drink of choice. Their love of the cocktail was how they'd first bonded despite disagreeing on whether to use Canadian Whiskey or Rye.

"And as you should have. I wish he would have accepted my offer of a security escort back to the Interstate to navigate the tricky roads that night. If he had, he might still be alive."

"If Lexi Mills is involved, I guarantee this was no simple accident," Keith said.

"I couldn't disagree, which makes me think a terrorist cell might have tried to get their hands on the locust technology. They may have mistaken Mr. Yarborough for me or thought he might have had it with him. Or it could have been someone from my past. I made several enemies during my black ops days. No matter the case, I've upped security at my compound."

"If you're increasing security, Agent Mills must be onto something. She wasn't specific about why she's interested in this case, but I can only assume it has something to do with explosives. I understand you weren't forth-coming with your answers to her questions."

"Her questions treaded on top-secret information," Benjamin said. "My counsel shut down the conversation to keep me from revealing anything classified. I suggested they go through DoD to get the proper clearance. When they do, I'll gladly share the information they asked for."

"They only wanted the names of the people at the meeting, for Pete's sake."

"I must protect my people. Once their names are linked publicly to a project of this magnitude, they could become a target, like Mr. Yarborough may have been. It's a shame he didn't live long enough to see it imple-mented. From what I could glean from his comments and the questions he'd asked that night, I gathered he was quite impressed with the limited prototype demonstration. We've implemented a backdoor protocol allowing DoD to disable a device if it gets into the wrong hands."

Something was odd about Benjamin's claim. Before the meeting, he hadn't mentioned the backdoor capability in his briefing. *Either he's blowing smoke up my ass, or the backdoor has another purpose.* Keith took a long sip of his drink.

"I'm sorry, Benjamin, but nothing you said changes the problem I have with the technology. Backdoors can be closed, leaving the same foundational risk. We have no affirmative defense against it that doesn't leave us completely blind. You develop it, and I will reconsider your proposal. Until then, I'm sorry, but I'm a firm no vote."

Benjamin shifted on the couch, narrowing his eyes in anger. A blind man could see he wasn't accustomed to not getting his way. "I think you're making a mistake, Keith. Technology is evolving at lightning speed, and micro-weaponry is the future. We need to stay on the leading edge."

"I don't doubt you're right, but not this way. This is as dangerous as a nuclear missile. There was no defense against it until we designed our multi-layered National Missile Defense System. Don't get me wrong. You have a great idea here, Benjamin, but the locust is a virtually invisible enemy. We must have a foolproof way of defending against it before unleashing it on the world."

"I still think this is the wrong decision, but we'll go back to the drawing board. Until then, I'd be careful. I have a feeling anyone who knows about the technology is at risk." Benjamin Foreman was known for using only measured words, and his point could have been construed as a veiled threat. Keith would have to up his security protocols as well.

"Unless they come after me with one of your little toys, I'll be fine. The Capitol Police provides world-class security." Keith downed the rest of his drink and stood. "I think we're done here. I look forward to seeing how you address my concerns."

Benjamin stood, too, turning his expression to its characteristic unreadable state. "You'll be hearing from me."

Keith buttoned his jacket and walked toward his security detail. Everything about the meeting came across as disingenuous, from Benjamin's concern about Darryl to this miraculous backdoor addition to the locust to his terrorist theory about who might be behind Darryl's so-called accident. Benjamin Foreman was someone Lexi Mills needed to scrutinize.

"Three minutes to spare, sir." Cameron smiled and led him from the lounge. "Let's get you home before Mrs. Jackson gives me a piece of her mind."

"We can't have that." After sliding into the backseat of his SUV, Keith pulled out his phone and dialed a number from his recent call list. It rang, eventually going to voicemail. "Agent Mills, this is Keith Jackson. I would like to discuss a concern I have. Please call my personal line in the morning."

Cameron pulled the SUV to the walkway leading to the front door of the Incline Village home. Her partner opened the back passenger door for Keith. "Thank you, Marcus. I'll see you and Cameron tomorrow morning."

A Capitol Police officer on the night shift was standing guard outside the door. "Evening, David. Everything buttoned down for the night?"

"As usual, sir. Mrs. Jackson is waiting for you in the kitchen."

"Uh oh. Is she baking?"

"I'm afraid so, Senator."

Keith patted him on the shoulder. "Thank you, David. See you in the morning."

He stepped through the door, discovering a dark living room—a bad sign. Wednesday was Peggy's night to binge her favorite television shows that had accumulated on the DVR from the past week. She would fast forward to the parts she was interested in, sometimes finishing a two-hour singing competition show in twenty minutes. It was her rarely missed sacred night of "me" time. And her baking this late at night was even worse. She only did so when she was worried. It was high time he allayed most of it.

Every light in the kitchen was on, the electronic panel on the oven said it was set to 350 degrees, and the granite island had batches of chocolate chip cookies lined up and cooling. Peggy was at the sink, washing something with her back to the entrance, so Keith eased behind her and slid his arms around her waist, pulling her close to him. At first, her body stiffened, but when he tightened his hold, she melted into his embrace.

"I was worried about you," she said, resting her head against his chest.

"I can tell by the number of cookies on the counter. A four-dozen night is pretty intense."

"Darryl's death has hit us both hard, but I know how much he meant to you."

He squeezed her tighter. "He was like another son to me."

"Which is why I'm so worried about you. I wish your cardiologist would have replaced your pacemaker the last time you were in there."

"It wasn't good timing. I would have needed up to two weeks off from my duties. It made sense to do it when the senate was in recess. Since control changed hands after the last election, we've had one vote after another. The majority leader has asked all Republican members to postpone optional medical procedures until the next recess."

"A working pacemaker is not optional. You'll be no good to them if it acts up again, and you end up in the hospital or worse."

Keith swayed her side to side for a moment. "Would you be less worried if I cut back on my office hours?"

"That would be a great start."

"Consider it done. I'll tell Judy only core hours for me and nothing on Fridays."

Peggy spun in his grasp, placing both palms on his chest. Her smile said he'd struck the right chord. "I've been trying to get you to take Fridays off for years."

"Well, I can't have you baking like this every day. My pants are already getting a little tight."

"That's because you stopped your morning walks. When was the last time Cameron took you for a stroll on the trail?"

"It's been too cold. I'll resume in a few weeks when the weather turns."

"Uh-huh. Sure you will." She wiggled from his grasp when the oven timer sounded. Armed with oven mitts, she pulled out what he hoped was her last batch for the night. "Did you take your evening pills?"

"On the way home from the lounge." The cocktail he drank earlier and the long emotional day he had with Darryl's father had taken their toll. Stifling a yawn was impossible. "I'm heading to bed. How much longer will you be?"

"Give me twenty minutes. I want to clean up and put most of these cookies into containers for your security team."

"They'll love it, especially Cameron. She has the world's biggest sweet tooth yet doesn't gain an ounce."

"Well, maybe these will put a few inches on her bones. I'll be in soon."

Keith snatched a cookie from a cooling rack and hurried out.

Peggy shouted, "And you wonder why your pants are feeling tight."

He waved a cookie over his shoulder in appreciation before biting off a sizeable chunk. *One cookie won't hurt*, he thought. By the time he reached the bathroom, the cookie was history. He brushed his teeth, washed his face, and changed into pajamas. Once under the covers, he grabbed the book on his nightstand, estimating he could get in a chapter or two before Peggy made it to bed.

Keith flipped to the last dog-eared page and settled into a high-octane action scene involving a bank robbery. A chapter in, he swatted away an annoying fly buzzing around his head. It flew away, only to return two pages later. He flung a hand at it again, but it persisted.

Odd, he thought. Flies at the lake usually didn't come out in force until mid-spring when the weather was warmer. It buzzed him again, but the little bugger landed on the breast pocket of his night clothes this time. It bounced twice, then something shocked him. It felt as if he was being tased. He dropped his book on his belly, sending the fly away. His heart felt like it skipped a beat, followed by a hard thump. His heart raced so fast he thought it might jump from his chest.

Keith's limbs became weak. He was unable to move them. His chest hurt. Pain. Pressure. Tightness like someone was squeezing it in a vise. His head wobbled. Staying awake became challenging.

"God, no." He heard his wife's voice moments before she appeared at his side. "Keith, are you okay?"

Unable to speak, he shook his head.

Peggy rushed to her nightstand and slammed her hand against the panic button. A siren sounded.

Keith gasped for air and struggled to remain conscious. He clutched Peggy's arm and pulled her toward him. When the room wobbled, he choked out, "Love...you."

"No, Keith. Stay with me." The tears streaming down her cheeks said she knew the end was near. He gasped for air, thinking this was how he wanted to die. He couldn't bear living without this beautiful creature. "Don't leave me, Keith."

He tried reaching out to dry her tears, but his arms had already lost their function. He tried to speak again to tell her she would be okay, that she needed to be the glue to keep the family together, but he hadn't the strength. Life was draining from him quickly.

He met her stare one last time, soaking in the warmth of her eyes and the curve of her lips. What he wouldn't give to kiss them once more.

Then.

The room went black.

16

A moan escaped Lexi's lips. She closed her eyes and leaned back farther, bracing herself on the bed with straight arms, her palms down, careful to not lay her wet hair from her earlier shower on the mattress. "You're so good at that."

"I should be. I do it for a living five days a week," Nita said, kneading her thumbs against the flesh of Lexi's residual limb to work out the accumulated edema since yesterday.

Usually, Lexi would have performed her limb care before going to sleep last night, but she followed Agent Lange's suggestion after returning from their interview with Benjamin Foreman in the mountains. A romantic dinner at the hotel restaurant was the perfect precursor to the tender rounds of making love back in the room before falling asleep.

A cold sensation broke her recollection of their perfect night when Nita applied the prosthetic salve. Nita inched up the corners of her lips and said, "You're content."

"I should be after last night. I love spending time with you like that. It makes me feel..." Lexi paused, trying to find the right word.

"Connected," Nita said, rubbing in the lotion and studying Lexi's limb.

"Yes, that's it. It makes me feel that you're a part of me. I'm not afraid of letting go when I'm with you."

In the wake of her mother's passing, she'd made the mistake of letting herself feel her grief while in the office, and as a result, her concentration slipped, forgetting details and minor tasks. But once Lange had sent her on a disposal mission, Lexi knew she had to lock away her emotions. The slightest lack of focus was a death knell for an explosives expert. One inaccurate assessment or wrong move could cost lives, including her own. So, she spent the working day in command of every thought and emotion. The practice was effective but also hard to turn off when she returned home. For sanity's sake, Lexi allowed herself one circumstance of vulnerability— making love to her wife. She relinquished control, letting Nita release her physically, emotionally, and mentally to the point of losing herself, and their resulting union was unshakeable.

Nita raised her gaze, meeting Lexi's. The corners of her lips turned up slightly, reaching toward her eyes. "I feel the same." She returned her focus to her work. "It looks much better."

"It *feels* better. Thank you." Lexi kissed Nita on the lips before glancing at the alarm clock on the nightstand. It was a little before seven. Senator Jackson should be up or would be soon, which meant his assistant in DC might send her the names of the Falcon Industries people working on the nameless, classified project at any time.

Lexi began rolling the liner onto her residual limb. "Nathan and I might have to take off soon, but I promise to make it up to you."

"Oh, I'm sure of it." Nita rose to her feet and removed her tank top and sleep shorts, leaving only a delicious thong covering her body. The queen of tease, she licked her index finger and jogged it down her sternum between her breasts, slowly, seductively, drawing in Lexi like a moth to a flame. Her skin tingled, making her rethink the proper order of things for the morning. Nathan and the investigation would have to wait. Then, like a switch had flipped, Nita gave Lexi a wicked smile, spun on her heel, and stepped toward the bathroom, adding an extra sway to her hips. "Just not now. I'm going to shower. Alone." She shut the door behind her and hollered, "I could use some coffee."

Lexi rushed putting on her prosthetic, eased the bathroom door open, and poked her head inside as Nita cranked the shower faucet on. "You're evil, woman." Nita angled her head slightly, revealing a self-satisfied grin.

"Would you like a pastry or some fruit from the lobby?" Lexi asked.

"I'd rather have a sit-down with you." Nita stepped inside the shower, letting the water cascade over her breasts in a show fit for Hollywood. The only thing missing was the sexy music. "Now go."

Yes, Lexi thought. *The queen of tease.* "Coffee coming right up."

She returned to the bed and properly donned her prosthetic, applying three layers of socks over her leg, one more than her typical complement since last month's tune-up with her prosthetist. Chasing the Raven required every precaution. Once dressed in cargo pants and a loose T-shirt, Lexi grabbed her paddle holster with her service Glock and slipped it into the waistband. She also snatched her phone from the nightstand without inspecting the screen, stowed it in her pocket, and exited the bedroom to the main suite, finding her father pouring a cup of coffee in the kitchenette.

"Hi, Peanut," he said in a quiet morning voice. Since last night, he'd trimmed the ends of his handlebar mustache, bringing Lexi back to her adolescent years when he'd worn it shorter during his driving days.

"Wow," she whispered back, retrieving a coffee mug from the countertop. "What got into you?"

He wiped his upper lip with his index finger and thumb. "Do you like it?"

"Surprisingly, yes. It makes you look younger."

"Well, it wasn't what I was going for, but I'll take it."

"What *were* you going for?"

"Just different." Her father sniffled and concentrated on dressing his coffee with cream and sugar. The same distant, glassy-eyed stare inhabiting him since the weeks following his wife's death had returned. It had appeared less often in recent weeks, but those few bouts lasted worryingly longer each time. She got the impression injecting change into his life was his way of trying to turn the page.

Lexi ran a hand through her hair. A pushed-up pixie had been her default hairstyle for years. Maybe it was time for a change for her too. Flipping the emotion switch only during private moments with Nita couldn't be healthy. "I've been thinking of letting my hair grow a bit."

He eyed Lexi more closely, focusing on her face. "You were cute as a button in pigtails."

"Let's not go crazy." Lexi cringed whenever her mother brought out the family photo albums. Each of her class photos up to the fourth grade and those of her posing for her T-ball team featured her in tight twin bundles of long, straight hair with a smile so wide it would hurt to replicate as an adult. "I was thinking collar length, so I won't be so cold in the winter."

A grin appeared on his lips, and a twinkle returned to his eyes. "Just how your mother wore her hair. I'd like that." The comforting nostalgia in his voice made her think he'd be okay soon.

"Is Nathan up yet?"

"He was in the shower when I came out for coffee."

"How was it sharing a room with him for the second night?"

Her father shrugged. "He's quiet and tidy. Just the opposite of Gavin when we were on the road."

Lexi recalled the lean years of the Jerry Mills racing team. Everyone doubled up in their rooms without exception. Room assignments had varied, but her father and his best friend were the one constant. They were inseparable on the road. Lexi chuckled, realizing Nathan was only the third person with whom her dad had shared a bedroom in decades.

"I understand you had a talk with him the other night."

He shrugged again. "He's your partner. He needed to know the type of person you are."

"I was surprised you told him about our difficulty until last year."

Her father sipped his coffee before he locked his stare on Lexi, his expression turning more serious. "I figured if he knew I was honest about a personal thing like that, he'd believe me about the rest." He nodded, forming a slight grin. "If he mentioned our talk, I guess it worked."

"I think it did. Thanks, Dad."

Her father's bedroom door opened, and Nathan stepped out, worry etched on his face. "Did you see the news?" he asked.

"No. Why?" Lexi knitted her brow. Whatever happened, it couldn't have been good.

He showed her the news alert notification on his phone. It read, *Senator Jackson (R-NV) dead from apparent heart attack.*

Her mind went to the senator's promise to get her the names of the Falcon Industries people. She fished her phone from her pocket and swiped the screen awake. The email app had no new notifications, confirming the senator's assistant had yet to respond. Toggling back to the notification screen, she noted a missed call from Jackson's private number. Lexi opened the phone app and played the waiting voicemail on speaker. Senator Jackson had said he had a concern he wanted to share, and she should call his personal line.

This was no coincidence, and Lexi's gut told her Benjamin Foreman was behind it. She locked eyes with Nathan. "We need to go."

17

Nathan shifted taller in the driver's seat when he crossed the state line into Nevada at the old Cal Neva Casino. He'd vacationed in California with his son and ex-wife twice, once to visit Disneyland in the southern part of the state and once to visit the Redwood Forest and the Northern Coast. He'd done all the driving and had racked up substantial miles on the Golden State highways then, but the amount of back and forth he and Lexi had done in the last few days might qualify them as honorary truckers. Maybe it was because Lexi wasn't needy like his ex-wife, or he didn't feel obligated to provide for her and do all the driving, but he gladly shared those duties with her. In hindsight, he realized his control issues played a major part in the demise of his marriage.

"I feel bad not stopping to see if Jan was at his office," Lexi said.

"He didn't answer his phone. We couldn't wait." Nathan left out the part about not leaving a voice or text message telling him where they were going. Besides finding the metal fragments in Yarborough's wreckage, Jan hadn't added anything to the investigation of the Raven. He'd read the initial accident report. It was top-notch. Hopkins was an excellent investigator, but his skills weren't the issue. This was now an ATF case. In Nathan's experience, straphangers only slowed things down.

"Still," Lexi said, "he deserves to be in the loop. We wouldn't have a lead on the Raven without him."

The guilt of not leaving a detailed message magnified as Nathan began to understand what made Lexi Mills tick. Jerry had told him on their first night sharing a room that his daughter looked tough and did a job requiring nerves of steel, but she was all heart. Nathan had believed Jerry when he'd said Lexi cared only about two things: her family and saving lives. And when those two things collided, God help the person who put her family in danger. But he took it with a grain of salt when Jerry said she did things because it was right, not for the accolades or some power trip. Today, Nathan Croft was a believer. Lexi Mills was the real deal and cared more about the people around her than making a name for herself. If she wasn't, Nathan would be in Austin, licking his wounds over her stealing his case.

"Maybe you should try calling Jan again." Nathan twisted the steering wheel wrap, thinking he'd make it up to Jan at the first opportunity.

"I would, but cell service has been spotty since we went over the summit."

Nathan pressed the gas pedal a little more, remembering cell service was better where they were headed in the exclusive part of Incline Village among the lakeside mansions. Soon, they reached the access road to Senator Jackson's home, but it was blocked by two dark SUVs with federal government plates. Two Washoe County Sheriff cruisers flanked the feds on either side of the entrance, and two deputies controlled access. Three news vans were parked across the street, and their satellite antennas were up for conducting live feeds to the local stations and national networks. Camera operators and reporters with Hollywood good looks were nearby, milling about. Further down the road was a Nevada County Sheriff's vehicle. When Nathan stopped short of the barricade, Jan Hopkins exited the SUV and jogged toward them.

"Glad you made it, Jan," Lexi said.

"I saw the news alert this morning and Nathan's missed call after my morning jog. I figured you'd come right up here, so I waited."

Persistent but respectful of boundaries, Nathan thought. Jan wasn't the straphanger. Nathan was, and probably the asshole, too. "Sorry I didn't leave a message, Jan."

"Things are moving fast. I get it. Just calling meant you didn't cut me out."

"Let's see if we can find out how he died," Lexi said, leading the way to the barricade. She approached a deputy, showing him her badge and credentials. "I'm ATF Agent Lexi Mills. I'd like to speak to the agent in charge of the scene."

The deputy's eyes widened with recognition. So did his grin. "One moment Agent Mills." He pressed the mic attached to his shoulder epaulet and called for Agent Stewart. "She'll be right out, ma'am." The deputy's expression turned sheepish as he pulled out his cell phone. "Agent Mills, would you mind? It would be an honor to get a picture with you."

Nathan snickered. *A selfie? This was a first*, he thought. He'd seen law enforcement types firsthand clamor to shake her hand and bend over backward to accommodate a request. She'd tried to hide it, but he could tell she was uncomfortable with the attention. This should prove to be an interesting encounter.

Lexi touched his lower arm, glancing at his nametag. "I'm flattered, Deputy Lewis, but there are enough pictures of me on Twitter and Instagram."

"Agent Mills." A woman in a dark suit stepped around the SUVs and joined their group. Her eyes were a bit red, as if she'd been crying. "It's good to see you again. We weren't formally introduced Tuesday evening. I'm Agent Cameron Stewart, chief of Senator Jackson's Capitol Police protective detail. How can I help you?"

"Do you mind if we talk to you privately?"

"Of course." Stewart invited their group several yards inside the control point outside of earshot of the deputies and the curious media across the street.

Lexi's expression turned soft. "First, I'm very sorry for your loss. This can't be easy on you."

"It's been hard on the entire team. The senator was a good man and quite charming. He was a delight to protect."

"I'm sure he was." Lexi took a deep breath, signaling a pivot to get right to business. "The senator left me a voice message last night. He said he had a concern he wanted to pass along to me. Do you know what it was about?"

"I'd love to help you, Agent Mills, but much of the senator's meetings were sensitive or classified. I can't release information about his comings and goings without authorization from the Capitol Police Chief and Senate leader." Stewart's defeated posture suggested she would provide the information in a heartbeat if her hands weren't tied.

"How about Mrs. Jackson? We met her Tuesday night. Is she up for questions?"

"I'm afraid not. The senator's children arrived overnight and have asked for privacy today."

"I understand. I felt the same when my mother passed away recently," Lexi said.

Nathan recalled Lexi's strength, pulling herself away from family the day after her mother died, two days after her wedding, to investigate a hit on the Raven. Though the leads they'd garnered failed to surface the target, they'd saved the life of a district attorney out to clean up corruption and put a killer behind bars. Those bars, however, weren't secure enough to protect the killer from the Raven, a disturbing fact that made Yarborough's death and now Senator Jackson's much more suspicious.

"Has the coroner issued an initial cause of death?" Nathan asked.

"We're still awaiting toxicology results, but the coroner on-scene saw no outward signs of trauma. Since it's an official record, I can relay Mrs. Jackson's statement to the responding deputy."

Finally, Nathan thought. All this secrecy and excuses about classified information posed one frustrating roadblock after another.

Stewart continued. "She said the senator had returned from the Emerald Club before nine and appeared fine. He went to bed, and she followed fifteen minutes later. When she entered the room, she found him clutching his chest. He passed out seconds later, and she called Agent David Ingram, who was on duty outside the house."

"Thank you," Lexi said. "This is quite helpful. I'll request authorization for your team to speak with us." She handed Agent Stewart a business card. "Please call when Mrs. Jackson is up for a few questions."

"Good luck, Agent Mills." There was following the rules but also doing the right thing. Agent Cameron Stewart was full of surprises.

Nathan slipped into Lexi's rental car, feeling certain that answers awaited them at the club. Lexi jumped into the driver's seat.

Jan entered the back and closed the door. "This is good news. The Emerald Club is a private restaurant and lounge for the jet-set crowd on the North Shore. Without a court order, they won't give up information or show us their security tapes."

"How is this good news?" Lexi asked.

"I need to make a call." Jan dialed his phone and put the call on speaker. It connected on the third ring.

"You left your earbuds on the nightstand."

Jan's cheeks blushed with embarrassment. Whoever was on the other end just solved the mystery of why he didn't answer his phone this morning. "I have you on speaker, Micha. I'm with Agent Mills and her partner, Agent Croft."

"Thanks for the warning, Jan."

"You didn't give me a chance."

"Well, the cat is out of the bag now. Hi, Lexi. Good morning, Agent Croft." Micha didn't sound the least bit sheepish.

"Hi, Micha," Lexi said.

Jan's impish grin hinted he might be sleeping alone tonight. "I'm calling to find out if your cousin still works at the Emerald Club in Incline Village."

"Yes. Why?"

"We need to check the security tapes from last night. Can you see if she's working today and ask if she'll help us?"

"I expect a very expensive dinner after this."

"It goes without saying. Joe's?" Jan said, looking as if his prospects for a repeat of last night had improved.

"Seven o'clock. I'll call Gina and let you know."

Jan disconnected the call and opened his car door, preparing to exit. "Follow me. It's only a few miles from here."

The entry room of the Emerald Club fit Lexi's expectation of a restaurant Senator Keith Jackson would frequent. It matched his public persona—luxury in a rustic wrapping. Every accent, fixture, and piece of furniture reflected the vibe of the majestic Lake Tahoe basin, but each flawlessly polished piece screamed money and exclusivity.

Jan stepped up to the host station. The tuxedo-clad twenty-something eyed the group up and down. His raised eyebrows told Lexi their casual attire didn't meet the club standards. He offered a forced smile. "Good afternoon. Welcome to the Emerald Club. Do you have a reservation?"

"I'm looking for Gina. She's expecting me. Can you tell her Jan is here?" Jan played it smart by not flashing his badge. If Gina was about to do them a favor, Lexi didn't want to jeopardize her job.

"Of course, sir. Give me a moment." The host scurried off, deeper into the restaurant.

"That was awkward," Lexi said.

"I feel like Jack Dawson sneaking his way onto the first-class deck of the Titanic," Nathan laughed. Jan and Lexi joined in.

Moments later, the host returned with a short woman in her forties. The designer suit fit her like a glove. She greeted Jan with a handshake. "Hi, Jan. Follow me to my office."

Gina led them down a short corridor to a door labeled "Concierge."

Interesting, Lexi thought. This was a one-percent club with an on-site concierge to cater to their clientele's every need and want.

After closing the door, Gina circled her desk and woke her computer with a jiggle of the mouse. "We don't have much time before the manager returns. What timeframe are you looking for?"

"We're not sure," Jan said. "We know Senator Jackson met someone here last night sometime before nine. Can you scroll through the tapes starting at about seven?"

Her head twitched at the senator's name. "I heard he died last night. Are you investigating his death?"

"We're working on another case and need to know who he met with."

"Sure. Sure. He was a regular and always sat by the fireplace in the lounge. That should narrow down my search to one camera feed." The speed and ease with which Gina punched commands into the keyboard reminded Lexi of Kaplan Shaw. When that woman got on a roll at her computer, her fingers were a blur.

Within seconds Gina had something. "There. That's Senator Jackson."

The video image showed him entering the lounge with Cameron Stewart and another man, presumably his security detail. The male guard went ahead and greeted another man whose back was to the camera near the fireplace and checked him with a metal detector wand. Once the male guard returned, Jackson joined the man at the fireplace lounge. When they shook hands, the man turned enough for the camera to catch his face.

"I'll be damned," Jan said.

"This makes two people who have died after meeting with him," Nathan said.

"With whom?" Gina asked.

"Someone who thinks he's covered his tracks," Lexi said. But Benjamin Foreman's mistake was working with a man who left calling cards. The Raven would be his undoing.

18

The driver brought the Town Car slowly to a stop at the curb of the Falcon Industries Building in Sterling, Virginia. Benjamin peered out the tinted side window, noting the vacant sidewalk. The last time he'd stepped onto this stretch of real estate, protestors carrying "Baby Killer" signs had pelted him with buckets of red dye, claiming his technology was responsible for the accidental bombing of a daycare center in Iraq. That was fifteen months ago.

Yes, special operators had used his product to take out the home of a suspected Taliban leader, but missing the target was a factor of faulty intelligence, not the equipment, as the official statement had read. The insulting day had precipitated his solitary life at his mountain retreat. He'd designed Shangri-La as a secondary headquarters during the summer months and holiday season, but the infuriating attack had convinced him to stay full time. Doing so was the best decision he'd made in years. The self-imposed solitude had given him more freedom to work on projects in secrecy.

Minutes later, Benjamin stepped from the elevator to the executive floor. Andrew Bohm exited a step behind, barking orders to his legal assistant through his cell phone. Everything seemed foreign on the floor, from the people to the furniture to the paintings on the walls, much like it had felt reopening the office after the extended forced COVID lockdown.

Every person in the corridor did a double take when Benjamin passed, and hushed whispers filled his wake. His impromptu visit was no longer secret. He pushed through the double glass doors of the CEO's suite, finally discovering a familiar face. His personal assistant, who served as Benjamin's eyes and ears and provided him with regular updates on the power struggles within the company, was dutifully standing by her desk, holding a leather folio.

"Good morning, Mr. Foreman. Everything is prepared per your specification." Smartly dressed in a dark pencil skirt and matching jacket, Leiha Walker was the poster image of a professional assistant. Not a hair was out of place, and her perfect posture was the envy of every charm school instructor. She handed him the morning briefing folio.

"Thank you, Ms. Walker. Any change of plans?"

"Yes, sir. Only Mr. Sutton is in the conference room awaiting the start of your noon meeting. The control center reports the senator is at the venue where the president is slated to speak later today."

A glance at the wall clock confirmed he'd arrived with ten minutes to spare.

"That is fine," Benjamin answered. Jack Sutton was Senator Majority Leader Ed Gotkin's chief of staff, but he was also the driving force behind the senator's policy stances, including a strong surgical strike capability. Their mutual tip of the spear experience in the Army also gave them a bond, one only warfighters shared. Ed was the real power in the Senate. His approval was all he needed to unlock the log jam.

"You'll find this week's status report on the Locust Program on top, followed by the financial projection you requested overnight," Leiha said. "Refreshments and snacks are on your credenza."

"Perfect as usual."

"May I get you anything else for the rest of your stay, sir?"

"Congressional approval and a three-year DoD contract would be nice." Benjamin winked. "Thank you. You've outdone yourself, but after a year in the mountains, I find the Beltway suffocating. I'll be leaving shortly after my meeting."

Following her soft nod, he stepped into his office. Except for the fresh flowers on the coffee table, the space was exactly as he'd left it last year, down to the autographed picture of him with Clint Eastwood during a chance meeting at Pebble Beach. Clint kindly couriered the signed copy to his office after speaking at the GOP convention.

Andrew completed his call and slid his phone into his suit breast pocket. "We revised the Locust Program proposal to allow immediate field use of the prototypes."

"Good. Good. I want to be prepared now that our biggest stumbling block is out of the way."

"This next meeting should get the program off the ground."

"Let's hope so. Otherwise, I'm prepared to act." Benjamin glanced at the wall clock next to the picture of him and Clint. It was time to see whether the country would be at war by next week.

He circled his desk and entered the conference room through his private entrance. Andrew followed.

"I'm glad you're here, Jack." Benjamin shook his hand. "The landscape is changing rapidly with Senator Jackson's passing." His friend's long expression suggested his hopefulness was premature.

"Not as much as you might think, Benjamin. I'm confident I could wrangle the votes to get your project out of committee if not for the roadblock living in the White House. President Brindle has signaled privately that she will veto any military spending bill increasing the lethality of our weapons arsenal or containing any new weapons projects. The Locust Program hits both of her red flags. She mentioned your project by name during her first meeting with my boss, citing she would never approve it. We currently don't have the votes to override a veto in the full Senate, which explains why Senator Jackson sat on your proposal. We're working on a deal with the minority leader to insert funding for the Locust Program under the black ops umbrella to mask it from the president. Unfortunately, it will take time and might not happen before the midterms. If it doesn't happen, we'll have to see how the next presidential election shakes out."

"That's not good enough." Benjamin pounded his fist once against the table. "You're turning into one of them, Jack. They all think it's easier to accept defeat than to act."

Benjamin shook his head to expel the bitter taste of disgust. No matter the issue, season, or time of day, politics and politicians turned his stomach.

Few had the backbone to place what was right before the party, and those who did were eaten alive by their own, given crappy committee assignments without a single leadership role. "This is very disappointing, Jack. Microtechnology is the future of warfare, and our adversaries aren't far behind. If we don't lead the way, we'll lose the tactical advantage and be at greater risk."

"I don't disagree, but to get things done in Washington, we have to play the game, or the game plays us."

"Live to fight another day type of thing," Benjamin said. *It's a loathsome philosophy reserved for cowards*, he thought.

"That's right. Some hills are worth dying on, but the Locust Program isn't one of them," Jack said, raising his eyebrow as if he'd thought they'd reached an agreement, but that couldn't be farther from reality. The program was Benjamin's Iwo Jima. Before he died on this hill, he would take out as many of the enemy as he could.

Benjamin stood. "Then I think we're done."

Jack rose to his feet too. "I'll do what I can to keep funding research, but we'll have to wait until after the midterms to see where we stand. If we can pick up three seats, we're golden."

"The midterms might be too late. Mark my word, if another nation starts using similar technology, it will be years until we can even the playing field."

Benjamin retreated to his office with Andrew Bohm steps behind him. He made a direct line to the corner wet bar and poured a double scotch. All the money and time he'd poured into the program was now wasted. He'd leveraged the company, taking out loan after loan to fund research and prototype development. If he didn't turn a profit soon, Falcon Industries could be on the brink of bankruptcy.

He downed his drink in one gulp, tightened his grip around the glass extra hard, and shattered it against the wall, missing Clint by an inch. "Jack and his boss have made their choice, dammit. Now it's war."

"Forgive my ignorance, Benjamin," Andrew said in a calm voice, "but how can a war help us in the immediate time frame? Fanning the flames of war in the right place will take months. Even if you did, this president is a political dove. She won't take this country to war even with enough Congressional support."

"I've considered the inevitability." Benjamin watched the flames dancing between the logs, comforted by their warmth and the meaning of his next words. "We need to kill someone high up, someone the country loves, and make it appear like a political assassination. It has to be the president."

The leather creaked when Andrew shifted in his chair—his tell he was uncomfortable with the suggestion. "Who do you plan to set up for the blame?"

"Maduro. His anti-American policies make him an easy target. And since he's sided with China, Russia, and Cuba, the administration won't risk starting an all-out war, but they will want to retaliate. That's when we present the locust as their only option. Even with Maduro's virtually impenetrable security, the locusts will find a way in and give them their revenge without the world knowing. And we'll give them the technology in exchange for the fat contract they're holding up in committee."

"I must say, your plan is brilliant, Benjamin. We get rid of a president who will take our country to the brink of irrelevancy, and we get the contract. How do you plan to pull it off?"

"The attack needs to be public with cameras rolling."

"During a speech or special appearance would be ideal," Andrew said.

"Perfect." Benjamin smiled. "I know the right fall guy we can use to be caught at the scene."

"The FBI will need to find a tie between him and Maduro," Andrew said.

"I'm ahead of you. The sniper will be a Venezuelan national on visas sponsored by Chevron." Benjamin glanced to his right, discovering a broad smile on Andrew's lips. "I take it you approve."

"Very much so. He won't have to take an accurate shot with the locust, only pull the trigger."

"Exactly." Benjamin pulled out his cell phone to set things in motion.

19

Fort Washington, Maryland

A man in a dark blue Herrington jacket shuffled forward in line for the step-through metal detector controlling access to the convention hall. His clean-cut appearance helped him blend into the crowd of three thousand presidential supporters for today's speech, but to Secret Service Agent Dante Cole, he stood out like a sore thumb. The man hit all the profile markers—white, male, twenty-five to fifty-five, traveling alone, and carrying a backpack. The exact profile of the man who put a bullet in his leg six years ago. The targets changed every four to eight years, but the type of radical nutjob stayed the same.

Dante issued hand signals to the uniformed agents operating the security checkpoint, flagging the man for extra scrutiny. His team would search every inch, coming short of a public rectal exam.

The radicals had remained on the sidelines during the campaign, but once the election results pointed toward the United States having its first Black woman president, death threats picked up from the typical extremist groups. But those didn't keep Dante up at night. The number of potential lone wolf reports from every state had spiked the week before Brindle's inauguration, which terrified him.

Every agent who joined the Secret Service had fantasies of diving in front of a bullet meant for the president. Most never made it to protection details, and even fewer made it to the president's side. Dante's chest had rightly brimmed with pride the day Director Woods tapped him to head up the new president's personal security detail, but the euphoria was short-lived. He'd become responsible for a president with the biggest target on their back since Lee surrendered to Grant in Appomattox, and he hadn't slept through the night since.

Today was particularly nerve-racking. Since the local coroner had yet to determine the cause of Senator Jackson's death last night, he considered the possibility of it being an assassination and had taken no chances with the president. He'd added extra agents at the stage, limited the public entry point to one door with two lines, and had double the amount of casually dressed agents and local police officers in the crowd.

"Twitcher One, you're needed in the nest," Dante's number two announced over the radio comms.

"Copy," Dante said through his mic. "How long until Bluebird is ready?"

"In ten."

"Copy. Twitcher One returning to the nest." Dante thought the code-name understated the new president. He understood why she chose it. Dark blue suits were her trademark, and she was born and raised in St. Louis, Missouri, where the Eastern bluebird was the state bird. However, he thought a woman who flew jet fighters and spacewalked while raising four children deserved a more majestic codename to reflect her fierce nature.

He glanced at the checkpoint again before stepping away. His instincts had been spot on. One uniformed officer put the man in the Herrington jacket in handcuffs, and another placed a switchblade into an evidence bag. The suspect might not have been there to target the president, but he clearly intended to make trouble.

Dante skirted the gathering crowd in the Gaylord's main hall, following the perimeter of the speech hall for the best full view of the room. This would be his last chance to spot possible attackers before Bluebird took the stage. Nothing caught his attention, so he slipped through the backstage door, acknowledging the agent stationed there with a firm nod on his way past.

Bright fluorescent lights lit the empty corridor, but he sensed the ceiling-mounted security cameras following him every step of the way. A pesky fly hissed around his ear, prompting him to swat a hand at it. He pushed open the door to the office suite where the president was getting ready. Aids were scattered about the outer room, most pulling their hair out while staring into a glowing tablet or laptop screen. The Naval officer with the football was in the corner, talking to the president's emergency physician. A newcomer raised his curiosity, so he approached his number two in the opposite corner with the comms controller.

Dante whispered, "What's Senator Gotkin doing here?"

"That's why I asked you here. He's asked for a word with Bluebird, but the chief of staff said no interruptions."

Oh boy, Dante thought, rolling his neck to release the tension. President Brindle had told him on her first day in office that the majority and minority leaders of each chamber of Congress would have unfettered access to her, day and night. As the majority leader, Senator Ed Gotkin was on her list. She'd never say it aloud, but after his second private meeting with her last week, it was abundantly clear he was her least favorite visitor.

"I'll handle this." Dante approached Gotkin. "Senator, what can I do for you?"

"I need a word with the president before she makes her speech."

"Can this wait? We want her on stage in a few minutes. The networks are covering this live."

"No, it can't." Gotkin turned his stare hard, baking in the accusation of *"how dare you block my access to the president."*

"Give me a moment, sir." Dante was one hundred percent sure the senator's arrival minutes before what might prove to be a controversial speech was not the right time for a chat. However, the president had made it clear on their first day together. His job was to protect her from threats, not thorny political adversaries to whom she'd promised unrestricted access. But of all the people she'd placed on her unfettered list, including her family, Gotkin came across as the most entitled by a mile.

Dante had seen his share of entrenched career politicians, and most turned his stomach. It didn't matter which side of the aisle they came from; they were all out for one thing—power. And political power was a hideous drug. Once tasted, it had them coming back for more. Gotkin, the king of backdoor deals, was the worst of the lot. Reelection and the balance of power were more important than actual lawmaking, and Dante suspected another grand bargain in the making.

He knocked on the meeting room door where the president, her chief of staff, and speechwriter were going over their final notes for her speech explaining her plan for a major troop withdrawal from the Middle East and eastern Europe while stressing the importance of stable oil-producing nations in the wake of last month's attempted coup in Venezuela. After hearing a muffled voice on the other side, he opened the door and stepped inside, closing it behind him. The stylist was putting the final touches on Brindle's flawless makeup.

"Madam President, Senator Gotkin is in the next room. He's asked for a moment of your time."

The president had few outward shows of frustration, but a deep intake of air was top of the list. This one was particularly long and breathy. "That man has no sense of timing."

Offering to run interference crossed Dante's mind but doing so might start him down a slippery slope. He remained silent and waited for the president's cue.

Chief of Staff Torres bit his lower lip—his annoyed look. "I wish you'd never given him full access. He's abusing it."

"I know he is, Martin, but I promised myself to prioritize mending fences over my peace and quiet. I will, though, discuss boundaries with him." Brindle glanced at the clock on the wall. "After my speech."

Dante couldn't hold back a grin. "Ready when you are, ma'am."

The president removed the protective tissue covering the collar of her blouse and pushed up from the director's chair. "Let's do it."

Dante opened the door, holding it open for the president and her small entourage. Gotkin stood and stepped toward her, extending his hand. "Madam President, thank you for seeing me. May we speak in private?"

She shook his hand with a firm grip but let go quickly. "Yes, but it will have to wait until after my speech. Unlike my predecessor, I won't keep the media waiting. Everyone's time is valuable." Brindle turned her focus to Dante. "Please see to it that he's comfortable until I return."

"Of course, ma'am." Dante waved over his number two and whispered so only he could hear. "Find him the hardest seat in the room." Number Two acknowledged with a wink. Dante then spoke into his mic. "Bluebird flying the coop."

President Brindle continued out of the suite without giving Gotkin time to object. His dazed expression reminded Dante of the time his brother banged his head on the monkey bars when they were kids. Gotkin's head must have been spinning.

Dante caught up with the president quickly. He wasn't tall at five feet eleven inches, but he towered over her by half a foot. Their height difference meant taking shorter strides at a slower pace, which had both advantages and drawbacks. While he had more time to assess threats, the president was exposed to danger for longer periods in transit. And during a rapid egress, her shorter stride could cost them precious seconds unless agents lifted and carried her.

Chief of Staff Torres stayed by her side, reminding her to first mention the passing of Senator Jackson and her condolences to his widow. He cocked his head and waved a hand over his ear. "Damn fly."

The fly floated higher before returning to Dante for a second round of taunting, convincing him his girlfriend was right. His recent choice of aftershave smelled nice, but its faint floral undertone might attract bugs. He made a mental note to toss the bottle out when he returned home.

They would reach the stage door in three more steps, and the show would begin. Every agent in the room would have eyes on the crowd. Two in the hotel security office would watch the live feeds, looking for anything out of the ordinary.

Torres stretched his legs longer, getting one step ahead to open the stage door.

The fly returned and hovered.

The president wobbled, her foot slipping on the polished linoleum. Dante reached out, grabbing her by the elbow before she hit the floor. Brindle went limp. "Are you okay, ma'am?"

20

Once over the summit and traveling west on the main interstate, Lexi checked her phone, discovering she and Nathan were in the best pocket of cell reception until they reached Shangri-La. She dialed the one person sure to help her quickly navigate the political red tape snarling her investigation.

"Lexi, I half-expected your call after hearing of Senator Jackson's death this morning," Maxwell Keene said. "Do you suspect it's linked to the fatal accident of his chief of staff?"

"Yes." Lexi outlined how she learned about last night's meeting between the senator and Benjamin Foreman and her meeting with him. "First, Yarborough. Now him. My gut tells me he didn't die from natural causes. I'd bet my last dollar Foreman caused it. The Capitol Police security detail here can't answer my questions without authorization from their chief. If I go through Lange and the ATF, her request will have to navigate layers of management and could take days."

"You need me to grease the wheels."

"That and help me shake the trees. Senator Jackson was supposed to provide me with the names of Falcon Industries personnel involved in some unnamed classified project before his committee. Like Jackson, his chief of staff had met with Foreman the night he died."

"If it's top-secret, it will be harder to wrangle, but I'll reach out to Senate Majority Leader Gotkin."

"Thank you, Maxwell. I hope I'm wrong about this."

"Considering how cagey you said Foreman was, I'd say you're on the right track. Before I let you go. How are Nita and Jerry faring with their Secret Service protection?"

"Nita is catching up on reading, but Dad feels cooped up."

"Knowing how you work, I'm betting this won't last much longer."

"I hope not." Lexi completed the call and re-pocketed her phone, mulling over what she might encounter during her second meeting with Benjamin Foreman. She expected more evasive responses to her questions or the runaround from his lawyer.

Jan leaned forward from the backseat. "If you don't mind me asking, Lexi, who's Maxwell?"

"Maxwell Keene, the Deputy Director of the FBI. I worked for him on a joint task force last year, and we've kept in touch." Jan didn't have to know Lexi had become close to the Keenes after saving his wife from falling prey to one of Tony Belcher's deadly traps. Nor did he have to know Maxwell would move heaven and earth to help her, and she would do the same for him.

"You're being modest, Lexi," Jan said. "Your task force stopped the Las Vegas dirty bomb. But the deputy director of the FBI. He must have some serious pull."

"He does and knows how to get things done. If anyone can cut through the red tape to get us answers, Maxwell can."

An hour later, Nathan eased their rental car up to the pole-mounted speaker on the access road several yards from the gate at Shangri-La. He pressed the button. A voice answered. "Good afternoon, Agent Croft, Agent Mills, and Detective Hopkins. How may I help you?"

"We need to ask Mr. Foreman a few more questions. Can you let us in?"

"Stand by." Several moments of silence passed, stretching into minutes. Finally, the gate clanked, and the sides rolled open. The voice returned. "Please drive to the main house."

Nathan rolled through the gate, following the asphalt until it turned into a path of pavers at the circular driveway. After he parked, the front door opened when the group stepped under the portico. Harold appeared, again dressed in his dark suit. He waited until they reached the top step. "Please come in. Mr. Foreman will speak to you soon."

Interesting choice of words, Lexi thought. Not "see you."

Harold escorted them through the great room where they'd first met Mr. Foreman and ushered them into the dining room. The rustic accents complimented the entry room decorations, creating a warm, cozy atmosphere. "Please have a seat. Mr. Foreman won't be long." He gestured toward the polished dark oak table. A serving tray holding a pitcher of ice water, a coffee carafe, glasses, and ceramic mugs was at the center. Another tray with a variety of cheese, crackers, fresh fruit, and pastries was next to it. Harold disappeared through a walkway past a fireplace with a large screen television above the mantle.

A glass of water would have been fine, but the entire spread was an attempt to put them at ease. To lull them into a trance with hospitality so Lexi would throw him only softballs when she opened the questioning. That wasn't going to happen. Instead, she remained standing and crossed her arms over her chest. Jan mirrored her stance. Nathan did too, but not before popping a grape into his mouth. She gave him the side-eye.

"What?" Nathan shrugged. "I'm hungry."

Several minutes passed. Lexi scanned the room, looking for surveillance cameras but didn't find any obvious ones. Their visual absence didn't mean they weren't there. She felt the unnerving weight of being watched. That Foreman was sizing up his visitors before showing his face.

The television flickered to life, and Foreman's image appeared on the screen. Everyone focused on it. The picture blinked and garbled in spots, suggesting it was a satellite feed. "Good afternoon, Agent Mills," Foremen said. "Forgive me for not being there in person to greet you. I trust Harold has been an excellent host in my absence."

"Yes. He's been very gracious," Lexi said. "May I ask where you are?" She wouldn't be surprised if he were heading to some country without extradition to the United States.

"I had critical business in Washington, DC, and am flying back as we speak. How can I help you?"

"Have you heard the news of Senator Jackson's death?"

Foreman's lawyer appeared on screen, leaning in to whisper something into his employer's ear. "Yes. His death prompted my return to Falcon Industries Headquarters to discuss the future of several projects."

"With whom?"

"Those involved with the projects or with a vested interest in them."

"I see," Lexi said. His responses were still guarded, including only vague answers. "How did it go?"

"The jury is still out. Things are in flux until the senate sorts out the leadership and committee assignments."

"I understand you met Senator Jackson last night at the Emerald Club. What can you tell me about the meeting?"

"We talked about several Falcon Industries contracts and proposals falling under the purview and oversight of his committee. The discussion was quite cordial. He had one drink and left with his security detail. I'm sure they can confirm everything I've told you. They had eyes on him the entire time."

"The last time we met with Senator Jackson, he mentioned that the names of the Falcon Industries people associated with your projects weren't classified. His staff is slated to provide us with those names. Why weren't you forthcoming with the information when I requested it?"

The lawyer appeared on screen again, whispering into Foreman's ear. Foreman nodded to him and said to Lexi, "I disagree with the Senator's assessment. The names were part of a highly classified package presented to DoD and the committee. If those names become public, my people could become targets of adversaries who want to get their hands on the technology. I won't put them in danger. It's my job to protect my people. If the Senator's staff or DoD provides you with the names, so be it. Otherwise, you'll have to subpoena me to get them."

And there it was. During their earlier meeting, Foreman was cautious, measuring every response and hiding behind the cloak of classified information while appearing cooperative. His legal line in the sand meant Lexi was getting close to something.

The lawyer entered the screen. "Agent Mills, my client is done answering questions. Please go through my office if you need to speak with him again. I'll send you my contact information."

The television went blank, and Harold reentered the room, looking crisp in his tailored suit and perfect posture. "You're welcome to stay to enjoy the refreshments."

"Thank you, Harold," Lexi said. "I think we'll be going."

He extended a hand toward the entry room. "May I escort you to the door?"

Once in the car and past the gate, Lexi couldn't hold back her satisfaction.

"What's the smile for?" Nathan asked after glancing at her from behind the wheel. "Foreman gave us nothing."

"He may have thought he'd covered all his bases, but he made one mistake. He said the senator's death prompted his trip to DC. The media didn't pick up the news until this morning. If Foreman is already returning from his meetings, he must have known about the senator's death before the rest of the world. Think about it. Even in a private jet, it takes five hours to fly across the country. It's noon here. He would have left about six o'clock in the morning. The first media alert didn't hit until six. You can't convince me he heard the news and hopped on a plane minutes later. That begs the question: How did he know? Either someone told him, or he learned about it firsthand."

"Someone may have leaked the information," Nathan said. The only people who knew he died last night were his wife, his security detail, the first responders, and the on-scene coroner.

"In that case, we need to check if his pilot filed a flight plan with the FAA. The timestamp might tell us when Foreman first knew."

"I bet he flew out of the Nevada County Airport. I'll call," Jan said, checking his cell phone, "as soon as we're in range of a cell phone tower."

"How far is the airport?" Lexi asked.

"About twenty miles."

"Hit me with directions," Nathan said. With any luck, they would soon get answers.

21

Dante tightened his grip around the president. His heart pounded harder when she became dead weight in his arms. "Are you okay, ma'am?"

Her eyes were closed, making it impossible to tell whether she was unconscious or, worse, dead. The worst flashed in Dante's head. Not since Freedom Square in Tbilisi, when some nut threw a Soviet-made hand grenade at the speech podium that failed to explode, had a would-be assassin gotten close enough to do harm to a United States president. He couldn't live with himself if he was the agent who let something slip by, and the country lost its first president since Kennedy.

Each passing agonizing fraction of a second without a response terrified him. He imagined his official photo being splashed on every news outlet and social media platform around the world as the Secret Service agent who lost a president. His planning and security procedures would be dissected at the Rowley Training Center by future agents for decades and become the standard for what not to do.

"Madam President." Dante shook her gently.

Then.

Brindle's eyes opened. "These damn heels." She struggled to straighten herself, but Dante was frozen with relief. The president was alive. The nation wouldn't dive into turmoil. And he wouldn't be the

Secret Service poster child for failure. She wiggled again. "Do you mind, Dante?"

"Sorry, ma'am." Dante brought her upright and steadied her by the elbow. "Are you okay? Did you hurt yourself?"

"Only my pride." She adjusted the shoe on her right foot. "I should have scuffed the bottom of these damn things with my nail file."

"You gave me a fright," her chief of staff said. "I'll get your aide to scuff the bottom of every shoe in your closet."

"Don't you dare. No one touches the Jimmy Choos. Never in my life have I spent a thousand dollars on a pair of shoes. Frankly, I never understood spending that much on wardrobe, but the stylist said they were a must."

"It's all about image," Chief of Staff Torres said. "The media is brutally critical about the wardrobe of women politicians. We want to give them one less thing to hate about you."

"Well, once this speech is over, I'm heading back to the residence to put on my sweats and Chucks."

Dante preferred the relaxed president in her knock-around clothes over the flawlessly dressed one in public. When she swapped her blazer for a sweatshirt, she relaxed and reverted to the fun-loving, French fry-eating woman from the campaign. Dante recalled the night after Super Tuesday when it had become clear she'd won the party's nomination. The Secret Service had assigned her a protection team a month earlier after her campaign appeared to be a runaway and had received a credible threat.

The hotel suite her campaign had rented was rowdier than Animal House, with more champagne ending up on the floor than in glasses. She'd sneaked into the kitchen for a moment of quiet and had almost turned around when she saw Dante had gotten the same idea.

"*Stay, ma'am,*" he'd said. "*Other than the bathroom, this is the only quiet place in the suite. I'll wait in the hallway.*"

"*Don't leave.*" She'd pointed to the Coors Light longneck in his hand. "*Do you have another? I sure could use a beer.*" She'd unbuttoned her blazer and removed her heels, slinging them on the counter. She'd downed half the beer in several consecutive gulps and slammed it next to her shoes. "*Dante, right?*"

"*Yes, ma'am,*" he'd said.

"*I'm not sure if I'm up for this. There's a good chance I might become President of the United States.*"

"*It's a little late for second thoughts. But if it's any consolation, I've been doing this for a long time, and you're the first candidate I've enjoyed protecting. You're not full of yourself, a rare quality in this business. I hope you don't lose this side of yourself when you become president.*"

Sadly, Dante had seen that side of President Brindle less and less since her election. Her nonstop schedule didn't allow for many moments of sweats, Chucks, and longnecks with her husband and youngest child. Every day had her at a meeting or an appearance requiring she wore her Sunday best, as she'd called her suits. The only time he'd seen her relaxed in the last month was following her half-hour on the treadmill or the one day a week on the golf course. He wished she'd make more time for it every day.

President Brindle locked gazes with Dante again. "Let's go win some hearts and minds."

Dante opened the door leading to the stage, where someone announced the entrance of the President of the United States. The crowd roared. Dante took his post in the wings. The president walked out onto the stage with her signature bright smile, waving to the masses.

"... and may God bless America." Meghan ended her speech with more cheers and applause than expected from this crowd. She'd predicted the convention of Democrats would hail her troop withdrawal plan, and they had, but the electricity in the room was spine-tingling. The attendees hung on every word, even clapping for her support of the United States promoting stability in oil-producing countries until the country retooled its ground transportation infrastructure, replacing fossil fuels with electricity. The second part was a long-term goal with California setting the example for the rest of the country.

She stepped away from the podium, acknowledging two high-roller donors at the back of the stage who had organized the event with firm handshakes and the promise to appear at a future gathering later in the year. When she turned and entered the stage wing, Dante spoke into the mic in his sleeve, telling every agent in the room that Bluebird was taking flight.

Meghan liked the Secret Service code name she'd picked from the list her security detail had provided. They'd added Bluebird as an homage to her St. Louis roots and her signature blue wardrobe, but those factors weren't why she picked it. Native American tribes associated bluebirds with the return of spring after winter and prosperity. That's how she wanted her administration to be received. She wanted the American people to consider her presidency a period of hope, happiness, and growth.

Martin Torres met up with her and kept pace as she left the stage area and reentered the corridor where she'd come close to breaking her neck earlier. "The sound bites should play well in the evening news cycle," he said. "The SecDef tasked the Joint Chiefs to have a detailed three-year plan to you within ninety days."

"Were they kicking and screaming?"

"There were grumblings, but she got the impression the chiefs planned to wait you out," Martin said.

"If they do, I'll accept anyone's resignation who doesn't provide an implementation plan on time and replace them with someone who will. This is the one issue I won't compromise on." Meghan expected resistance but was willing to take any legal measures to implement her primary platform issue.

"I made your stance clear, but they think your veto threat is a bluff."

"Reelection is no guarantee. The American people gave me four years to make changes, and I won't break a promise to them. Our overseas presence will be limited to traditional strategic strongholds. If I hope to complete it by the end of my term, withdrawal must begin next fiscal year."

They reached the door to her staging room. Meghan paused and lowered her head, dreading the conversation she was about to have with the person waiting for her on the other side. Senator Gotkin was a power-hungry man. Not winning his party's nomination made him publicly resentful of Meghan's success and positive reception around the country. Privately, he acted just as aggrieved, testing how far he could push the President of the United States.

She understood his gall. The Democrats had a razor-thin majority in the House, his party had a seven-seat control of the Senate, and the Supreme Court was stacked six-three in favor of conservative justices. Considering their ages, she estimated it might take a decade or more before liberals could claw back control of the court. He was under the misimpression she would bend to pressure to reach a consensus, but a career as a naval aviator and raising four teenagers gave her a backbone the size of his home state of Texas.

Dante, who could read her mood like a book, leaned in and whispered so only she could hear. "You look tired. Shall I tell him you've been called away and have him see you in the White House tomorrow?"

"Thank you, Dante, but I keep my promises," she whispered back. He retreated, offering her a silent nod. She pushed the door open, half-hoping Gotkin had given up waiting, freeing her to return to the residence and dump her heels for some Chucks, but her favorite tennies would have to wait. Gotkin was sitting in the corner, scrolling through his cell phone, and several assistants were milling about.

Meghan straightened her posture, put on her best game face, and shook his hand. "Senator, I'm glad you stayed. Now, what would you like to discuss?"

"May we speak in private, Madam President?"

In his letter to Meghan on her first day in office, the outgoing president had detailed some pitfalls uniquely associated with the office. One stuck out. He'd said holding private meetings with a political adversary without a trusted advisor by his side was his biggest regret. He'd written his words had a way of being twisted and being leaked to the press. While she disagreed with his brand of politics, the subtle advice was sound.

"Follow me." Meghan opened the door to the secondary room where her speechwriter and stylist were chatting and sipping coffee. They stood when she entered. "Can you give us the room?"

"Of course, ma'am," both said and left.

Martin followed her into the room with Gotkin, following her standing order to never leave her alone with a member of congress, no matter their party affiliation.

"I meant alone, ma'am," Gotkin said. He was testing her again, but it was time he learned boundaries.

"Mr. Torres stays. He's my memory, so I won't forget any action items that might come from our talk. This is the price of unfettered access, Senator. If you have a problem with my stipulation, my door is no longer open to you."

The skin above his collar turned a blotchy red. Meghan had heard stories of Gotkin's hot temper but had pushed those aside as sensationalism. She was beginning to think the report of him throwing a coffee mug through his office aquarium and sending water and exotic fish to the plush carpet was true.

"Fine," Gotkin said.

Martin closed the door.

"Madam President, Senator Jackson's death has changed the playing field on the Emerging Threats and Capabilities committee he chaired. We both know his seniority earned him the seats, not his record of toeing the party line. I'm moving up Mullins and added Green from Mississippi. We both know what effect their loyalty will have on the votes. Every project Jackson was sitting on will make it out of committee and through the senate, including the Falcon Industries' program you'd labeled dead in the water."

"We discussed this, Senator. No new weapon systems while we withdraw our forces from overseas."

"Your plan will decimate our intelligence-gathering capability in those countries you're abandoning. Even more reason to approve the program."

"I agree with the need to enhance intelligence gathering, but I agree with Senator Jackson's assessment on this one. I won't authorize a lethal system for which we have no defense. If the technology got into the wrong hands, no official or head of state would be safe."

"You're not following, Meghan. We've already brokered deals in the house to peel off three Democrats. We have the votes."

"Don't insult me, Senator. And do not presume an open door equates to informality. You may not respect me or my policies, but you will respect the office. This will be the last time you call me by my first name. Have I made myself clear?"

"Very."

"You may have the votes to pass the legislation, but you don't have the numbers in the Senate to override a veto. My stance on our military posture is the one issue on which I won't bend."

"We have a plan for that too, Madam President." The disdain in his voice was thick enough to clog the drains. His neck turned redder than when she'd shut down his private discussion. He crowded her before raising his voice loud enough to rattle the window. "I won't let you cut this country off at the knees and destroy the standing we've built as the world's superpower."

Meghan was shorter than him by at least half a foot and lighter by seventy pounds, but since her two sons' teenage growth spurts resulted in them towering over her, she knew how to handle a tantrum from someone bigger than her. She stood toe to toe with him and put on her mom face, sensing the fire in her eyes growing. "You picked the wrong woman to try to intimidate. You may think you're the big man in the Senate, but you'll never be so big I can't knock you down an inch or two."

The door flew open, and Dante rushed in with his extendable baton in hand. The determination in his eyes meant he was ready to crack Gotkin in the ribs for getting too close to her. Before she could tell him coming to her defense wasn't necessary, he had the senator by the collar and pulled him back several feet. Gotkin flailed his arms to keep his balance.

"Dante, it's okay," she said. "We were having a simple disagreement."

"Take your hands off me," Gotkin ordered. He tried shaking Dante loose, but his training and superior strength allowed him to maintain a firm grip.

"It sounded and looked like more than a disagreement, ma'am."

"It's all right, Dante. Senator Gotkin was just leaving." She turned her attention to him. "Don't test me, Senator. You will fail, and a media friendly to me will make sure you end up looking the fool. Now, if you'll excuse me, I have a country to run."

Ed Gotkin stormed from the small conference room, leaving the smug, ignorant Meghan Brindle at his back. Not since he was sixteen, standing in front of his mother after sneaking the car out of the garage without permission and backing into the neighbor's mailbox, had someone shorter than him given him a browbeating. It was embarrassing and infuriating, especially after her guard dog handled him like a rag doll. He should have insisted his personal security detail come in with him instead of volunteering them to augment the eyes in the auditorium for the president's speech.

That woman and her entire crew of advisors and Cabinet members spelled death for the country in terms of national security and world standing. Brindle didn't understand China, Russia, and every Islamic State in the world needed to be kept in check, and the United States was the only nation capable of doing so. She was pulling out American presence from Africa, west and central Asia, and eastern Europe, leaving Diego Garcia in the Indian Ocean as the only jump point between theaters.

Her plan was dangerous, creating a massive gap in intelligence gathering in Russia's and China's proxy countries—Cuba, Pakistan, Afghanistan, Libya, North Korea, Iran, and Iraq. She seemed incapable of learning from the hard-learned lessons from the Khobar Towers, the USS Cole, the twin towers, the Pentagon, and a dozen U.S. embassies around the world. But Ed wouldn't let her dishonor the memory of those who died to teach her those very lessons, including that of his only son, who was one of nineteen airmen killed in Dhahran in the Khobar bombing. The pain of losing him still stung more than a quarter century later, and he was determined to prevent other parents from suffering the pain he'd endured because of a lack of intelligence gathering on the ground.

Ed texted his security detail, telling them to meet him at the control point inside the Secret Service secured zone for the president and her entourage. Once they linked up again and started marching toward his waiting Town Car, he regained his confidence and sense of importance. Today would be the last time Meghan Brindle embarrassed him. Despite what she'd said about picking the wrong woman to intimidate, she'd picked the wrong man to piss off. She may hold the highest office in the land, but he had the right friends in the right places.

After boarding his Town Car in the back with his security team in the front, Ed scrolled through his contacts list until he found the number that could change the course of the country. He dialed, but the call went to voicemail. He opted to hang up and send a text message to keep his guards from hearing what he had in mind. He typed out a text and hit send. *We have a problem, Need to talk ASAP. Money is no object in solving it.*

22

While driving to the executive airport where Benjamin Foreman kept his jet, Lexi realized this part of California was nothing like how she'd envisioned the state before coming here. Movies, television shows, and commercials mainly featured the sandy beaches of San Diego, the metropolis of Los Angeles, the Bay Area bridges, Napa Valley vineyards, and Lake Tahoe's high mountain basin. But the Sierra Foothills were the state's hidden gem. The rolling hills brimmed with ponderosa, gray pines, and multiple varieties of oak trees, and the forest's underbelly was dotted with the red hue of manzanita and white streaks of buckeye and deer brush.

Jan had told her this region had four distinct seasons and was high enough to escape the Sacramento Valley heat in the summer but low enough to only get rare, light dustings of snow in the winter. It was the perfect retreat for those escaping the bustle of city life and the monotony of suburbia.

Lexi kept her stare fixed on the passing rustic scenery. "You're right, Jan. It's beautiful." This area reached the top of her list of possible retirement places for her and Nita when they were ready to grow old together. She could easily overlook the large flies like the one she'd seen at the bank.

"I've traveled to all fifty states," Jan said, "and fallen in love with many areas, but this place is simply magical."

"I get the same vibe," Lexi said, thinking Benjamin Foreman got it right by naming his compound Shangri-La. This part of the state was simply serene.

Nathan pulled into the parking lot of the Nevada County Airport. Along one side was a monument with an Air Force jet mounted at a forty-five-degree angle with the nose pointing toward the sky. Curious about the display, Lexi exited the car and walked down the sidewalk to the plaque. It said the jet was a retired F-104 Starfighter, the exact supersonic model Chuck Yeager, a local long-term resident before his death in 2020, had flown during an ill-fated test flight featured in the film adaptation of the *Right Stuff*.

"Lexi," Nathan shouted from farther down the sidewalk. "You coming?"

"Yeah," she said. While jogging toward him, she thought about her dad. He loved things like this. She would have to bring him up here once this case was over.

The airport reception area was no bigger than her hotel suite back in Napa. A small grille, similar to those found in golf course clubhouses, was on one side, but the counter on the other side brought Lexi back to her high school days. It was the exact configuration of the attendance office she would report to when she'd arrived late for class.

A man in a red flannel shirt perked up when they walked in. "Morning, folks. How can I help you?"

Jan stepped up and displayed the badge he had clipped around his waistband. "Detective Hopkins of the Nevada County Sheriff Department. I called ahead."

"Ah, yes." The man reached beneath the counter and brought out a set of stapled sheets. "I printed the flight plan notice you asked for and added today's return flight."

"When is it due to arrive?"

"In an hour." The clerk handed him the flight plan printout the pilot had filed for Benjamin Foreman's impromptu trip to the DC area.

"Do you mind if we wait for his plane to land?" Lexi asked.

"Knock yourselves out."

Jan scanned the papers and handed them to Lexi. She visually sifted through the data in the sheet, showing a flight to Leesburg, Virginia, focusing on the times listed. The projected and actual departure times weren't as important as when the plan was filed. The FAA received the flight plan at 0223 hours Pacific time. Unfortunately, the early hour raised suspicion but didn't prove guilt. Foreman could explain the timing by claiming someone at the scene had leaked information about the senator's death.

Lexi scanned the rest of the form-like printout, noting the number of people onboard was listed as four. She also noticed several unfilled data fields for a section labeled "For International Flights Only." One area left room for a list of passengers and their passport information for Customs, which gave Lexi an idea. She walked up to the counter.

"Excuse me, sir." She showed him her ATF badge and credentials. "Can you check if any international flight plans were filed for Mr. Foreman's plane in the last year and print them out for us?"

"Sure," the man said. "Give me a minute." When he rotated on his stool to face the computer monitor on the counter, the creaking metal told of its age. He worked the keyboard, using the hunt-and-peck method with only his index fingers, reminiscent of her father's technique.

"What are you looking for, Lexi?" Nathan asked.

"I don't know. I'm fishing."

"There's only one, miss." After the clerk dramatically pressed his finger on the Enter button, the familiar sound of a printer sounded from below the counter. He handed Lexi the sheet.

Her focus drifted to the bottom, where the passenger manifest would be listed for international flights. Besides the pilot, one passenger was listed. The name might not amount to anything, but it was worth checking out.

"Find anything?" Nathan asked.

"Foreman flew one man to Mexico City two months ago. His name is Robert Segura. I'll have Kaplan check him out." Lexi's stomach growled, reminding her she'd skipped breakfast. She glanced at the food counter on the other side of the room. The menu tacked to the wall said they offered hot dogs, hamburgers, and a limited variety of grilled sandwiches. "How about some lunch while we wait for Foreman?"

Fifteen minutes later, the man who helped them with the flight plan grilled up and served three burgers with fries and sodas.

Between bites, Lexi pulled out her phone and dialed. "Hi, Kaplan. I need your help." After explaining the day's events, she added, "Maxwell will try to get the names of the Falcon Industries employees. Meanwhile, I'll need you to dig around Foreman's and Falcon Industries' finances and see what you can come up with."

"That's a tall order, Lexi. Falcon Industries is like Fort Knox with its servers and information. I doubt I'll find anything on their systems, but—" Lexi could almost hear the wheels spinning in Kaplan's head—"I'll check their SEC filings and tax returns. If I can find out what banks Foreman uses, I can attack the search from that end."

"I have faith in your abilities, Kaplan. One more thing." Lexi snapped a picture of the bottom of the international flight plan and texted it to Kaplan. "I'm sending you a photo of a name with the man's U.S. passport number. Can you do a background search and send me his passport photo?"

"Let me open the State Department system. Give me a second," Kaplan said. Lexi heard keyboard clicks over the phone and imagined her friend's fingers moving at lightning speed. "Got him. I'll text you his photo and email you his passport application and travel records."

"Thanks, Kaplan. You're a gem. Keep me posted on your search."

"Will do. How are Nita and your dad doing with their bodyguards?"

"They're coping, Nita much better than Dad. This isn't how I envisioned my honeymoon, even after we asked my dad to come along."

"At least the ATF is picking up the bill since you went back on the clock. You'll have to schedule another one."

"We'll see." Lexi thought she and Nita might never get a proper honeymoon. They had rescheduled after Lexi's mother died, and now the Raven had shown up. At this rate, their first anniversary might arrive before they could take an uninterrupted vacation.

"You better do better than 'we'll see,' Lexi. You both deserve it."

Lexi completed the call and took another bite of the burger before her phone chimed with an incoming text. She opened Kaplan's message with the promised passport photo of Robert Segura. The image took her breath away. She gasped.

"What is it?" Nathan asked.

Lexi showed him the photo. "I know this man. He was at the bank hostage scene with the vest bomb two days ago. I thought he might have been the triggerman, but another man in the crowd was. I had him in my hands." She shook her head, thinking her instincts were right. He *was* involved, but the action on the ground was moving too fast for her to vet the other men she suspected. Lexi harrumphed. Segura was sly, bringing up a game of solitaire on his phone to misdirect her. In retrospect, she was right to be leery of his cool reaction when she pressed the muzzle of her service weapon against his back. "I can't believe I had my gun on him and let him go," she said, letting out a heavy sigh of failure.

"Don't be hard on yourself, Lexi," Nathan said. "You had no way of knowing who he was."

"We have to find him again," Lexi sighed. "He's linked to Foreman, and my gut tells me the bank bomb was the work of the Raven." She studied the photo, memorizing every feature of his face. "I'll find you again, Robert."

A half-hour later, following Nathan and Jan outside, Lexi leaned against the back wall of the airport greeting center under the metal awning covering the dining patio. The late-winter mild temperature and humidity were similar to those in Ponder this time of year, but there wasn't a place in Texas with the majestic scenery found in the Sierra foothills. She would have to move to the Rockies to find anything comparable. But the Rockies meant harsh winters, and Nita wasn't a snow person. She'd once said snow was something to visit, not live in.

Soon, a Learjet landed and taxied to the parking markers painted on the tarmac near the back patio. The tail number matched the identifier the man in the greeting center had provided Lexi and her group earlier. When the engines wound down, a passenger door sprung upward and a set of metal stairs unfolded, reaching the asphalt. That was Lexi's cue. She pushed herself from the wall and stepped to the edge of the cement patio, remaining under the awning. Nathan and Jan silently joined her side by side, blocking the walkway.

Several moments passed, making Lexi think Foreman was weighing his options and getting his story straight with his lawyer before stepping out. Six minutes after the door opened, Foreman finally appeared in the doorway. He'd exchanged his jeans and flannel shirt for a tailored silk and cashmere suit, which screamed money and power. His robust, confident stride didn't fool Lexi. She smelled fear from twenty yards away.

His lawyer caught up, carrying a leather satchel. The sweat beads on his forehead in the cool air confirmed Lexi's assessment. They were both nervous about her poking around, which boded well for her. Edginess set the stage for mistakes, and she'd be there to take them down when they slipped.

Foreman and his lawyer stopped several feet short of Lexi. Bohm eyed her up and down as if sizing her up for a harassment suit. "Agent Mills, I told you to go through my office."

"You're here, so I'm going through you." Lexi brought out her cell phone and opened the screen to the picture Kaplan had sent her. She first showed it to Foreman. He remained silent, but the barely there eyebrow arch suggested he recognized the photo. "Do you know this man? His name is Robert Segura."

"Over here, Agent Mills," Bohm said.

Lexi pivoted and showed him the picture. "Does your client know this man?"

"Why do you ask?"

"He was at the scene of a hostage situation involving an explosive device at a bank in Penn Valley on Tuesday. He was also a passenger on your jet on January 15th for an overnight trip to Mexico City."

"Are you suggesting this man had something to do with the hostage event?" Bohm had yet to answer Lexi directly, responding with questions. It was an effective avoidance tactic Lexi had used many times but found annoying when on the receiving end.

"We don't know, but we're looking into people who were there that day."

"My client often loans his jet to friends and associates. This man might have been a guest of one of them." Bohm carefully worded his response to toss suspicion elsewhere without directly answering the question. This man was good.

"The manifest listed only two people on board, him and the pilot. If your client didn't let this man onto his private jet, who did?"

"That was two months ago, Agent Mills. We'll have to review my client's records and get back to you."

"All right," Lexi said, doubting he'd get back with her in her lifetime. She turned her attention to Foreman. "During our last conversation, you had said Senator Jackson's death had prompted your trip to Washington, DC. News of his death didn't hit the media until the six o'clock hour this morning. However, your pilot filed a flight plan shortly after two. How did you learn of his death so quickly?"

The question failed to rattle Foreman. He remained still with not as much as a twitch to give Lexi a read. Bohm answered for his client, but Lexi kept her focus on Foreman. "My client misspoke earlier. He'd planned the flight to tend to pressing business. The senator's death made the trip much more necessary. Unless you issue a subpoena, my client is done answering questions, Agent Mills."

Foreman buttoned his pricey suit while giving Lexi a condescending nod. "It's been a pleasure, Agent Mills." He pushed past Nathan and Jan and walked into the building with Bohm.

Jan crossed his arms, focusing on the door Foreman had disappeared through. "That was the biggest pile of manure I've heard in a long time."

"I couldn't agree more," Lexi said.

"What's next?" Nathan asked, assuming his frustrated stance with his hands on his hips.

"Until Kaplan comes up with something, we wait at the hotel for Maxwell to come through so we can interview Senator Jackson's security team and maybe his widow."

23

A Falcon Industries' Lincoln Navigator was parked outside the airport reception building, idling at the curb, when Benjamin stepped through the main door. Andrew was still grumbling at Agent Mills' ambush, mumbling about the balls on her, but Benjamin wasn't angry. He was worried. Mills knew Robert's name and was on the trail of linking the locusts to Mr. Yarborough's death, and if his instincts were right about her, she also suspected him of the senator's death. She was getting too close to discovering how far he'd gone and would go to protect the Locust Program. Bugging her phone and tracking her location wouldn't be enough if this went on much longer.

The front passenger door opened, and a member of his security team exited the SUV to open the curbside rear passenger door. Benjamin slid inside while Andrew swung around the back to enter via the other side. After the doors slammed shut and everyone buckled in, the driver took off toward Shangri-La.

Andrew escaped by answering emails and missed text messages sent during their flight. Unlike his lawyer, Benjamin never felt attached to his electronic devices, considering them only as tools to get work done. He was an anomaly in today's world, but his phone contained not a single game, social media, or entertainment streaming app. Unless he felt his phone vibrate, Benjamin never checked it until he started the day in the morning or left a classified meeting where electronic devices weren't allowed.

Ten minutes later, his phone buzzed with the distinctive chime from his personal control center. Their notifications were one of the few interruptions he tolerated. He removed his cell from the interior breast pocket of his suit and checked the screen. His control center had reported the guests he'd requested meet him at Shangri-La had arrived, and Agent Mills and her partner were returning to Napa for the evening. Things were falling into place for him to put his plan for war in motion within a day or two.

Before re-pocketing his phone, Benjamin noted he'd missed one call and two text messages. Few people had his personal number, so anything missed was important. He swiped the notifications screen, ignoring his son's plea for another infusion into his trust fund to get him through the end of the semester at Yale. That was a discussion better held in person. Benjamin focused on the other notifications. Ed Gotkin had called and left a text message over an hour ago while he was on the plane from Virginia. Since he didn't leave a voicemail, Benjamin clicked on the missed text. The Senate Majority Leader always had a problem, but the part about money being no object in solving it caught Benjamin's attention.

He dialed Gotkin's number. The call connected.

"It's about time, Benjamin."

"What's wrong this time, Ed?"

"I met with the president. She's making it her life's mission to kill the Locust Program while implementing her insane plan of withdrawing our troops from Africa, eastern Europe, and the Middle East. If she does both, the country will be in untold danger. We need to stop her."

Benjamin liked the direction of this conversation. If he could create the right trail by using the Raven as the middleman to hire the Venezuelan with Gotkin's money, his hands would appear clean. Mills would go after those two, not him. Even if Mills linked his program to either death—the president's, Senator Jackson's, or Yarborough's—Benjamin could claim he knew nothing of Robert Segura's association with the Raven. He could say Robert had gone rogue, using the technology without permission like he did at the bank.

"What do you have in mind?" Benjamin asked. "Jack mentioned you plan to hide the Locust Program in black ops funding."

"Yes, but we still need to give her an indisputable reason to stop her foolish plan," Gotkin said.

"And what is that?" Benjamin pushed. He needed Gotkin to say the words. For him to think that what came next was his idea.

"Short of war, I don't know," Gotkin said the magic word.

"That's brilliant, Ed. We need to give the country a war in such a way that withdrawing troops would be impossible."

"How do you propose to do it?"

"Leave that part to me. But the man I have in mind to pull this off comes with a hefty price tag."

"How hefty?"

Benjamin thought, *one more push, and I'll have Gotkin where I want him.* "If you have to ask, maybe you should rethink what you're asking of me, Ed?"

"No, no, no. This needs to be done. Can you give me a ballpark figure?"

One little twist to make himself endearing, Benjamin thought. "I don't think the Raven would get involved for less than five million. I can front you the money if you can't raise it in time."

"No, no. I can raise the cash. This was my idea, so I need to foot the bill. I know of the Raven. He'll get the job done. Tell me when and where you need it."

"I'll be in touch." Benjamin ended the call, thinking if he played his cards right, everything would be in place within the hour.

Soon, the driver pulled through the main gate of Shangri-La, Benjamin's sacred retreat. Yards inside the fence, they passed the original log cabin that came with the land, a piece of history he didn't have the heart to tear down. The property had been in the family for four generations. The grandson of a Gold Rush 49er, his great-grandfather had bought the land in 1915 when traveling through this area after visiting the World's Fair in San Francisco. The little shack was a reminder of the Foreman men who came before him. He and his son were their legacies. All of this would one day be Harrison's if he could ever get his head out of his butt and graduate from business school.

The driver stopped at the foot of the portico leading to the main house's entrance. A black Escalade and two large men in dark suits were several yards ahead. They had to be the Raven's men.

Anxious to get things rolling, Benjamin didn't wait for his security team to get the car door. The front door opened before he was halfway there. Ever the impeccable manservant, Harold stepped out, holding a glass tray with Benjamin's traditional options of ice water or scotch on the rocks, his preferred cocktail following a long trip.

Considering who was waiting for him, he chose the scotch and took a healthy sip. The Raven was no fool and was known for keeping a tight ship among his clients. Though Agent Mills never mentioned finding the Raven's calling card—raven DNA—embedded in the locust remains, he'd overheard her discussing it with her colleagues. He could leverage the tasty tidbit against the Raven.

"That's perfect, Harold. Where are my guests?"

"They chose the game room, sir. Mr. Segura has missed using your billiards table."

"Of course he has." When Robert wasn't busy in the capsule lab solving the locust problem, he was honing his skills on the custom table. Benjamin stepped inside while Andrew caught up and swigged the orphaned glass of ice water from Harold's tray. "Follow my lead inside, Andrew. This might not go over well with our guests."

"What do you plan to do, Benjamin?"

"Get the Raven to do my bidding."

Benjamin heard the crack of billiard balls colliding off the break as he strode through the great room. He swigged the rest of Harold's lovingly prepared drink and dropped the glass on the corner bar as he passed. Until today, the Raven had only been a voice on the other end of the phone. After five more steps, Benjamin would finally meet the man to whom he owed solving the flight problem with the locust in person. The Raven was also the man who would become his fall guy.

He turned the corner into the game room. Robert, the engineering genius who'd made the locust operational, leaned over the side of the table. He gripped the tail of the cue stick with his left hand and rested the head between the thumb and index finger of his right with the hand arched against the red felt, lining up to hit the seven ball in a corner pocket. After analyzing the table's layout, Benjamin would have started with the shot too.

Motion from the dark corner of the room caught his attention. He turned, not surprised by the man standing there. Benjamin had conjured up an impression of the Raven months ago—dark, mysterious, and threatening—and his imagination wasn't far from reality. He expected the Raven's black clothes, long black stringy hair, and pale skin, but the bloodred eyes surprised him. The name matched the persona brilliantly to instill fear in clients. If Benjamin hadn't the intelligence resources of the CIA and a small, well-armed private army at his fingertips, he might have cowered under the Raven's intimidating presence. However, controlling the locust technology made Benjamin a stealthier threat. He stepped toward the man, offering his hand.

"It's a pleasure to meet you in person. Benjamin Foreman."

"Likewise," the Raven said, shaking his hand.

"Thank you for coming. A serious matter has come up. While the discussion might not be pleasant, I find it better to look a man in the eye, especially one I respect and am doing business with."

"I follow the same principle. It's the only way to judge a man's honesty and sincerity."

Benjamin gestured toward the seating area beneath the wall of his grandfather's mounted tennis rackets. They were a prized family possession. Before being drafted into WWII, he was the top-ranked amateur player in the country in 1943. Sadly, he returned home in a flag-draped casket, never reaching the professional level.

"Please, let's sit." Benjamin sat in his favorite leather chair, leaving the one across the table for the Raven. "I discovered what had caught the ATF's interest in Mr. Yarborough's death. They found raven DNA on the locust fragment. That was a concerning turn of events."

"Robert," the Raven said while keeping his stare on Benjamin. "Join us, please." His expression remained stonelike, but his chest rose and fell at a more rapid pace. He was visibly upset.

Robert returned the cue stick to the wall rack and sat on the end couch cushion closest to the Raven. His stiff posture suggested he was nervous.

"Robert is very proud of his work and has a practice of placing our mark into some of our products." The Raven turned his attention to him. "Please tell him which devices have it."

"Only the first ten units in the prototype run. It was the batch I used during development."

Benjamin rolled his neck, wondering how an arms maker of the Raven's caliber could leave such a damning trail in his work. The vanity, however, could play into Benjamin's favor. He would use one of those units to start the next war, effectively linking the Raven to the terrorist act, not him.

Benjamin focused on Robert. "I need you to send a list of the serial numbers to my control center so we can isolate those units from the rest of the prototypes." While Robert retrieved his phone, presumably to locate and send the information, Benjamin turned to the Raven. "This is very disappointing. Trust me when I say you don't want me disappointed."

"How can I make it up to you?" The Raven appeared uncomfortable being on the weaker end of a high-stakes business arrangement.

"I have another job for you, and we need to set up the Venezuelans to take the fall."

The Raven entered the backseat of his Escalade. Robert sat next to him and his guards took the front seat. When they were clear of the gate, the Raven turned toward his oldest friend in the world. He remembered the young boy who had arrived at the orphanage. He was scared and filthy from living on the streets of New York for the better part of a month after his family's apartment building had burned down, killing his parents, before Child Protective Services caught up with him. His innocent smile was why he protected the younger boy from the others his age. His act of kindness had earned him the nickname Starshiy, the beloved elder brother, from the shy boy who turned out to be an engineering genius. Robert had never stopped adoring him, but his devotion might be their undoing.

Robert searched his eyes. "You're angry with me."

"Can you blame me? What were you thinking, adding raven feathers to the product?"

"You had it right with Mr. Foreman. I'm very proud of my work, but I'm more proud of working for you. I had to leave your mark on everything we produced."

The Raven took a deep breath to calm the storm brewing inside him. "How long has this been going on?"

"Since the beginning, when you chose the raven feather as your calling card," Robert said.

"I use it only to drive a point home for special occasions." The Raven dug deep to temper the seething anger brewing in his belly. He hadn't been this enraged since the Russians he'd aligned himself with years ago tried to double-cross him by stealing the weapons he'd sourced from Iran and leaving him for dead. The scar on his chest reminded him to never leave a trail for someone to find him, yet Robert had done so in spades. "Can't you see you've given the authorities a way to track us?"

Robert lowered his head. His contrition meant he was beginning to see his blunder. "I'm so sorry, brother. I won't do it anymore. You have my word."

The Raven turned to peer out his passenger window at the dark evening sky. The thick rows of pine trees hid the moon and stars except in certain spots. He recalled how Robert was afraid of the dark when he arrived at the orphanage. He'd given the boy his only flashlight so he could fall asleep comfortably at night. He had to do something to punish Robert, especially after the bank robbery fiasco when Robert had gone after Lexi Mills on his own. Death was the proper sentence, but they were brothers. He would have to think long and hard before passing judgment.

"Your word might not be good enough, brother."

24

A cool, moist gray marine layer had collected along the Napa Valley hilltops overnight, adding a chill for Nita's stroll with Lexi along the golf course walking trail. It was sad to think that on their honeymoon, this was the most time in days she'd spent awake with her wife. She gave Lexi's hand an extra squeeze, recalling the day they'd arrived at the resort for an eight-night stay with many day trips planned to explore the area.

Saturday had been physically tiring from the travel and emotionally taxing from the memories of their last trip to this area, starting when they landed at Sacramento International Airport. The journey through the terminal and waiting for their luggage at the carousel had triggered awful recollections of the previous time she and Lexi were there. Their plane hadn't even landed last summer, and Lexi had already been called into action for a bomb threat in the town of Gladding. Lexi had hit the ground running, and that day had ended with her barely escaping three of Tony Belcher's traps alive and Nita taking a drink and gumming cocaine for the first time in six years. The giant slip from her sobriety had nearly cost Nita the love of her life, but Lexi had surprised her with her capacity for forgiveness.

The first two full days of their honeymoon had been relaxing. Sunday had included a drive north along the coastal highway with Jerry to take in the rocky shoreline and dine at a restaurant overlooking the Pacific Ocean. They'd spent Monday driving through the Napa Valley, stopping in St. Helena and Calistoga to explore the quaint shops and local eateries. Lexi and Nita had made plans to return to Calistoga to bathe privately in their hot springs, but that never happened.

Tuesday had begun with Lexi's boss dragging her away to another bomb threat. Her early morning call marked the point at which their honeymoon had gone awry. Nita wondered if her life with Lexi would always be like this. They would plan a romantic getaway, but duty would call, ripping Lexi away to save the day.

"Thank you," Lexi said softly, kissing the back of Nita's fingers as they walked. She then stuffed their clasped hands into her jacket pocket, protecting them from the morning cold.

"For what?" Nita asked.

"For being so patient and understanding. I sense we're getting close to some answers and the Raven."

Nita slowed, bringing them to a stop to search her wife's eyes. Regret filled them, but Nita needed to say her piece. "Understanding? Yes. Happy with it? Not so much. When I married you, I married your job, but understanding you can be called away at a moment's notice doesn't make it easy to accept, especially when it disrupts our honeymoon."

Lexi opened her mouth to respond, but Nita placed an index finger over her lips to delay it.

"Yes, I'm disappointed, but I'm not upset. How can I get mad when you're saving lives and protecting us from another madman? I'll get over it. Eventually. But I am worried about your father."

Lexi knitted her brow with worry. "How so? He seemed fine this morning when he got his coffee."

"Without his usual distraction of working on cars, being cooped up is taking its toll. He's become more withdrawn over the last few days and spaces out for longer periods. He misses Gavin and Jessie, and now he misses you."

"But when I get back here at night, I'm tired and want to spend time with you alone." Lexi lowered her head, her outward signal of guilt—the last thing Nita wanted to add to her wife's plate.

Nita raised Lexi's head by the chin with an index finger. "I get that, but he needs you more right now." She let go when Lexi met her gaze. "I know you two are uncomfortable drinking in front of me, which I get, albeit an unnecessary gesture. My urges are under control. But you should take your dad out for a beer at the hotel bar. He would love spending time with just you."

"He would enjoy that. He and Gavin used to hang out in hotel bars during their NASCAR days." Lexi smiled and stared far off as if knocking a memory loose "The stories those two used to tell of the early days on the circuit. It's a wonder they never ended up in jail with all those bar fights."

"It's settled. Take your dad out and swap some stories to let him know he's not alone."

Lexi pressed her hand against the top of Nita's left breast. "This is why I love you. You have such a big heart with the capacity to love everyone around you."

Nita placed a hand over Lexi's. "That might be true, but this belongs to you, Lexi Mills."

Lexi's phone buzzed with an incoming phone call. Nita recognized the custom ringtone. "You better answer. If Maxwell is calling this early, it must be important."

Lexi leaned in for a kiss while fishing for her phone from the seam pocket of her leggings. She let her lips linger through an extra ring before bringing the phone to her ear, making it sexy as hell. She pulled back far enough to speak while keeping her eyes locked on Nita. "Please tell me you have good news."

Lexi had the volume of her phone up high enough for her to hear Maxwell say, "The Capitol Police Chief approved your interview of the senator's security detail, but you better hurry. They're pulling up stakes at his house by the end of the day."

"That's great. We can get up there by noon."

"Talking to them will only get you so far, so I called in a marker with the chief. He talked to the senator's detail lead. Mrs. Jackson has agreed to answer questions before she goes to her son's house in California."

"Thank you, Maxwell."

"No need to thank me. The death of a sitting U.S. senator makes this a top priority. I trust your gut on this. If talking to the widow would bring you another step closer to capturing the Raven, I'd call in every marker I have."

"I'll let you know how things shake out." Lexi disconnected the call and slipped her phone into her thigh pocket. The excitement dancing in her eyes said she expected something in the case was about to break. "Nathan and I have to go back to Lake Tahoe."

"I heard. Do you think the senator was murdered?" Nita asked. "The news reports all say it might have been a heart attack."

"The coroner listed it in his preliminary assessment, but I have a hunch there was more to it. I suspect a rich, powerful defense contractor hired the Raven to supply him with the tool to kill the senator. And the bank hostage scene I went to on Tuesday is also tied in. I think the Raven is behind that too. But we've kept our suspicions under wraps until we can find proof."

"Assassinating a United States senator is insane. This man needs to be caught."

"That's exactly what I plan to do."

25

Feet pounded against the treadmill, and arms swung in a compact motion to the beat of Redbone's "Come and Get Your Love." Meghan wasn't a fan of science fiction movies but had to give the writers of *The Guardians of the Galaxy* props for cobbling together the perfect Gen X-er workout playlist.

The distance counter clicked higher, nearing her mark of two miles. Meghan had stopped breathing through her nose several minutes ago, a sign her age or the job had caught up with her. When she'd retired from the Navy, putting jets and spacewalks behind her, she'd thought about how her life would change without a physical fitness test looming every year.

During her active duty years, staying in running shape had been a daily routine, but she had feared without someone looking over her shoulder, her practice would wither like her husband Austin's had. She couldn't remember the last time he jogged for time, let alone laced up his favorite pair of running shoes. Meghan hadn't lapsed as much as Austin but finding the time and motivation to do more than keep the pounds off had become problematic.

Get real, she thought. Finding both had become impossible. She loved jogging around the pond near their Florida home, but Dante had placed outdoor runs on the forbidden list due to the increasing number of confirmed threats against her. Sweating in the residence's small gym and sucking in filtered, conditioned air was not her idea of a pleasurable work-out. She'd had enough during her three months on the International Space Station.

The counter finally clicked to two miles, causing the treadmill to slow automatically to a cooldown pace. Her respiration rate decreased enough to allow her to close her mouth and begin breathing through her nose again. But with her mind not engrossed in lasting to the finish line, her thoughts drifted to the overflowing things on her already enormous plate.

Every week since her inauguration, her daily schedule of meetings and public appearances had focused on a different policy area—border secu-rity, inflation, abortion rights, relations with Russia and China, and now military drawdown. She wouldn't get through Martin Torres' initial list for another five weeks to set the stage for her administration's top ten issues. Maybe she should find more time for jogging, if only for a few minutes daily away from the constant grind of presidential work.

When the treadmill slowed to the pace of a leisurely stroll, a familiar tune interrupted the music playing through her headphones. She smiled every time the *Hogan's Heroes* theme song, the perfect ringtone for her husband, played on her cell. Austin and his brother had grown up on reruns of the show, and they challenged each other at every family gath-ering to identify which episode a particular piece of dialogue came from. The loser did the dishes after their cookout.

She pressed her left earbud to accept the call. "Hey, you. How did the talk with Sophie go?"

"She's pissed." The slow cadence of Austin's voice meant pissed was an understatement.

Sophie was their rebellious child, and angry was her default state. Meghan could only imagine her reaction when Austin delivered their ulti-matum. She'd expected her youngest to act out her freshman year at Sacra-mento State. All the Brindle kids had during their first two years at their chosen colleges, but Sophie was the only child of hers who had to contend with a Secret Service detail shadowing her every movement in college. However, ditching her security detail for the third time, this instance to smoke legal pot at a house party, was dangerous. If Meghan had known becoming the President of the United States would mean putting her adult children on a shorter than expected protective leash for four years, she might not have thrown her hat in the ring.

"How did she react when you told her about the death threats?" she asked.

"It only made things worse. Sophie said you signed up for all this security, not her. She thought it unfair to rip her from her dream school because she wasn't willing to give up her freedom. She called it very un-American." He laughed.

The treadmill stopped, and Meghan wiped her face with the towel draped over the machine's side safety bar. She let out a guffaw. "Oh, please. She chose the college because it's as far away from us as possible."

"You'll get no argument from me."

"Do you think she'll shape up?"

"I know she will. You should have seen her face when I told her if she gave her detail the slip one more time, we'd move her to the White House and put her in community college. She knows this is her last chance."

Meghan blew out a loud breath. "I hate manipulating her like this, but it's the only way to keep her safe."

"We talked about this, Meg. She only responds to nuclear options. I wouldn't have flown out here if I didn't think it the only way forward."

"Is she coming to Napa tomorrow? I'd like to see her after the event."

"Uh, that would be a big no. If she doesn't screw up, don't expect her home until summer break."

Meghan lowered her head. She had a good relationship with her adult children, except for Sophie. However, it wasn't always that way. Throughout Sophie's middle school years, Meghan was her hero. She was the parent to brag about among friends at school after her name had been floated as a presidential hopeful. Fifteen, though, was the age when everything changed. Maybe it was her new school after moving or too much time on social media, but suddenly everything Meghan said or did was wrong, stupid, or mean in Sophie's eyes. Meghan hoped this phase would be over soon, and they could get back to giant hugs and bingeing *Grey's Anatomy*.

"At least she'll be safe," Meghan said. "Are you still coming?"

"Wouldn't miss it. Call me a groupie, but I'm not passing up the opportunity to meet Tiger Woods."

"Not because it's our wedding anniversary? I'm hurt." Meghan ended in a lighthearted manner.

"Well, that too." Austin's tone was playful. In thirty-four years of marriage, he'd never missed an anniversary.

"I'll tell you a little secret," Meghan said.

"I'm not sure if I have the security clearance for the type of secrets you're privy to these days."

"For this one, you are. I didn't want to do this event until Martin said Tiger would be there. He's on my bucket list of people to meet before I leave office."

"He is, is he? Who else is on your list? Should I be jealous?"

"I'll share who's on mine if you tell me who's on yours. Should I be jealous, too?"

"Let's not get crazy. Every marriage should have a touch of mystery."

"Fair enough," Meghan chuckled. "I wish I could stay to play eighteen with him, not just the first hole." Her phone buzzed with an incoming message. Martin must have been getting anxious to start the day. "I gotta run, Austin. Martin is already at it this morning."

"See you tomorrow, dear," Austin said, closing with his usual, "Love you."

───────

Showered and dressed, Meghan stepped from her and Austin's suite into the main corridor of the residence. Dante stood patiently at his traditional position near the elevator at the far end of the hallway and cocked his head toward her. It might have been the product of his training, but the man cued on every little sound. She issued him a good morning wink because once the man sitting next to him in a high-back armchair, reviewing something on a tablet, realized she was out of the bedroom, she wouldn't be in control of her day.

Meghan squared her shoulders, preparing for chaos, and stepped toward them. "Good morning, Martin."

He stood, respecting her new position. They'd been colleagues and friends for years, since her NASA days. However, once she swore her oath as president, he stopped treating her like a friend when they weren't alone by standing when she entered the room and not using her first name. He'd slipped once or twice with the name but quickly corrected himself to set the right tone among the staff.

"Good morning, ma'am. We have a full day before our trip to California tomorrow. The schedule has changed since Gloria emailed you last night before going to bed."

"Do I have anything in the next twenty minutes?"

"No, ma'am."

"Join me in the dining room. The cook sent up my favorite omelet this morning."

"Southwestern?" Martin's eyes widened at the prospect of tasting what had become her go-to breakfast at naval flight school. She'd ordered the dish in every state and at least six countries, but the one here outstripped them all. The White House chef added something extra, giving each bite an extra kick. One day, she would have to find her way to the kitchen and shake loose the special ingredient from the chef.

After they stepped into the private dining room, Martin's eyes rounded with surprise. "You ordered two."

Meghan closed the door. "I knew you wouldn't pass it up."

"Thanks, Meghan. By the way, I tried, but the kitchen staff is still closed-lipped about the recipe. The chef treats it like nuclear codes and keeps it under lock and key."

"Somehow, I'll wrangle it out of him before I leave office."

While they ate, Martin reviewed the schedule change, noting the shuffle was needed to accommodate an impromptu joint briefing from the Defense and State Departments on the overnight developments in Venezuela.

Meghan sighed. That country had become increasingly unstable under Maduro's reign. His anti-American rhetoric had heightened rebel opposition within the government. Venezuelan military leaders had opposed the country's closer alignment with Russia and China, citing the "One Hemisphere, One Alliance" philosophy that had gotten traction last year during Meghan's presidential campaign. Her hope was to win the hearts and minds of the Venezuelan people to promote slow change. A military coup, however, would defeat her goal and send the country into chaos, disrupting the production and exportation of thirteen percent of the world's oil.

"What happened overnight?"

"Rebels from the interior hit the Port of Cabello and disabled a ship at the mouth of the harbor. It might take a week before authorities can clear it and reopen the shipping lane. At your meeting today, advisors will present military and diplomatic options on moving forward with your stance on the country."

"I won't reverse course less than a day after my speech. It's a sound policy. We just need the backbone to stay the course."

"I won't disagree, but Senator Gotkin is already making hay with it. He's saying your speech fanned the flames of revolution, inspiring the rebels to act."

"Of course he did." By striking Meghan at every turn, Gotkin was positioning himself for another run for his party's nomination. She was betting the country would eventually tire of him, or the Republican Party power brokers would neuter him when he took things too far. If he didn't get his way with funding bills, a government shutdown was not the way to build alliances in Washington.

Martin swiped his tablet screen. "That brings us to the California trip. We're scheduled for a 0600 takeoff, so you'll need to be ready for Marine One by 0530. Housekeeping has programmed your alarm for 0430."

"Please tell me I don't have anything scheduled past eight tonight."

"I got you covered, Meghan. I know you're grumpy on travel days without a full night's sleep, so I bumped drinks with the House leaders to Sunday after the Capitals' game."

"You're a good man, Martin," Meghan laughed. "By the way, I spoke to Austin this morning. Sophie won't be at the golf course tomorrow, but he'll meet me there as planned. I'd like a few minutes with him alone before things start."

"Of course. I had the scheduler build a forty-minute buffer after Austin flew to Sacramento to see Sophie. I thought you might want some time with him for your anniversary. We can bring him aboard Air Force One before you deplane."

"Thank you, Martin. You've thought of everything."

"I could claim credit for the idea, but Maria suggested it."

"Give that wife of yours a big kiss. Austin and I haven't spent an anniversary apart since right after 9/11. We'd like to keep the streak going."

"Well, who am I to stand in the way of love?" Martin paused at her pert smile. "Also, per your request, we arranged for you to meet with Senator Jackson's widow at her son's home tomorrow afternoon before our return flight to Andrews. Dante nearly blew a gasket over it."

"Heavens, why? He's the calmest man I know."

"Your add-on gave him less than twenty-four hours to scout the route once Mrs. Jackson agreed to a meeting location. The logistics of getting you there have been a pain in the butt to coordinate. He had to arrange for an Air Force C-37 to shuttle you to the nearest airport and a second presidential limo to get you to the son's home."

"I realize the difficulty in arranging this, but the country hasn't had a sitting senator die in office since John McCain. I need to pay my respects to the Jackson family. No matter the difficulty, this needs to happen."

26

Detective Jan Hopkins slid into the backseat of Lexi's SUV. "Thanks for picking me up," he said. He'd laced tremendous patience and humility in those few words, expressing his appreciation for Lexi including him in the interview.

This was as much his case as it was Lexi and Croft's, if not more, and he deserved to see it through to the end. Sure, she had jurisdiction and pull at the federal level, but Jan had done much more. Lexi was sure he harbored some resentment at her for taking over the case, but he never showed it, and she respected him for showing such grace.

"Thanks for meeting us on the way. I wouldn't think of working this without you," Lexi said, pulling out of the gas station parking lot and back onto the interstate.

"I'm surprised you got us in so quickly," Jan said. "It would have taken me days."

"It helps to have good friends who can cut through the red tape." Lexi glimpsed his kind face in the rearview mirror. "I include you among that exclusive list. We couldn't have gotten this far without you." They briefly locked eyes in the mirror, and he nodded respectfully.

"I got the coroner's initial findings back on Yarborough early this morning. He found wounds on his face that could have been caused by a small explosive charge, but he found only sodium azide residue, which may have come from the deployed airbag. He listed the cause of death as trauma to the head."

"Well, that's no help," Nathan said.

"I still think there's more to his injuries," Lexi said. "The coroner just couldn't find it."

"Then you'll like this. We got back analysis on one of the pipe bombs Lexi disarmed at the bank hostage scene. It contained the same raven DNA found at Yarborough's crash site."

"Now, that's the best news I've heard in days," Nathan said, turning his head toward Lexi in the driver's seat. "You were right. It was the Raven's work."

Lexi's phone rang through the car's Bluetooth connection. The ringtone and name flashing on the entertainment console alerted her to Kaplan's call. She pressed the Accept button on the dash screen. "Hi, Kaplan. I have you on speaker with Nathan and Jan."

"Good morning, everyone. I did the digging you asked for. Are you ready for an update?"

"Absolutely, but talk fast. We're on our way to interview Senator Jackson's widow and might lose phone service in the mountains."

"Got it," Kaplan said. "First is Robert Segura. Information on him was light. His tax returns list him as a Texas resident with a trailer park address in Houston. He's an independent contract engineer who performs temporary work for several companies."

"Is Falcon Industries one of them?"

"Yes. I dug into the direct deposit account Segura has on file with the IRS and found several deposits from the company, dating back for three months."

"How much?"

"Twenty-five thousand a week, always paid on Friday."

"We're in the wrong line of business," Lexi said.

"But that's not the interesting part," Kaplan said. "He received what appears to be two bonus payments this week of two hundred fifty thousand dollars each, one on Sunday and the other Tuesday night."

"Interesting," Lexi said. "Both payments were one day before Darryl

Yarborough and Senator Jackson died. Did you dig around Falcon Industries' finances?"

"I couldn't break into their servers, so I started sifting through their SEC and IRS filings, but it will take some time. I dug deeper into the accounts feeding Segura money and an interesting picture formed. Every company he provides services to except Falcon Industries uses the same bank."

"You think they're fronts."

"That's my suspicion. It will take time to unravel the layers. I'll keep monitoring the account and will update you once I know more."

"This is great stuff, Kaplan. It confirms that Foreman, the Raven, and Robert Segura are all connected."

An hour after finishing the call, Lexi pulled up to the access gate at Senator Jackson's lakeside mansion. The police and media that had swarmed the property yesterday were gone. She pressed the button on a control panel on a stone pillar below the camera.

A voice came through the speaker on the panel. "Agent Mills, this is Agent Stewart. Drive on up. I've held my team here so we could talk to you, and Mrs. Jackson is ready for you too."

"I appreciate that," Lexi said.

The gate clicked and retracted behind the stonewall, opening a clear path to the home. Two dark SUVs and a van with United States Government license plates were parked along the access road near the house. Two men in Capitol Police windbreakers were carrying file boxes to the back of the van. The boxes were sealed and marked "Classified."

She parked short of the activity and exited her car with Nathan and Jan. Cameron Stewart appeared at the front door and met them on the lushly landscaped walkway. She shook Lexi's hand. "Glad you navigated the roadblocks before we closed the shop. I'm happy to answer any questions you and Agent Croft might have, but Detective Hopkins doesn't have the proper security clearance."

"I understand," Jan said without a hint of anger or disappointment. "I'll wait by the car."

"Can he come inside when we speak to Mrs. Jackson? He was with me Tuesday evening when I first spoke to the senator and his wife."

"Of course," Cameron said before leading Lexi and Nathan up the walkway toward the house.

Once they were out of earshot, Lexi said, "Thanks for the unofficial nod yesterday. Thanks to Detective Hopkins, we got the security footage from the Emerald Club and learned the senator had met with Benjamin Foreman Tuesday night. What can you tell me about the meeting?"

"It was impromptu. The senator added it to his schedule late that afternoon."

"It makes sense. We talked to Foreman earlier that day, and I'm betting we spooked him."

"Senator Jackson met with many congresspeople, donors, policymakers, and military bigwigs. Foreman was a regular. I wasn't privy to their discussions, but he left most meetings in a good mood."

"Most?" Nathan asked.

"All but the one Wednesday night. Their talk got heated, and I almost stepped in, but the senator calmed him down."

"How was the senator after the meeting?" Lexi asked.

"He seemed fine, more worried about his wife giving him the cold shoulder for going out so late than he was about Mr. Foreman."

"He called me and left a message that night. Do you know what it was about?"

"I think it had something to do with his meeting with Foreman," Agent Stewart said.

"We're having difficulty getting information on the meeting between Foreman and Darryl Yarborough the night he died due to its classified nature. Would you know anything about that?"

"I don't, but Agent Buckner might." Cameron waved over an agent at the van. "David, come here."

The man jogged over. "Yes, ma'am?"

"Weren't you with the senator in DC when he last talked to Darryl Yarborough Monday afternoon?"

"Yes, I was."

"These agents have questions about the meeting Mr. Yarborough took for the senator on Monday."

"Ma'am?" Agent Buckner regarded her with questioning eyes.

"It's all right, David. The chief cleared them." He nodded.

"What can you tell us about the meeting?" Lexi asked.

"Only that it was about a classified military project and the senator had doubts about approving it."

"This is great," Lexi said. "Every bit helps.

"Is that all?" Agent Buckner asked.

"Yes, thank you," Lexi said.

He pivoted to return to the van but stopped. "I almost forgot. I'm not sure what it meant, but I heard the senator used the word locust that night."

"Locust," Lexi repeated. She hadn't come across the term related to military weapons systems before, but perhaps Maxwell might have a line on someone who had. "Thanks, Agent Buckner."

Lexi waved up Jan after Buckner stepped away, and the group entered the senator's home. Several file boxes were stacked in the entry hall, ready for the Capitol Police agents to store them in the van.

"Excuse the mess," Stewart said. "We have orders to clean up the senator's office and take everything to Washington. Someone will sort through it there. This has been very upsetting for Mrs. Jackson, which is why her son is taking her to his place until the funeral."

"I understand. We won't be long."

"She's with her daughter in the bedroom. I'll get her." Stewart disappeared down the hallway.

Lexi recalled when she and Jan were there Tuesday night. Mrs. Jackson had appeared visibly shaken, having learned of Mr. Yarborough's death minutes earlier. She prepared herself for the possibility Mrs. Jackson might be too devastated to offer anything beyond what she'd already learned.

A television mounted above the fireplace was on with the volume low, tuned to a national news station. Footage from President Brindle's speech yesterday at a Democratic event in Maryland was playing. When a picture of Benjamin Foreman in front of the Falcon Industries logo flashed on the screen, Lexi walked over to listen better.

The newscaster said the president had singled out Falcon Industries as the poster child for what was wrong with our military-industrial complex. It focused on increasing weapons systems' offensive lethality instead of bolstering a defensive posture. The story went on to draw a parallel between the part of her speech calling for the United States to support stable oil-producing nations and last night's sinking of a tanker, blocking a key Venezuelan shipping harbor. The senate leader was calling for a complete reversal of the president's policies, calling them unforgivable for weakening the country on the world stage.

Moments later, Stewart returned with Mrs. Jackson and another woman in her thirties, presumably Jackson's daughter. Both women had swollen, red eyes from recent crying, but Mrs. Jackson looked exhausted. Her sunken face, contracted posture, and unkempt hair were signs of a distraught widow.

Lexi shook her hand, but before letting go, she cupped it with both hands. "I met your husband only that night when you two learned of Mr. Yarborough's passing. I could tell his first concern was for your well-being. In those few minutes with him, it had become clear how much he loved you. I'm truly sorry for your loss, Mrs. Jackson."

Mrs. Jackson's lips trembled when she thanked Lexi. "How can I help you, Agent Mills?"

"Your husband left a message for me after his meeting at the Emerald Club, saying he had a concern he needed to discuss with me. Did he mention what he was worried about?"

"No, he didn't. I nagged him about not getting his pacemaker replaced when he last saw his cardiologist." Mrs. Jackson covered her mouth briefly with a hand. "He'd said the timing wasn't right. That he was waiting until the Senate was in recess."

"Had the pacemaker been a problem?"

"It had triggered once and kept his heart rate elevated for half an hour, but a thorough check determined it was functioning fine." She clenched her hand into a fist. "I begged him to have it replaced."

"I understand from your statement to the police that you followed him to bed after finishing up in the kitchen. Can you walk me through what happened when you went to the bedroom?"

Mrs. Jackson inhaled deeply and let the breath out slowly before beginning. The pain in her eyes was heartbreaking. "I walked into the room, and he was in bed clutching his chest." Her knees buckled, but Lexi steadied her by the elbow.

"If this is too much—" Lexi started.

"No, I'm fine," she said. "I know Keith wanted to help you, so if there's anything I can do, I want to continue."

Lexi issued a soft nod. Instinct told her his death wasn't merely a heart attack. "Was he on his laptop or tablet?"

"No." Mrs. Jackson stared into the distance with sad eyes as if recalling a painful memory. "He must have been reading. After I pressed the panic button on my nightstand, I went to him. I remember shoving his reading glasses, a book, and a huge fly from the bedding. Then he was gone."

A big fly. The entire region must be home to them, Lexi thought. She remembered swatting at one at the bank robbery scene. "Is the fly still here?"

"No. It flew away."

"Thank you, Mrs. Jackson." She handed the widow a business card. "If you think of anything else, please call."

Nathan took the wheel for the drive from the senator's home. After Lexi buckled in and updated Agent Lange over the phone, Jan said, "There are so many puzzle pieces in this case it's hard to make sense of it all."

"I know what you mean," Lexi said. She closed her eyes, visualizing the events since Willie Lange called her Tuesday morning about the bank hostage scene.

Lexi now knew the bomb vest was made by the Raven and the sniper shot directed at her proved she was the real target. But the operation seemed sloppy, unlike something the Raven would concoct. And yesterday, she learned the person she'd thought might have been the triggerman worked for Foreman.

She moved from the bank scene to looking into Yarborough's car crash after Jan had found raven DNA on the metal remnants. Those two incidents, twelve hours and sixty miles apart, were linked. They were both the work of the Raven but very different. The car crash was better planned.

She focused on Senator Jackson next. When he was poised to release information about Yarborough's meeting with Foreman less than an hour before his death, the senator died from apparent heart failure. But Lexi didn't buy that cause for one minute. Foreman knew about the senator's death before the media had gotten wind of it.

Benjamin Foreman had his virtual fingerprints over all three incidents. She knew Yarborough and Jackson were connected to whatever Falcon Industries' weapons program was before the senate committee. The Capitol Police agent had said the senator had reservations about approving it. Could that have been the program the president referenced in her speech yesterday? Was that the locust the agent had heard the senator mention?

Lexi circled back to the Raven. Yarborough and the bank scene were connected to him. She couldn't figure out why Foreman would need his services for those events. Foreman had tremendous resources, including access to high-tech weapons systems. It made sense if the Raven had something Foreman didn't have, but what? Technology? Material? Expertise?

And how did Robert Segura fit into this? He was an engineer on Foreman's payroll and received bonuses immediately following Yarborough's and Jackson's deaths. Was he Foreman's weapons maker? His hitman? Or was he the Raven's? That was it. Segura was the missing link between Foreman and the Raven. If he engineered the bomb vest at the bank scene, he worked for both men.

"I think I have it figured out," Lexi said. She spent the next few minutes explaining her reasoning and how Robert Segura must have been the Raven's engineer.

"It all fits," Nathan said. "We find Segura, we find the Raven, and take down Foreman."

"We still haven't figured out how Yarborough and the senator were killed," Lexi said. "My guess is Segura is the key. When I had him in my grasp at the bank scene, he was holding a phone sideways with both hands. He made me think he was playing a game, but who plays solitaire at a police scene? I think he was controlling something remotely."

"That's brilliant, Lexi," Jan said. "Now what? How do we find Segura?"

"We dig, which means pulling in Kaplan Shaw again." Lexi's phone buzzed with the ringtone she'd reserved for Kaplan. "Speak of the devil." She swiped the screen and placed it on speaker. "Hi, Kaplan. You're on speaker again with Nathan and Jan. Were your ears burning?"

"No. Why?"

"We think Robert Segura is working for both Foreman and the Raven. We need to direct all our energy into finding him."

"I think you're onto something. I set up notifications for Segura's account and all the accounts feeding it money. I got a hit on a big transaction."

"How big?"

"One million was transferred into Segura's account from one of the shell companies he supposedly consulted for. I tracked it to part of a five-million-dollar transfer from a Cayman Islands account."

"Who owns the account?"

"I don't know yet. But until this transaction, Falcon Industries was the source of all deposits into his account. The money was later funneled to a dozen other Cayman accounts. I have a feeling this is going to take time to unravel. If this is another bonus, something really big is about to go down."

"I think you're right." Lexi completed the call with Kaplan and turned to Nathan. "I have a bad feeling about this. That amount of money could only mean Foreman or the Raven are going after a high-value target tomorrow."

"What's going on tomorrow?" Jan asked.

Every puzzle piece linking Foreman and the Raven swirled in Lexi's head and two questions popped into her head: Why here? Why now? Only one answer came to mind. The president was scheduled to appear at the charity golf tournament at her Napa resort tomorrow.

"They're going after the president."

"The golf tournament," Nathan whispered.

"We need help." Lexi dialed her phone. The call connected. "Maxwell, we need to warn the president."

27

Benjamin placed the next sixteen-inch-long round of dried oak carefully atop the chopping stump. Once it steadied, he raised the Michigan axe over his head with a firm two-handed grip and slammed its blade through the wood with a well-practiced stroke, splitting the log down the middle. One uneven, splintery half flipped in the air, rotating twice before landing a foot away. He tossed both lengths into the freshly cut pile, taking care to line them horizontally with the other cuts he'd made that morning.

Cutting wood in this spot in the cool mountain air had centered him since his adolescence. His father had sent him outside every day during their winter and summer month-long stays to prep the fireplace wood for the cabin for cooking and heating. This site, wielding the very same axe, was where he'd first envisioned the life he wanted. Forty-five years later, he nearly had it all.

The land had belonged to him since his father's death twenty years earlier, but he hadn't the time nor enough money to develop it as he'd envisioned it until he'd retired from the army and built up Falcon Industries a decade ago. And now that he had his dream house on the land of his ancestors, it felt empty without a family to fill it.

Though still legally married, his wife hadn't filled that role since he pinned on his first star. The lack of a prenuptial agreement made it too expensive to divorce, and if not for the never-ending drama known as their son, he would have no contact with her at all. That was one circumstance he wished he could have changed. Tessa couldn't accept the long absences, not knowing where he was or when he might return. But such was the life in the black ops world, even after he'd transitioned from field operator to control center commander, directing covert teams around the world.

Only in the last three or four years, when he moved into Shangri-La and returned to his roots, had he settled into a schedule somewhat resembling banker's hours. But the trouble with the Locust Program had him reverting to his old ways of late-night meetings and circling the globe on a jet on a moment's notice, a troublesome circumstance bringing him to the axe this morning.

Benjamin scooped an armful of freshly cut split oak and cradled it against the flannel shirt covering his chest. He opened the door of the original log cabin using a tempered kick from his right foot and added the load to the built-in storage area next to the fireplace. After tossing three pieces into the fire, he poured a cup of coffee from the kitchen and returned to his father's old leather chair, placing his feet on the ottoman.

When Benjamin wore the uniform, never in a million years would he have pictured himself in this position under any circumstance, but Gotkin and Brindle had backed him into a corner. Neither had the backbone to lead the country as they should—as the world's only military superpower. Russia was revealed as feckless in Ukraine, and China was more focused on establishing economic dependency as their weapon of choice, leaving the field wide open for the United States to maintain, if not grow, its military might. But a coward was in the White House, and an ineffective career politician controlled the Senate. At least Gotkin didn't fool himself into thinking he could work with the president. There was no negotiating with someone delusional. Replacing Brindle was the only way forward.

Benjamin glanced at the pictures on the cabin wall. He hadn't replaced the aging frames, opting to view the images of the Foreman men who had come before him in their original displays. He felt more connected to his great, great, great-grandfather, looking at the picture of him next to his massive gold find along the South Fork of the American River in the same frame as all the other Foreman men had.

He tipped his mug toward the wall of pictures. "I hope you understand my choices, Silas." Silas and his sons, as did each of his grandsons, and so on, had been patriots by helping build the frontier or with military service. Benjamin would be the first in a long line of good men to go against his ancestors' traditional view of right and wrong on such a large scale.

A knock on the door broke his solitary communion with the past. Only two people had the temerity to interrupt his private time without electronic devices tethering him to his business. He doubted Andrew had returned yet from his Sacramento law offices, so Benjamin was left with only one choice.

"Come in, Matthew," Benjamin shouted.

The door creaked open, and his control center manager appeared through the opening. He stepped inside, closing the door behind him and keeping in the hard-earned warmth from the fireplace. He was holding a tablet. "My apologies, Mr. Foreman, but you'd asked me to let you know if there was any new movement with Lexi Mills. She's en route to Senator Jackson's Incline Village home to interview his security detail and widow." He handed Benjamin the tablet. "I cued a conversation she had in her car with her intelligence agent over the phone that I think you should hear."

"Thank you, Matthew. I'll be in the main house soon."

Once Matthew retreated out the door, Benjamin swiped the tablet alive and brought up the Falcon Industries executive app. An alert with a link to the audio recording Matthew had mentioned flashed on his dashboard. He clicked it.

Benjamin recognized the voices as belonging to Lexi Mills and Jan Hopkins. He smiled when the detective explained that Darryl Yarborough's injuries found during the autopsy were likely caused by the car's airbag.

"You're a genius, Robert," he said, recalling he'd used a particular compound for the explosive trigger to mimic the airbag deployment. His glee was short-lived, however, learning the police had found the same raven DNA in the bombs used at the bank hostage scene. It was the same event at which Robert had watched Lexi Mills through a locust device. Benjamin was more upset learning the DNA matched the trace evidence found at

Yarborough's crash site. That man's arrogance would be his downfall, and perhaps Benjamin's if they weren't careful.

Benjamin listened to the recording, waiting for Kaplan Shaw to chime in. His research into her background revealed she was one to watch. Her skills at ferreting information were top-notch. If he'd thought she would accept, he would offer her a position at Falcon Industries in a heartbeat.

"Dammit," he whispered. Kaplan had tracked the payroll payments to Robert, keying on his bonuses for launching locusts on the senator and his chief of staff.

Benjamin switched to the live feed of the listening app on Mills' phone and placed the tablet on the side table next to his father's chair. He leaned back, sipped his coffee, and listened with his eyes closed. Without voices to listen to, the faint white noise of the car tires rolling against the highway asphalt and gravel relaxed him enough to fall asleep. He woke startled when voices broke the stillness in the cabin. It took a moment to acclimate to the conversation, but he still couldn't discern who was speaking. He picked up the tablet and clicked on the live transcript feed, listening in as Mills talked to Senator Jackson's lead officer on his security detail.

Moments later, Benjamin heard a disturbing tidbit. Another security detail officer mentioned the senator had said the word locust the last time he was on the phone with Yarborough. Every effort Benjamin had taken to keep the name of the project from Agent Mills was all for nothing. Mills was bright, and her training as an explosives expert meant she thought through puzzles logically. She would eventually piece things together, but by the time she did, he was betting it would be too late to stop the coming war.

He continued to listen and perked up when Kaplan's voice returned. His breathing turned heavy with every word she said. He sensed the walls closing in, cringing at the mention of a five-million-dollar transfer, but his breath hitched when Kaplan said, "*If this is another bonus, something really big is about to go down.*" His anger built like a volcano on the precipice of erupting. Benjamin threw his mug against the stone fireplace, sending pieces and ceramic shards flying in all directions.

Mills was onto him, the Raven, and the bones of tomorrow's attack plan. He had two choices: Cancel the attack and hope for another opportunity or roll as scheduled. But once Lexi Mills passed along her suspicion and mentioned the word locust, the Secret Service would alter their security posture to leave the president less vulnerable to his technology. Benjamin doubted they would get another chance to prevent Brindle from making the United States irrelevant. The attack had to go as planned.

28

Late afternoon traffic approaching the Silverado Resort was congested. Crews had erected tents and temporary structures for tomorrow's charity golf event throughout the week, but their trucks had only created brief slowdowns on the access road. Today, however, the rest of the prep crews showed up. All at once, it seemed. Lexi counted a dozen trucks and vans lined up for caterers, food service, special event merchandise, media, and the players. The traffic control crowd directed vehicles to their designated location, turning away several visitors.

Nathan finally eased their rental to the control point, rolled down his window when a man wearing an orange reflective vest approached the car, and displayed his ATF badge and credentials. "We're guests at the hotel on official business."

"Unless you're on the pre-approved list or are cleared by the Secret Service, I can't let you through."

Nathan rolled his neck as his face turned an amusing shade of red. "Do you want me to arrest you for interfering with a federal officer?"

Lexi leaned closer to Nathan toward the open window, placing a hand gently on his forearm. "There's no need for a standoff, but we're not turning around. I'll call Agent Humphries." She dialed his number. He picked up.

"Hey, Lexi. Your wife and dad are fine."

"Thanks, Scott. I appreciate the update, but I need your help to get through security at the front of the resort. We're at the checkpoint."

"Sure thing. Hold on." Humphries issued some commands in the background before returning to Lexi's call. "I sent a team from the entrance. They should be there in a minute."

"Also, we'll need to talk to your supervisor for a critical update. Can your team take us to him?"

"He's swamped today. Can it wait until we're ready to bed down for the night?"

Lexi shifted back to her side of the car and spoke more quietly to prevent the traffic guard from overhearing. "Tell him I stumbled on a credible threat after interviewing Senator Jackson's widow today."

"Got it, Lexi. I'll let him know. Until he can meet you, I suggest you return to your suite."

"Will do."

Moments later, a Secret Service agent approached their vehicle and leaned in to get a better view of everyone in their rental car. Lexi recognized the face as one of the agents who scouted the resort during the week, but she never learned his name.

"Hi, Agent Mills. Agent Croft." He glanced at the backseat.

"He's with us," Nathan said.

Jan held up his deputy badge. "Detective Jan Hopkins, Nevada County Sheriff's Department."

The agent nodded and returned his focus to the front seat. "Parking is a nightmare with the delivery trucks and setup crews. Head to the section marked off for GOVs. If you get any guff, tell the parking guys Sampson okayed it."

"Are you Sampson?" Nathan asked.

"No, he's the agent in charge who flew in today." He focused on Lexi. "His orders were to treat you like one of us."

"I'll have to thank him," Lexi said before the agent waved them through.

After they parked, the chaos from people moving things about for tomorrow's event grew more intense around the main building. Lexi thought about what the property would look like tomorrow when spectators arrived. She envisioned hundreds of people lined up at the security checkpoint to run through the metal detectors and thousands more milling about the course and pop up gift shop, waiting to see their favorite players and the president. The sheer number of people would be Lexi's worst nightmare if she had to deal with an explosive or similar threat. If the stampede didn't set off a device at the onset, a straggler with a remote control like the one Segura had at the bank scene might.

Lexi, Nathan, and Jan entered the hotel through a side entrance nearest their parking spot by using her hotel room keycard. The corridor was industrial, lacking an ornate carpet and decorations like the ones in the main part of the resort. It had the distinct smell of laundry drying. Once through a set of double swing doors and the housekeeping area, they walked past a series of conference rooms. One had its doors open, and Lexi glanced inside on her way by. The space was filled with communication equipment, trunks large enough to hold a small arsenal, and Secret Service agents. Some faces she recognized as being on the advance team.

Before she reached the end of the corridor to enter the lobby, someone called out her title and name from behind. She stopped and turned, discovering an unfamiliar agent in casual clothes walking toward her.

"Agent Mills," she repeated, closing the distance between them. "Agent Sampson would like to meet with you ASAP."

"Of course." Lexi gestured for Nathan and Jan to follow, but when they stepped toward her, the agent raised her hand in a stopping motion.

"I'm sorry, ma'am, but he only asked for you. Space is tight in the room he's using as an office."

Lexi turned to Nathan, apologizing with her eyes, and handed him the room key. "I'll meet you back at the suite." The more prominent creases in Nathan's forehead meant he wasn't happy with her benching him, but the Secret Service had been doing her a favor by keeping watch over Nita and her father. Pushing against Sampson would be a slap in the face.

Nathan snatched the card but gave Lexi a respectful nod before continuing up the hallway with Jan.

Lexi followed the female agent into the hectic temporary operations room and guided her toward the far end. A dozen laptops, paper coffee cups, and loose papers littered three eight-foot-long tables in the room's center. Four flatscreen monitors on mobile carts displayed dozens of security camera feeds from the resort and golf course. The room murmured with multiple conversations and chirping from the radio console on a table against the wall.

The agent stopped at an open door and craned her head around the frame. "Agent Mills is here, boss."

"Send her in," a male voice said from inside. It sounded vaguely familiar, but Lexi couldn't place it.

Lexi stepped inside to a pleasant surprise and smiled. "Jacob Sampson."

Jacob circled the makeshift desk in the cramped office and pulled Lexi in for a firm hug. "It's great seeing you, Lexi."

She pulled back. "I haven't seen you since FLETC. How have you been?" It had been twelve years since she'd seen Jacob at the Glynco training center. He'd put on a few pounds of muscle, and his face had creased in spots with age, but there was no mistaking her tablemate during the two-month class.

He rubbed his hair which was a bit thinner than she remembered. "Other than losing most of my hair, I've been doing damn good." He squeezed her upper arms and shook his head, smiling. "But you. I've been reading incredible things about you. And to think I knew you when you were just a cadet." The corners of his lips dropped. "I was sorry to hear about your leg." He released his grip.

"I nearly quit after losing it, but once I found Nita, she helped me find the strength to work my way back."

"Ah, your wife." He nodded and gestured for her to sit in the only guest chair. She did when he circled around to his chair. "I'm glad my advance team could keep them safe while you investigate your case."

"Yes, thank you for the help. After someone took a sniper shot at me, I wasn't about to take chances when I suspected the Raven was involved."

"You told Scott Humphries about an imminent threat. Do you think this Raven character is involved?"

"Yes, I do." Lexi explained how she'd linked Yarborough's and Jackson's deaths to Benjamin Foreman and about the money transfer to Segura, the engineer associated with Foreman and the Raven. "One million dollars was transferred into his account today, four times more than the deposits following the other deaths. This tells me something big is about to go down. If you saw the president's speech yesterday, you know Foreman has a legitimate beef with her. I know Senator Jackson was going to pass on some big project of Foreman's, and now he and his chief of staff are dead. If he killed a sitting senator like I suspect he did, it's not a giant leap to think he'd go after the president with the help of the Raven."

"How did he kill the other two?"

"I haven't figured out that part yet, but I know Yarborough had trauma to the head, and the senator's pacemaker may have been targeted."

"This isn't much to go on, Lexi. My boss passed along a similar alert from the FBI as informational only."

"That would have come from Deputy Director Maxwell Keene. I looped him in this afternoon."

"His call had a lot of juice behind it, but I'll tell you what my boss told him. Other than canceling her appearance tomorrow, which her chief of staff promptly vetoed, there's nothing we could plan differently. A public event like this is one of the times when the president is the most vulnerable. We've been scouting the area all week and have implemented every precaution at our disposal, including different options for her arrival."

"I don't like this, Jacob. My gut tells me Foreman or the Raven will attack tomorrow. Who do I need to convince to get the president to cancel?"

"At this point, President Brindle is the only one."

"Can you arrange for me to talk to her?"

"That's a big ask, Lexi." Jacob glanced at his watch. "But it will have to wait until morning. The president is already in the residence, which means we can only disturb her for emergencies. The most I can do tonight is to message her lead agent on her protective detail. She listens to him."

"Thank you, Jacob." Lexi stood and pulled a business card from her hip pocket. "Can you keep me updated?"

"Save it." Jacob waved off the business card, pulled out his phone, and swiped the screen. He handed it to her. "Dial your cell so we have each other's number. If you get any new information, I want you to call."

Lexi called her phone and let it ring until she felt a vibration in her pocket before handing it back. She asked, "Whatever happened to the woman you dated during FLETC?"

A grin slowly formed on his lips. "I married her, and she blessed me with a son and daughter."

"Good for you, Jacob. I'm very happy for you."

"By the way, you should know we reassigned the agents I had watching your family. We closed the resort to the public and check everyone before letting them through the checkpoint, so I didn't think leaving a team there was necessary tonight."

"That makes sense."

Minutes later, following a second hug, Lexi returned to the corridor and turned toward the lobby to go to her suite. Passing the hotel restaurant, she glanced inside and spotted a man at the bar with his back to her. The mirror behind the display of top-shelf liquors reflected his image. Though it was shorter recently, Lexi would recognize the mustache anywhere.

She pulled out her phone and sent a text to Nita. *Spotted Dad in hotel bar. Staying to have a drink with him.*

Nita returned her text in seconds. *You're about to make him very happy. See you soon.*

Lexi slipped her phone into her cargo pocket and walked inside the restaurant, gesturing to the woman at the host station that she was headed to the bar. The tables were sparsely occupied, and another man was sitting at the bar at the end opposite her father. The wall-mounted television in the corner was tuned to a sports channel replaying the NASCAR Truck Series race from earlier that evening. Without question, it was her father's doing. His stare was fixed on the screen.

Lexi stepped behind her dad. He was nursing the remnants of a glass of light-colored beer. "Mind if I join you?"

He cocked his head to see her better. His eyes sparkled with joy as he patted the neighboring stool. "Have a seat, Peanut."

Lexi got the bartender's attention, signaling him to bring over two more beers. He acknowledged with a firm nod. "What brings you to the bar before dinner?" she asked.

"Since Scott left, Nita and I are no longer tied at the hip. I thought I'd give her some time alone in the suite." Her father's curt tone made Lexi think a problem might be brewing between them. Asking him directly would be futile. He'd only deny it, so she would have to drag it out of him.

The bartender dropped off their drinks, and Lexi and her dad each took a sip.

"That's very thoughtful, Dad. Cooped up in the hotel hasn't been easy on either of you, but I still think the Raven is close."

"And after what the Belcher character did to Nita, your mother, and me, I get why you've tethered us to the hotel." His long face showed more than understanding. It revealed frustration.

"You get it but don't like it." Lexi sipped more of her beer. "I think you were the one who needed alone time. Am I right?" Her father wasn't the type of man to discuss his feelings unless whatever had brought him down came to a head and gave him no choice but to talk.

"Maybe," he said. "But I hate drinking alone, so I'm glad you stopped by."

"I am too." Lexi racked her brain but couldn't think of a time when she and her father had hung out at a bar for a drink. She had left his racing team before her twentieth birthday after he disowned her for coming out as gay. It was a shame that the thought of going to a place like this with him alone hadn't come to mind since their reconciliation.

"I think Mom would approve of us having a beer together."

He raised his glass, his eyes misting over with sadness. "I think she would too."

29

The wheels of Air Force One touched down smoothly onto the tarmac of the Napa County Airport. The plane coasted along the taxiway toward the secured apron area where the armada of vehicles made of steel and bullet-proof glass awaited the president's arrival in the airport's largest hangar. The moment the plane stopped and the engines wound down, Dante Cole's job began again. While walking toward the front, he barked orders into the microphone hidden under the cuff of his jacket sleeve, telling his team to implement plan Delta.

After last night's warning from the FBI and ATF about a potential attack on the president today, Dante held back announcing which route and motorcade he'd assign the president until the plane's wheels hit the asphalt. He ran a tight ship and was sure no one on his end would compromise the president's travel plans, but he also had to rely on local law enforcement to supply motorcycle sweepers and the rear guard on both routes he'd picked out for today. There was no telling what pillow talk might have transpired if a local motorcycle cop knew last night he was assigned to the president's actual motorcade, not the decoy.

The plane rocked, the sign the passenger boarding stairs had locked into place. The Air Force flight attendant opened the hatch, and Dante's team sprang into action, taking their assigned positions on the ground to watch for threats. Dante peeked outside, determining everything was in place. He spotted two rows of vehicles waiting to exit the field. One set was for the actual motorcade for the president, and the other was for the decoy. They were identical on the outside but were very different on the inside. Each decoy vehicle was staffed with a skeleton crew big enough to make it appear it was part of the real deal.

He waited near the opening while the media and the president's support staff exited from the rear and boarded their assigned vehicles in the two waiting motorcades. Minutes later, the president's husband ascended the boarding stairs. "Good morning, Mr. Brindle," Dante said.

"Good morning, Dante. How is she this morning? Did she get enough sleep?"

"I believe so, sir. She was chipper most of the flight."

"Unfortunately, I think it has more to do with her playing partner today than her life partner."

"You have nothing to worry about, sir."

"I know, but I don't plan on letting her off the hook just yet. She's meeting her bucket list man." Mr. Brindle formed a wry grin and continued toward the president's office.

Thirty minutes later, the president, her husband, and her chief of staff appeared from her office and stepped down the corridor toward the hatch. She stopped. "Everything set, Dante?"

He considered the message Jacob Sampson had sent him overnight, relaying ATF Agent Mills' concerns and her request to speak to the president before landing this morning. The president's orders about Dante not acting as a filter applied only to elements of her duties as president, not his as her protector. Chief of Staff Torres had already shot down canceling the event despite the FBI's deputy director's warning, and Dante had to agree with his assessment. If the president canceled events based on every nonspecific threat, she would never leave the White House. Being realistic, however, didn't exclude being cautious.

"Yes, ma'am. All set, but we're going with a full decoy today and want you to board the Beast inside the hangar."

The president furrowed her brow. "Should I be worried?"

"Let me do the worrying. It comes with the territory. I felt like throwing a curveball today."

"Your curveball will piss off half the media on board if they miss a photo op."

"They'll get over it." Dante raised his left wrist to his mouth to alert his team. "Bluebird leaving the nest."

She patted his shoulder on the way by and descended the stairs holding her husband's hand before making a straight line for the hangar. Two presidential limousines were idling inside, and Dante guided her to the one with the open door. Once she, her husband, and Torres boarded, Dante closed the door and hopped into the front passenger seat. He picked up the radio microphone mounted on the dashboard. "Package on the move."

Both limos fell in line behind their lead car from the hangar and were followed by the Halfback, an SUV with its rear window up for quick response by the tactical agent sitting in the rear-facing third row. The rest of the SUV in the actual motorcade was filled with a well-armed tactical response team, while the decoy contained dummies. Once each three-car package emerged from the hangar, the drivers lined up behind their route and pilot cars, leaving a twenty-five-yard gap for the motorcycle sweepers to fill in once they left the fenced-in area of the airport. The other vehicles filled in behind.

The decoy had an operational Watchtower, providing electronic countermeasures and a support vehicle for the staff, but the president's doctor rode in the actual motorcade. The only operational Hawkeye Renegade with a counter-assault team, ID car providing communications to all the vehicles, and Hazardous Material Mitigation Unit were with the actual motorcade. Both rows had a press van, a White House Communications Agency vehicle, and an ambulance to complete the appearance of two identical convoys.

Once every vehicle was in place, Dante radioed, "Overwatch, sit rep."

The helicopter pilot from Travis Air Force Base, who would follow their route from above, said, "All clear."

"Copy. Green light." On Dante's order, both lines of cars headed toward the main access gate simultaneously. Once past the entrance and on the blocked-off two-lane road, one route car turned left at the first intersection while the other turned right. Each led the motorcades in opposite directions to pick up their motorcycle sweepers and rear guards, consisting of local police cruisers, for added protection.

If the driver in each pilot car did their job and traveled at their designated speed, the caravans should arrive three minutes apart, one approaching the resort from the south, the other from the west. The southern route was ten miles to the resort, and the western one was thirteen and a half. Each had over two dozen intersections to contend with to keep the sweepers busy, but the shorter southern route passed through rural areas, which posed a greater risk for roadside IEDs at the shoulder drop-offs.

Choosing the route for the president was the tricky part for Dante. Most experts would select the longer, safer way, but he wanted to get the president into a secured building quickly. Accordingly, he chose plan Delta—twin motorcades with the actual package approaching from the south. The president would arrive first.

The conversation between Torres and an aide in the backseat grew louder when the line of vehicles reached the midpoint. The aide caught the fallout after a staffer failed to provide an executive summary for an upcoming meeting on the revived Keystone XL Pipeline.

Dante glimpsed the president in the two-foot-long horizontal rearview mirror. She rolled her eyes before locking stares with him and wagging her thumb upward—his cue to roll up the privacy divider. It wasn't soundproof, but it often drowned out heated discussions the president rarely engaged in. He focused on scanning the terrain to the west and east, searching the horizon in both directions for movement. Every passing bird gave him pause until they reached the last turn at the back of the Silverado Resort.

Once the driver lined up the Beast with the temporary canopy at the rear hotel entrance and brought it to a stop, Dante flew his door open, stepped out of the car, and scanned the area in all directions. He swatted a pesky fly floating near his left ear. Before exposing the president, he wanted confirmation the area was clear.

Dante activated his cuff mic. "Ground Watch, sit rep," he said, asking the comms center to review the live feed from the cameras his advance team had installed around the hotel, providing 360-degree coverage of every location the president would travel to or through before hitting the golf course.

"Romeo Eighteen, green light." The response included the day's arrival code, confirming the control center hadn't been overtaken.

Dante opened the rear passenger door, allowing the aide, chief of staff, and Mr. Brindle to exit the limo first. The aide fast-walked inside. Meanwhile, Dante offered the president his hand to help her out. She had learned at the Capitol building minutes before her inauguration that sliding out from the leather seat made her skirt ride up and asked for his help. She was such a gracious lady in his eyes. Continuing the practice, no matter her day's wardrobe, seemed the proper thing to do.

He followed her inside, always staying six feet back while another agent held the door for the president. Her first stop was the staging room inside the security detail operations center, where her personal staffer would brief her on the blow-by-blow movements for the event.

The bothersome fly had followed Dante into the building, requiring him to swat at it again. *Strange*, he thought. He'd changed his aftershave to stop attracting bugs like day-old food scraps in the trash can, but they still followed him. If this kept up, he'd have to start going without, something he hadn't done since high school.

Once inside the operations center, the president and the others with her disappeared into the small office for her briefing. Dante scanned the room and spotted the advance team commander issuing last-minute orders to an agent. When Jacob finished, Dante waved him over.

"Any problems?" Dante asked.

"The mobile hazmat detection team picked up high gasoline readings near the maintenance shack before dawn. I sent a team to investigate. A groundskeeper got distracted while fueling the mowers, and one overflowed. It's been cleaned up and poses no danger."

"Anything else before we let Bluebird fly?"

"Agent Lexi Mills from the ATF is standing by. She's asked to see the president before making her appearance."

"She is a persistent one, but I've made the call. Without more specificity, I won't shut this down."

"At least hear her out. She convinced me something is in the air." Jacob's worry lines became more prominent, which was a rare occurrence.

Dante checked his watch. Bluebird wouldn't be on the move for another six minutes. Listening to Lexi Mills couldn't hurt. "Send her in."

30

Waiting was never Lexi's strong suit, especially when she had to do it by sitting in a stiff, armless chair like she was next in line to see the vice principal for socking the middle school bully and giving him the shiner of a lifetime. At least she only had to defend herself twice in school, once for punching Teddy Bain and the other for doing the same to his older brother a week later, who had ambushed her after class in a misguided attempt to uphold the family honor. After those two unfortunate incidents, word spread quickly to never tease Lexi Mills for her short hair or for dressing like a boy.

She shifted in Jacob's guest chair for the hundredth time in the last hour while waiting for the president to arrive. She insisted Nathan take Jacob's desk chair with the arms to not aggravate his lower back pain. He'd said becoming a parent was the best and worst thing to happen to him. That having a child had taught him the true meaning of unconditional love and brought him more joy than he'd thought possible. But carrying an oversized toddler around amusement parks for hours on end had also ruined his back.

She rechecked her phone to see if Maxwell had pulled the right strings to get her a quick meeting with President Brindle, but the notifications screen was empty. Her mentor and friend was the second highest ranking agent in the FBI, but even he didn't have the clout to wake the president over a hunch.

The door swung open, and Jacob appeared at the opening. "I got you a few minutes with the president's protective detail chief." His eyes turned sad. "That's the best I could do."

Lexi sprang to her feet. "It's something."

Jacob shifted sideways, pressing his back against the door. A tall man appeared in the entryway. His trim frame, business-cut hairstyle, and crisp suit suggested federal agent. "Lexi, this is Special Agent Dante Cole."

Lexi shook Cole's hand. "It's a pleasure, Agent Cole. This is my partner, Nathan Croft."

"Your reputation precedes you, Agent Mills," Cole said. His posture was relaxed, the first good sign he might listen. "I have five minutes before the president is on the move again. Can you give me any specifics about this threat involving Falcon Industries?"

He knew the company name, so he'd read Maxwell's or Jacob's warnings. It was a good sign he'd taken Lexi's concern seriously. "Senator Jackson and his chief of staff had threatened to kill a classified Falcon Industries program this week, and both were found dead the day after money was transferred to an account we're tracking. The president made such a threat in her speech, and the amount of money transferred yesterday tells me the target is high value. If I'm right, Benjamin Foreman and the Raven have already killed a sitting senator with a security detail. Considering the cutting-edge technology those two develop, it's not farfetched to believe they'd go after the president."

"You've sold me on the possibility, but I need more to go on. Do you know how those two killed the two victims?"

"Not precisely. I believe whatever device was used, someone controlled it remotely. Your best defense is a signal jammer."

"That's something I can act on. I'll make sure jammers are disbursed among my agents."

"I also believe it has something to do with a weapons program under consideration by Senator Jackson's committee, but I can't cut through the red tape to learn more about it. The only thing I know is someone overheard the word locust."

"Locust? I'm not familiar with the term. I'll ask Mr. Torres to release everything on the program to you today."

"Thank you. It will help my investigation but won't lessen the risk to the president. I'm convinced an attempt will be made on her life today. I just don't know how."

"I agree there's a possibility, Agent Mills, but we receive a dozen threats like yours daily and guard against them appropriately. The president needs to govern, and supporting wounded warriors today is part of it." Cole checked his watch. "I'm sorry, but I must go."

"May I send you a photo of a man we suspect has engineered whatever device killed Jackson and his aide?"

"Yes, please do. I'll work on getting you the information on the weapons project as soon as possible."

Lexi thanked Cole for his time before he left. After sending Jacob Robert Segura's photo, she'd never felt more sure of a gut feeling. Everything she knew about Foreman and the Raven added up. It might not have been enough to cancel the president's appearance, but even a remote chance of Segura or the Raven showing up was enough for Lexi to stick around.

Stepping out of Jacob's office, Lexi retrieved her cell from her pocket and dialed Detective Hopkins. "Jan, the event is going on as scheduled. The advance team lead said we could shadow him. Meet us at the outdoor platform near the driving range. The president will open the charity event from there with a few words."

"I'm in the lobby," Jan said. "I'll be right there."

Once Jacob signed out a portable signal jammer from the equipment bin, she and Nathan followed him outside with their badges and sidearms hidden beneath their clothing.

The marine layer had lifted over the coastal hills, revealing several stray clouds in the mid-morning sky and warming the air nicely for the event. A standing crowd had gathered at the roped-off area half the size of a football field, waiting for the opening ceremony and the president's speech. Stragglers were still filtering through the final security checkpoint, submitting themselves to another once-over with a metal detector wand. Photojournalists and local and national television stations were lined up with cameras on a raised platform at the back of the crowd.

They settled at Jacob's assigned post on the west edge of the crowd along the cart path, ten yards from the raised platform. Nathan was taller, so he stood in the grass behind Lexi while Lexi straddled the grass and asphalt. Jan joined them five minutes later, standing next to Nathan.

"I should have worn leather tennies today," Nathan said. "My toes are freezing."

Lexi glanced at her prosthetic foot, realizing her left shoe was soaked with morning dew. She tapped the socket of her prosthesis. "One benefit of not having toes."

Minutes passed while eighteen of the top men and women professional golfers filled the raised platform. Their amateur playing partners—NFL and NBA stars, movie and television actors, comedians, and musical artists —paired up with their assigned golf pros. The only golfer without a partner was Tiger Woods.

Lexi scanned the area, focusing on the center where the crowd was the thickest. Her breath hitched when she noticed two people. They were so recognizable she could have made out their faces from space. She leaned toward Nathan and said, "I'll be right back."

Lexi pulled out her badge dangling on a chain around her neck from beneath her jacket and pushed her way through the crowd. "Federal agent. Excuse me," she repeated several times. Her heart thumped harder with each step until she reached Nita. She grabbed her by the upper arm and flipped her around. "What the hell are you doing here?"

"Your dad would not stop bugging me about seeing the president and Tiger. He said this might be his only chance." Nita looked at her with confusion in her eyes.

"You shouldn't be here. It's too dangerous."

"What do you mean dangerous? There are twice as many cops here than were yesterday. You said we were safe at the resort."

"That was before—" Lexi caught herself before she caused a panic, just as she had held back last night to not frighten Nita.

"Before what?" Nita's narrowed eyes meant she wouldn't leave without an explanation, so Lexi leaned in and whispered into her ear so others wouldn't hear.

"I think I'm right about the president being a target. If she's not safe, no one is. Please take Dad back to the room and don't open the doors or windows."

Nita pulled back, studying Lexi's eyes. "You're scaring me."

"Please, just go. I'll come as soon as I can."

An event organizer stepped up to the podium, pulling on the microphone. "Good morning, and welcome to the Twenty-First Annual Wounded Warrior Pro-Am Golf Tournament."

Nita nodded in agreement, and Lexi pulled on her father's shirt sleeve to get his attention. He turned. "Hi, Peanut."

"Dad, I need you to take Nita to the room, and don't leave until I get back."

Confusion filled his eyes, but Nita backed her up. "Please, Dad. Let's go."

His uncertainty morphed into worry, but he responded with a quiet nod, took Nita by the hand, and disappeared into the crowd, moving toward the main hotel.

Lexi started making her way back to Jacob and the others while the announcer explained the event's history, highlighting the many life-changing items from high-tech running blades for amputees to a wheelchair-accessible home the organization had provided to thousands of wounded and paralyzed veterans. Lexi tried to move quickly, but the crowd had grown thicker, slowing her dramatically.

"Since its inception," the organizer continued, "this tournament has raised over one billion dollars, and nine out of every ten dollars raised today will go directly to the three thousand wounded veterans waiting to regain their independence." Three golf carts approached the platform. Lexi saw that one had the president and Agent Dante Cole.

The organizer concluded. "It gives me great pleasure to introduce today's eighteenth amateur player, the President of the United States, Meghan Brindle."

Most in the crowd cheered, while a few blowhards booed and hissed when the president walked onto the stage. Lexi never understood that brand of public disrespect. People had a right to a difference of opinion and political views, but booing a president, especially one who had yet to break in the new Oval Office chair, was simply an act of a sore loser. It said more about those doing the taunting than their target.

The president had ditched her signature blue suit for dark blue golf pants and a coordinating light blue shirt and sweater vest. The fingertips of a white golf glove were hanging from her back pocket. The outfit wasn't worn but didn't seem straight off the rack either, bolstering Agent Scott Humphries's tidbit about the president the first night he protected Nita and her father. President Brindle played the game regularly and was damn good at it.

Brindle blew off the haters, waved to the crowd, and shook the organizer's hand at the podium. Tiger Woods greeted her with a firm handshake, drawing out a broad presidential smile. Lexi suspected some fangirling was at play.

Still ten feet from Jacob, Lexi stopped to listen when the president stepped up to the microphone. She admired the woman for her long list of accomplishments and for her refusal to acknowledge the existence of a glass ceiling. It was a model every marginalized person should adopt.

"Welcome, everyone, and thank you for supporting our wounded warriors," the president said. "I can think of no better cause than honoring the commitment we made to our veterans after they swore an oath to defend our nation and came home injured. Their bodies may have been broken but not their spirit." She paused her speech to gesture toward the audience's front row of men and women in wheelchairs and others proudly displaying their prosthetic arms and legs.

Lexi admired their collective courage and respected each vet for their sacrifice, but she was particularly moved by those wearing their artificial limbs in full public view. She'd accepted her handicap and had gotten past her reluctance to adjust her prosthetic in front of her peers. She'd once thought it would make her appear weak... lesser. But she was wrong. Her artificial leg was her badge of honor and a constant reminder of the sacrifices sometimes required of her job. It shouldn't be something to hide, but in her line of work, airing her prosthetic for the world to see was distracting and often generated questions when she needed complete focus. She wished she had the freedom and courage of those in the audience.

Applause for the vets made the president pause. While waiting for it to die down, she waved a hand near her forehead as if swatting away an annoying fly. *A fly*, Lexi thought. That insect had come up a lot recently. She'd encountered a large one at the bank hostage scene, and the senator's wife said she'd knocked away a big fly from the covers when she found her husband dying in bed.

The president swung her hand in the air again. Then it clicked. The fly was a micro-drone. Segura was controlling the fly, not the bomb trigger. But the question remained: How did the fly kill its victims? A small explosion near the head could have killed Yarborough, but the senator had no injuries. The drone must have interfered with his pacemaker.

Lexi clawed her way frantically through the crowd to get to Jacob, but the people there were unforgiving when the president whispered something to Tiger Woods. Everyone had craned their necks to see.

Finally, Jacob came into view. "Jacob. Nathan. The fly," she yelled, still making her way toward them. She reached out and clutched Jacob's arm, repeating, "The fly. That's how they got to the senator. There's one near the president. You need to stop it."

Jacob cast his stare toward the raised platform and squinted as if focusing on the president. "I don't see it."

"It's there, I tell you. It's there."

Agreement swam in his eyes. He raised his left wrist to his lips while reaching into his inner breast pocket with his right. "Code Red. Code Red. Jamming comms." He pulled out and activated the portable signal jammer.

Two agents—one was Dante Cole—rushed the platform to gasps from the crowd, shielded the president, and ushered her off. More agents surrounded her with their guns drawn, creating a moving cocoon as they bolted toward the Beast.

Some in the crowd screamed and pushed in the opposite direction, seeking safety.

Jacob made his way toward the platform, fighting against several people who had jumped into the roped-off area. Lexi and the others stayed on his heels. Jacob stopped at the foot of the stage and steadied his focus on the microphone. "The fly is still moving. Shouldn't it have stopped?"

Lexi was confused. The jammer would have cut off signals to the drone, rendering the fly capable of only executing its last command. But the fly circled the microphone and landed on the same spot several times, suggesting it was a real fly attracted to some scent.

Jacob scaled the platform and followed the fly's motion. When it landed on a wood plank near his feet, he stomped on it and lifted his shoe. The discovery was a gut punch. Nothing but bug guts were on the wood. He radioed the all-clear.

Jacob flicked his stare to Lexi with fire in his eyes. "Dammit, Lexi. You really screwed the pooch on this one."

31

Benjamin placed three freshly split lengths of oak onto the fire using the long tongs, positioning each one by following the technique his grandfather had taught him to promote airflow and achieve the optimum burn. He returned to his father's leather chair, sipped his coffee, and brought up the executive app on his tablet. He hated bringing technology here, but today the country would undergo a sea change, and he wanted to experience it where he felt most connected to the legacy he was bound by blood to uphold.

Bringing up the live feed, he realized again Lexi Mills was too good. This was the second time he'd listened to her explain her theories to the Secret Service, but today's instance was notable. Her newest audience was with the lead of the president's personal protective detail, Agent Dante Cole. She'd managed to work through the layers of security and meet with the one man who could potentially thwart Benjamin's planned attack.

He cringed again at the mention of the word locust, but if the Raven came through like he suspected, Mills would not piece together the entire picture until it was too late. His tablet alerted him to an incoming text from the disposable phone he used to communicate with the Raven. The perplexing message had one word. *Mountain.* The attack would not come in Napa but during the president's trip to Senator Jackson's grieving widow.

Why he chose the president's private visit and not the public event was a mystery, but the security on the ground and the availability of a vantage point for the sniper must have factored in. Nevertheless, by the end of the day, Brindle would die from a sniper's bullet, and the Venezuelans would take the fall.

The show wouldn't start for some time, but with Robert Segura at the controls today, Benjamin was sure the Raven would hit his target. He envisioned the mountain operation as he'd discussed with the Raven. The president would exit the Beast, walk up to the senator's grieving widow to shake her hand or offer a warm embrace, and the Venezuelan national hiding in the treetops with a high-powered sniper's rifle would pull the trigger. The locust, loaded with fragments from a bullet already fired from the weapon, would float nearby the president. If the sniper missed his target, the locust would deliver its payload via an explosive charge through the eye. Death would be instant. The patsy in the tree wouldn't have time to climb down and escape from the remote area before the Secret Service and military swarmed the area. He would be arrested, and the media finger-pointing would begin.

Benjamin returned his attention to the live audio feed. He laughed when Cole issued mobile signal jammers to his agents. Those devices were useless against locusts once they locked onto a target. Constant communication with a controller wasn't necessary to complete its mission. The locust was the perfect weapon, and Benjamin needed only one unit to hit the president to light the fuze of war.

He continued to listen, letting the fire warm his body while the unfolding events on his tablet warmed his soul. The comedy was proving so rich, listening to it wasn't enough. He had to see it. He swiped the tablet screen, brought up the executive app dashboard, and clicked the link labeled "Lexi Mills Live Video."

He rewound the live feed from a national news outlet carrying the president's opening speech at the Napa golf tournament. Brindle had praised the wounded veterans, receiving a round of applause, and began swatting at a pesky fly. Knowing the agents were about to whisk away the president over a false alarm, he couldn't hold back his laughter seeing Lexi Mills make a fool of herself on the national stage. Mills had played her card and had blown it. She was now the special agent who had cried wolf, going ballistic over a living fly, which played right into Benjamin's hands. She couldn't possibly recover from this mistake in time to save the president from the actual attack.

Benjamin's joy was so pronounced he reread the message and played the video recording again, catching the dejection on Mills' face when she realized she'd jumped the gun. The combination was better than every childhood Christmas and birthday rolled into one.

His tablet alerted again to an incoming phone call to his private line. The caller ID said it was from Ed Gotkin. Benjamin considered observing his rule of no calls or text messages while in the old cabin by letting the call go to voicemail, but he knew the senator. He was the nervous type who had to have his thumb on top of every aspect of his pet projects, and killing the President of the United States had to be his all-time venture. It was for Benjamin, and that was saying something, considering the number of high-value targets he'd eliminated during his time in the black ops world. If he didn't answer now, Gotkin would only continue calling until he did.

Benjamin released a sputtering breath and pressed the Accept button. "Hello, Senator. I take it you've been watching the news."

"What in the hell is going on, Benjamin. I thought the Raven was a professional. I expected better from you." The panic and anger in Gotkin's voice were expected but not his dismissive tone.

"Tread lightly, Senator. If I don't take that tone from my wife, I certainly won't take it from you."

"Then please explain what just happened in Napa."

"The best thing we could have hoped for. That was not the planned attack. It was an exasperating agent making a fool of herself."

"You're not making sense, Benjamin. Just tell me what happened."

"It's called conditioning. The president's protection detail will ignore the locust when the actual attack occurs. Their complacency will give my man the seconds he needs to pull this off."

"You're sure?"

"I'm positive," Benjamin said. He would have preferred a public spectacle but had to trust the Raven knew what he was doing. "The Raven *is* professional. You have nothing to worry about. By tomorrow, the country will be in mourning, and every news outlet in the world will point the finger at Venezuela. We will be at war within a week, and the Locust Program will be in full production."

"If you're wrong, we'll both end up in prison for the rest of our lives."

Benjamin disconnected the call, laughing. The money trail and altered phone records all pointed to the senator. Right or wrong, Gotkin would be the only one going to prison.

32

Jacob pressed two fingers against his right ear and raised his left wrist close to his lips. "Repeat that...Copy. En route." He turned to Lexi with concern etched on his face. "You need to come with me."

Lexi followed Jacob toward the main building at a slow jog, shaking her head. The feeling of being sent to the vice principal's office returned in force, making her skin crawl with regret. How could she have gotten it so wrong? Every detail she and her partners uncovered this week told her the high-tech weapons Foreman used to kill Senator Jackson and his aide were drones camouflaged as horse flies. Had her gut finally failed her? She suspected her fixation with the Raven had clouded her judgment. If this was the case, it was time to relinquish her role and let Nathan take the lead.

Nathan fell in line right behind her while Jan brought up the rear. The silence was unnerving until Nathan placed a comforting hand on her shoulder. "Don't beat yourself up. I would have done the same thing if I was close enough to see it."

"I've never been this wrong about a case."

"I don't think you are. I didn't see the connections until you pieced it together. You have a gift, Lexi. Trust it." The certainty in Nathan's voice was reassuring to a point. Her reputation for having a reliable instinct had earned her the Secret Service's goodwill, but she had burned their trust the minute the president's agent rushed her off the stage for a damn fly.

"Thanks, Nathan, but Jacob is right. I really screwed up."

Jacob took an unexpected turn where the cart path split. Instead of going left to the hotel's back entrance, he turned right. They jogged to the edge of the building and rounded the corner, where several black SUVs were lined up. He stopped at the one in front and opened the rear passenger door. "The president wants to see you before her plane takes off. We'll take you to the airport."

The heavy load of guilt weighed Lexi down. Thousands of people had paid hundreds of dollars to watch the president play a hole of golf with Tiger for charity, but Lexi's hastiness ensured it didn't happen. "I take full responsibility, but can my partners come? They've been involved with the investigation from the beginning and could provide better insight into the case if she has questions."

"Hold on." Jacob spoke into his microphone and nodded to the reply coming over his earpiece. "Get in, all of you."

Lexi, Nathan, and Jan crammed into the backseat. Jacob slammed the door closed and pounded his hand twice on the metal, cueing the driver to take off. "Wait," Lexi shouted. The car stopped, and she rolled down the window. "Aren't you coming, Jacob?"

"My job is here. It was nice seeing you again, Lexi. Good luck."

Lexi was no stranger to barreling down city and rural streets in a government SUV with lights and sirens parting the traffic like a zipper on an old pair of jeans. She much preferred the Charger she drove during the high-speed pursuit in Oklahoma last year for its maneuverability, though she had to admit the way the agent handled this car in the turns was impressive. She made a mental note to ask Maxwell if he could pull some strings to sign her up for the Secret Service driving course.

The driver slowed at the industrial gate of the Napa County Airport but sped up again when a uniformed officer guarding it waved him through. Air Force One was parked in the distance and was surrounded by guards and an eclectic collection of service vehicles. Lexi expected the driver to slow and drive toward it, but he veered around it, revealing a smaller white and light blue Gulfstream jet with U.S. Air Force markings, utterly eclipsed by the president's plane.

When the SUV stopped at the foot of the smaller jet's boarding stairs, the three piled out from the backseat. The plane's engines were roaring, the noise almost deafening. Lexi greeted the agent standing near the entrance on the tarmac with a handshake and nod. He gestured his left arm toward the stairs, inviting her to board.

Lexi ascended the stairs, feeling her residual limb sink lower into the prosthetic socket. Thank goodness she had the forethought this morning to add a third sock layer, predicting this might stretch out into another long day. At the top, she turned right and waited. Once Nathan and Jan entered, she passed by the small galley and a leather bench where three agents were seated. The aisle opened to the main cabin with two four-chair seating areas with two chairs on each side of the aisle positioned back-to-back.

The president was sitting in the far back on the left, speaking to a man directly in front of her. His back was to Lexi. Chief of Staff Torres was across the aisle, and although she couldn't see his face, Lexi recognized Dante Cole sitting across from Torres.

When Lexi stepped into the seating area, President Brindle stopped her conversation and focused on her, locking her gaze for several beats. The silent, lasered stare was intimidating and sent the message she was not happy without coming across as terrifying. Lexi appreciated and respected her restraint.

The president touched the knee of the man across from her and whispered something to him. The man stood and entered the aisle. When he turned, Lexi recognized him as the First Gentleman, making her more nervous. She'd interrupted the president's trip with her husband. He took a chair in the first seating area, and the president waved Lexi forward, gesturing for her to take the seat directly in front of her. Nathan and Jan filled in the seats in the nearest area with the First Gentleman.

Lexi sat. Bracing herself for a dressing down by the President of the United States, she let out a shaky breath. "Madam President." She stopped when the president raised her hand in a stopping motion.

"You'll need to buckle in. We're about to take off."

"Oh." Lexi complied but was confused. She thought they would talk while the plane idled on the apron, not inflight to some unknown location. Lexi heard other seatbelts click when the plane started moving. *Shit*, Lexi thought, placing her phone in airplane mode. She was in some serious trouble.

President Brindle crossed her legs at the knees and shifted in her seat. "So you're the reason I didn't get to golf with Tiger Woods today."

"Yes, ma'am."

"No apology?"

"I never apologize for doing my job, Madam President. I had good reason to believe you were in danger, and I acted on it."

The president angled her head to her left, inspecting Lexi with her eyes. She grinned and released a single chuckle. "I can respect that, Agent Mills."

Lexi forced a lumpy swallow. "Thank you." Maybe she would escape this trip without an ass-chewing.

"Agent Cole filled me in on your theory about Senator Jackson's death. I understand you saw his widow yesterday. Did you tell Peggy about your theory?"

"No, ma'am. We questioned her about the evening her husband died."

"Tell me what she told you and how it ties into the case you're investigating."

"Mrs. Jackson told us about the senator's pacemaker and the presence of a large fly on the bed when she found him. I saw a similar fly at a bank hostage scene in the Sierra Foothills on Tuesday involving a bomb vest. I thought nothing of it then, but from what we've pieced together over the week, I believe the fly was a micro-drone developed by Falcon Industries in coordination with an illegal arms builder the ATF has been investigating. I believe a similar drone was used to sabotage the senator's pacemaker."

"You're suggesting a sitting United States senator was assassinated."

"Yes, and based on money transfers my intelligence team uncovered, we identified a pattern that led me to believe you were the next target."

"By whom and why?" the president asked.

"By Benjamin Foreman because you threatened to pull the plug on his military weapons project. Have you heard the word locust associated with any of his new projects?"

"This sounds like a project I was briefed on, but it's supposed to be in the conceptual stage, not operational."

"I think it's well beyond a concept. I believe Senator Jackson and his chief of staff were both killed after meeting with Benjamin Foreman about that classified weapons project, and I fear you're next. The man we think Mr. Foreman is working with, the Raven, is dangerous. He has already killed two federal agents. One of them was on my task force."

"So this is personal." The president's tone sounded accusatory, but Lexi couldn't blame her after this morning's fiasco.

"Yes." Lexi took no shame in admitting her motive. The criminals she chased were evil. They'd made it personal by going after people close to her, creating a fire in her belly hot enough to ensure she wouldn't stop until she'd brought them to justice.

"If I recall correctly, you headed up Task Force Zero Impact because Tony Belcher had become personal to you. We could all benefit from you taking things personally." The president shifted her stare to Dante. "Agent Cole, please tell her what you told me."

Dante shifted to face Lexi. "Twice in three days, I've encountered large flies, including one today after the president's motorcade arrived. I thought nothing of those incidents, but now I believe they might have been the micro-drone you spoke of."

Lexi let a small grin form. "So I was right."

"Just not during my speech, Agent Mills. It appears Mr. Foreman's technology was much farther along than he'd let on." The president focused on her chief of staff. "Mr. Torres, please have Senator Gotkin and the SecDef provide me information on current Falcon Industries proposals and anything associated with locust."

"I'm on it, ma'am." Torres pulled out his cell phone from his jacket pocket, dialed, and spoke with someone on the other end.

"May I ask where we're headed, Madam President?" Lexi asked.

"I'm going to visit Senator Jackson's widow to pay my respects at her son's home. Care to augment my security detail?"

"I'd be honored."

33

The president's Gulfstream landed and coasted toward a hangar, where a motorcade and another team of Secret Service agents and local police were awaiting her arrival. Lexi stared out her window. She couldn't be sure, but the building a hundred yards in the distance resembled the airport structure where she, Nathan, and Jan had ambushed Benjamin Foreman two days ago.

"Is this the Nevada County Airport?" she asked.

"Yes. Why?" Dante Cole said.

"Benjamin Foreman lives not too far from here." Thinking there were no coincidences when the Raven was involved, Lexi felt a chill prickle the skin on her arms.

Nathan looked out the same window and said softly, "This can't be good."

Lexi snapped her head toward Dante. "I have a bad feeling about this. We need to get out of here."

"We added this leg of the trip only yesterday," Dante said. "I doubt Foreman or the Raven could have planned for it."

"Those two have a longer reach than you realize. It's scary how much they know."

"I get what you're saying, Mills, but the motorcade has the newest counterattack measures. I have four teams continuously driving the sixteen-mile route. If they report anything unusual, we'll turn back."

The president reached across and touched Lexi's knee. "I appreciate your concern, but I won't be the president who cowers in a bunker. I need to pay my respects."

Lexi nodded, acknowledging the president's decision. Usually, she admired boldness like hers, but she knew the Raven, and from what she'd learned about Benjamin Foreman, they were much alike. Either could penetrate the president's defenses anytime they wanted. But now they knew what they were looking for and would be watching for it.

The president graciously invited Lexi's team to join her and her husband in her limo for the ride to the Jackson family home, taking up all three passenger seats in the back. With Dante in the front with the driver, her chief of staff boarded a support vehicle with the president's doctor between the Watchtower providing radar warning and the Hawkeye Renegade with the tactical assault team.

Minus the press vans, the caravan mirrored every presidential motorcade Lexi had seen. She suspected they had at least thirty armed personnel with advanced weaponry to repel an attack. But would that be enough against whatever the Raven and Foreman had in store?

A military helicopter flew overhead, and Dante issued the green light order to commence rolling. The caravan of cars exited the flight line underneath the overcast sky, passing the F-104 Starfighter on display in the airport parking lot, and picked up their sweeper escorts on motorcycles and two rear guards in Nevada County Sheriff patrol cruisers.

A half-cocked grin grew on Jan's face when he recognized one rear driver as they passed. "The guys will never believe me when I tell them I was inside the limo."

"Would a picture together help?" the president asked, adding a wink. Lexi liked her playful side. It was partly why the country elected her. On the campaign trail, she was a personable, knowledgeable, and eloquent speaker who knew when to add humor without appearing forced or idiotic. She was genuine then and was now.

Facing backward and sitting directly across from the president like on the plane, Lexi directed her gaze out the window, watching the passing pine and oak trees as the limo rolled through the forest, swaying through the mountain road's gentle curves. The motorcade entered a straightaway in an open clearing, where the tree line had retreated on both sides by at least a hundred yards. Newly formed dark clouds hung over the treetops of the western Sierra slopes like a blanket, hiding them from the sun's rays.

While the president and her husband talked, remembering when they met Senator Jackson and his wife on inauguration day, Lexi kept her stare on the horizon toward the rear of the caravan. It was their most vulnerable side and the ideal angle of attack.

The low clouds hanging over the trees at her ten o'clock, the driver's four o'clock, turned darker and appeared to grow at an alarming rate. Parts of the cloud broke away, creating dark horizontal ribbons in the sky in multiple directions. They reminded her of Carlsbad Cavern National Park when she was there chasing the Raven. She and Nathan had arrived minutes before sunset when the colony of Brazilian bats had begun its nightly migration, creating the same long ribbons for as far as the eye could see.

"What the hell is that?" Nathan said. He was on the other end of the rear-facing bench with a view out the driver's side of the limo. He must have seen the same thing, which meant something was coming at them from all directions.

"I'm not sure," Lexi said.

Each ribbon simultaneously veered toward their position. Whatever they were, they were moving fast. The radio crackled with chatter. "Watchtower to Ground One, I have multiple bogeys inbound from all directions."

"It's the locusts!" Lexi shouted.

Dante picked up the dashboard mic and barked orders. "Overwatch. Watchtower, launch countermeasures. Evasive maneuver Alpha."

The caravan picked up speed instantly. Lexi instinctively reached for her service weapon. Nathan and Jan did the same. The president clutched her husband's hand. The tension inside the cabin jumped off the charts.

White, fluorescent flares launched from the helicopter circling above and the SUV two cars behind the limo, lighting the cloud-darkened sky with bright flashes and long white contrails. Some locusts fell from the sky, but there were thousands of them, and most had gotten through and were attacking the motorcade vehicles. The countermeasures couldn't possibly deter them all. Lexi suspected one of their vehicles was employing a radar jammer, but she still heard radio chatter, which was alarming. Its presence told her they weren't blocking the right signals for the locusts.

Lexi craned her neck to speak to Dante better. "You need to jam the entire spectrum."

She looked out the front window and saw the motorcycle sweepers wobble and drop like flies, tumbling in violent crashes along the roadside. The military helicopter engine spat out smoke, and it spun wildly before crashing in a meadow west of the road, creating a giant fireball. Other vehicles slowed and steered oddly toward both shoulders. A brief glance through the rear window revealed that most of the motorcade's cars behind them had broken down too. The locusts were picking them off one by one, likely using electromagnetic pulse emitters and explosive charges. Individually, the explosive wouldn't amount to much, but the compounding effect could be devastating in a swarm.

"But we'll lose our comms."

"They're riding *your* comms." Lexi gritted her teeth. "Can't you see? Do it."

"Watchtower. Go wide. Go wide," Dante ordered through his mic.

Lexi glanced back again, but the SUV with the radar dish had fallen out of formation and was stranded on the roadside. "Your jammer is inoperable. Did you bring a portable?"

Dante dug into his jacket and slid the device over the cabin partition to Lexi. "Will it be strong enough?"

"It should help." Lexi manipulated the buttons on the screen to jam all frequencies and pressed the device against her window. The bulletproof glass would significantly limit the signal range, but it should be enough to block signals from getting to the micro-drones before hitting the limo. Without the ability to receive future commands, the drones couldn't change direction or deploy their EMP.

It was working. Locusts bounced off the roof and windows in rapid succession. The plinking noise was eerily reminiscent of machine gun fire. Lexi saw two problems. First was the limited signal jammer range. The limo was speeding away, so once they had moved out of range, if a fallen drone was still operational, it could receive commands again. As a result, whoever was controlling them could revive and return the locusts to action, creating an endless supply of attackers. The deployment was genius.

Secondly, blocking a wide range of frequencies created a rapid power drain. A portable unit couldn't sustain transmitting at such a pace for long. Lexi focused on the power level. It was already below sixty percent and dropping quickly. "Do you have another battery or charging cable? Power will drop quickly." Lexi kept emotion out of her voice to not panic the others.

"No. It had a full charge when I left. The damn thing is supposed to last for hours." Dante's sharp response meant he was on edge. They all were. The plinking noise was relentless, but the president and her husband, both retired naval aviators, remained calm. However, beads of sweat on their brows betrayed their underlying nerves.

"Blocking all frequencies is a huge power drain. We'll need to find cover or a power source ASAP." Lexi's breathing shallowed when the power dipped below fifty percent. "We have maybe fifteen minutes of power left." She snapped her attention to the person sitting next to her. "Jan, any ideas?"

He glanced out the window. "The only place close is Shangri-La."

"That's the lion's mouth," Lexi recoiled. "It's the last place we should go."

"Then we're dead ducks," Jan said. "Think about it, Lexi. From what I could tell, his mountain cabin is fortified with signal-jamming capabilities and is only minutes away. I've lived here all my life and know this area like the back of my hand. It's there or a grave."

"What's Shangri-La?" Dante asked.

"Benjamin Foreman's compound," Lexi said. "We can't go there."

"Foreman?" Mr. Brindle cocked his head back. "I overheard you talking earlier. He's the one you think is trying to kill my wife. We need to get as far away from there as possible."

"Hopkins is right, Mills," Dante said. He peeked out the front and back windows. "The only vehicles left are this limo and the SUV behind us. It has our security detail with heavy weapons. We'll have ten armed agents and two rocket launchers between the two vehicles. We can fight our way in and mount a defense until reinforcements from Beale Air Force Base come."

"When will that be?" the president asked.

"They're at least twenty minutes out."

"We don't have that much time." The president looked to Lexi for confirmation, and Lexi offered a slow headshake. Brindle then opened the storage compartment between her and her husband and pulled out two Beretta M-9 semi-automatic pistols. She handed one to her husband. "I'd rather die fighting than sitting on my hands."

Dante rested a hand on Jan's shoulder until Jan turned his head toward him. "Where is Shangri-La?"

Jan turned around on the bench seat, settling on his knees, and rattled off directions to the driver. Within a minute, they passed the scarred stretch of road Jan had pointed out as the spot where Darryl Yarborough had crashed and died after meeting with Benjamin Foreman. They were close, and the next few minutes would determine whether everyone in their two cars lived or died.

Lexi's thoughts drifted to what would happen if she didn't make it out of this alive. The Raven would have gotten his revenge and would have no reason to go after Nita and her father. Knowing her death would secure their safety was comforting and provided a sense of calm in the chaos.

Lexi closed her eyes, took a slow, deep breath, and imagined herself at the house in Ponder. She had returned from a long day working on a case and parked her car under the stars and shade tree behind the house. Then, glancing toward the garage, she had discovered the right door open and the light on. She had walked inside and had seen her father tinkering again with the '65 Shelby, a wedding present for her and Nita.

"Hey, Dad. I thought you were done with that thing."

"I wanted to adjust the carb. Make the mixture a little richer to increase your speed off the line when we take it to the track on Saturday."

She had thanked and kissed him on the cheek before going inside the main house, discovering Nita getting ready for bed. Her wife's hair had been wet and combed back, and only a cotton bath towel had covered her sexy body. Lexi had stood in the doorway to watch Nita rub lotion onto her leg. The grin on her lips had suggested she knew Lexi was there and had been paying close attention to her movements. Each graceful stroke of her hands had been a master class in seduction.

When Nita was done, she had stood at the foot of the bed and loosened the towel, letting it drop to the wood floor. *"Do you plan to watch all night?"* she had asked in a seductive tone.

"What do you think?" Lexi had said. She had stridden across the room, taken Nita into her arms, and kissed her languidly, passionately before lowering her to the mattress. She had lain on top of her, propping up her torso by resting her weight on her forearm. *"I've loved you since our first kiss,"* she had said before pressing their lips together in a second memorable one.

"I can see it," Jan shouted desperately as if he'd spotted a trickle of light at the end of a long, dark tunnel. The plinking of locusts trying to battle their way inside the armored limo had reached a crescendo like a steady, pelting rain against an aluminum awning. The repeating sound reverberated down to her bones.

Lexi woke from what might have been her final thoughts of Nita. She opened her eyes. The president's husband had wrapped a loving arm around his wife while holding a gun in his free hand. The juxtaposition of gentleness and violence was a jarring foretelling that the end was near.

Lexi twisted the wedding band on her left ring finger and whispered, "I love you, Nita."

She craned her neck toward the windshield and recognized the access road leading up to Shangri-La. The gate was closed, and the driver began to slow down.

"Ram it," Jan yelled, but the car continued to lose speed. "Ram it," Jan repeated, more frenzied than the first time.

Dante snapped his head toward the driver, twisting the man's right suit coat sleeve. "Ram it. Ram it!"

34

Coffee won't do, Benjamin thought. Lexi Mills was made a fool on the national stage, the country would soon be at war, and the Senate would green-light the Locust Program for full production. These incredible unfolding events deserved something more, so Benjamin padded to the old cabin's kitchen. He'd stocked the cabinet with two selections—hot cocoa for those cold mornings when he wanted something sweet to warm up by the fire and twenty-five-year-old scotch for the evenings to unwind. It was a chilly morning in the mountains, but the president's plane would land in minutes, according to his long-range radar, setting in motion a history-changing event. It was a momentous occasion deserving of celebration.

He grabbed the bottle of Rare Marriages and a glass tumbler and returned to his father's leather chair. A two-finger pour was conservative for a day like this one, so he went for three. He picked up the tablet and sipped on his drink, enjoying the sweet, creamy flavor that made the Balvenie easy going down. Most new money types fell for Macallan Sherry Oak, the supposed Rolls-Royce of Single Malts, for its hefty price tag, but Benjamin thought its flavor was overrated. Coming from the Highlands should not be the defining characteristic of a good scotch. Moray, where his ancestors originated, was a perfectly acceptable location for a distillery.

Benjamin opened both links of interest—the audio feed from Lexi

Mills' phone and the locust video feed the Raven provided. Both offered only static. Once the plane dropped altitude and Lexi was back in a cell service area, he would again be the proverbial fly on the wall for the president's private conversations. Depending on whether the meeting location with Mrs. Jackson was changed during the flight, the video would start when the president was on the tarmac or had arrived at the senator's family home a few miles away.

The fire had waned since Benjamin last added wood and needed more fuel. The stack he'd brought in earlier that morning had dwindled, so this break in the action was the ideal time to restock. After another sip of his Balvenie, he put on his jacket and went to the pile of pre-split wood stacked several yards from the cabin. He selected several lengths of various sizes, cradled them with his left arm against his chest, and started for the front door. He noticed several bugs flying above the cabin's roofline and tried to get a closer view, but they disappeared before he could focus.

Benjamin returned inside and stacked his load of wood in the storage cubby, saving three to place on the embers. Once satisfied with the fire, he returned to the chair and called his control center from his tablet.

"Yes, Mr. Foreman," Matthew said.

"Is anyone flying locusts in the compound?"

"No, sir. The board is clear."

Still suspicious, Benjamin said, "Please message me if any units are activated other than the ones we assigned to today's op."

"Of course, sir. You should know we experienced a momentary anomaly on the primary server an hour ago. We followed protocol, rebooted the system, and everything is functioning normally."

Benjamin's antennae went up. The control center's systems were inspected and tested routinely and received a clean bill of health two days ago. A hiccup today was a statistical improbability. Nevertheless, a disruption could affect today's operation. "What kind of anomaly?"

"IT investigated and determined the operating system hung on a minor subroutine. They completed a full diagnostic and recommended replacing a memory chip during the next tech refresh."

"Very good. Please see to it." Benjamin disconnected the call, still uneasy about the glitch. His control center hadn't experienced a problem since the last software upgrade months ago when the locust testing over-loaded the memory buffers. Maybe they hadn't worked out all the kinks.

His tablet crackled with noise from the live audio feed. From the conversation, he deducted Mills must have had her phone on airplane mode for some time and was already en route to the Jackson family home in the president's motorcade. After the mention of taking a selfie together—a loathsome practice that fed narcissism—someone asked, "*What the hell is that?*" Benjamin thought nothing of it until another voice reported, "*multiple bogeys inbound from all directions,*" and Mills shouted, "*It's the locusts!*"

What the hell was right. Benjamin sprang from his chair, knocking over his glass of prized scotch and shattering the crystal into a dozen pieces. Using the locusts to attack the motorcade was not part of the plan. The chatter in the car was nonstop, with the Secret Service radio going off with one report after another. The motorcade deployed defensive countermea-sures, which meant an overwhelming number of locusts were employed.

Heat flushed Benjamin's neck and cheeks as he activated the phone on his tablet again and dialed his control center.

"Yes, Mr. Foreman," Matthew said.

"What the hell is going on?" Benjamin paced the floor in front of the fireplace.

"I don't understand?"

"I'm listening to the Mills audio feed. Locusts are swarming the presi-dential motorcade right now."

"That can't be. The board is clear."

"That was no anomaly. The Raven hacked our system." Benjamin's survival instincts kicked in. If those were locusts above the cabin, its many penetration points made him a sitting duck. He clutched his tablet tightly, darted toward the door, and turned toward the main house. "Open the front door. Prepare for shields up and signal jammer. Returning to the nest."

"Copy," Matthew said.

Benjamin dialed the Raven on the run while staying inside the tree line for camouflage. The call connected. "What the hell are you doing, Raven? Why are you swarming the motorcade with locusts?"

"I'm following the orders of the man who paid me."

"I gave no such order."

"Not you, Senator Gotkin."

"Gotkin?" The call went dead. Benjamin almost stumbled at the realization the senator had double-crossed him but caught himself and continued toward the main house at a full sprint. He'd be most exposed at the curved driveway, so he paused at the edge of the trees and scanned the area up to the roof line, looking for locusts. After spotting no dangers, he darted across the asphalt to the portico and sprinted up the stairs to the open door. Once he was past the threshold, the door automatically shut and metal plates slid into place with sharp thuds, covering every window and door in the center building and cutting it off from the rest of the aboveground structure. He checked his tablet, but the signal was still strong. Something was wrong.

Benjamin slowed but didn't stop until he reached the waiting elevator with its door open. The instant he skidded to a stop inside, the door closed, and the car descended to the control center level. The ride down took too many precious seconds to be without information. He didn't know whether Shangri-La was under attack nor what was happening to the president's motorcade. This was an absolute disaster.

The elevator door opened, and Benjamin stepped out calmly. He couldn't let his staff see how unraveled he'd become. The giant screen wall was partitioned, displaying static from the expected Raven attack in the center. The audio feed from Mills' phone was noted in the lower left corner as offline. The rest of the screen displayed live exterior security feeds from Shangri-La, including the long-range cameras two miles out.

"Status report," Benjamin barked. "Why isn't the signal jammer working?"

Matthew was down from his perch on the upper level, hovering over the two-person staff while at their workstations. He turned to face Benjamin. "I have a man working on the jammer. As far as we can tell, the command was overridden by an embedded protocol in the server."

"What about surveillance?"

"All cameras and radar are operational and show no activity."

"The locusts are designed to fly below the radar at treetop level. They could be anywhere. Any luck in picking up their feed?"

"Not for any of the operational units. I brought out an alpha prototype from storage, and it checks out. We can control it and bring up the live feed on screen."

Benjamin smelled a rat in the form of Robert Segura. "Find a beta prototype developed by Mr. Segura and activate it."

"Give me a moment, sir." Matthew dashed up the steel stairs, each clanking step echoing throughout the command capsule. He returned seconds later with a locked metal container. He pressed his thumb against the biometrics reader, unlocking the case and exposing the locust model Robert Segura had developed during his tenure at his compound. Matthew powered it on and snapped his attention toward his controllers. "Bring up Bravo 218."

The controller typed something on his keyboard, changing the display on the screen wall, but the video feed was static, and the status bar read offline. "I'm unable to connect, sir."

Benjamin pounded his fist against a workstation, creating a loud thump. "I knew I shouldn't have trusted him." His heart pounded so hard his face flushed again. "Get Kyle Sands on the horn. See if he can override Segura's control."

"I'm on it," Matthew said, lifting a phone handset.

"We have incoming, sir," a controller said, switching the feed to the center of the screen wall. The two-mile-out camera picked up the presidential limo and an SUV barreling toward Shangri-La, staying close, virtually bumper to bumper. A minute later, another camera picked them up a mile out. This time the operator was ready for them and zoomed in on the vehicles. A swarm of locusts was pelting the cars without effect.

"Alert security," Benjamin ordered.

The control spoke into a microphone. "All teams, THREATCON Delta. Front Gate. One minute out. Repeat THREATCON Delta. Front Gate."

Teams reported in via the radio. The exterior camera feeds showed them moving to their assigned positions to defend Shangri-La with automatic weapons, rocket-propelled, fragmentation, and smoke grenades, all developed by Falcon Industries.

The screen wall changed, shifting from the camera pointing outward from the front gate to the center. The remaining elements of the presidential motorcade had made the final turn and were heading toward the weakest link in the compound's defenses. The limo appeared to slow but sped to ramming speed a moment later.

The Beast was essentially a luxury tank on a General Motors truck chassis. This armor-plated car weighed twenty thousand pounds and had eight-inch-thick doors. The only effective weapon against it in his arsenal was a direct hit from an RPG. Everything else would only make a dent. Though, if he had an entire colony of locusts, a swarm could envelop the undercarriage, the most vulnerable part, and penetrate the cabin. The exterior security team had neither. The RPG was their last defense inside the perimeter.

The team opened fire with their military-style automatic rifles, aiming for the front tires. Both took on direct fire, but the run flat feature engaged, and the car kept coming. The limo crashed through Shangri-La's reinforced metal gate like the two panels were toothpicks, sending them springing inward on their hinges. Several locusts peeled off. They attacked Benjamin's men, taking them out easily with explosions to their heads.

The SUV followed but accelerated when it received automatic rifle fire from the gate team and passed the Beast before the access road narrowed. The main body of the Locust swarm kept up its relentless attack.

Beyond the first bend, the interior team had set up with the RPGs, and when the first vehicle appeared, it fired. The two rockets soared in trails of smoke, both striking the SUV head-on in a violent explosion, engulfing the car in an orange fireball. The Beast continued forward, and his response team was out of rockets. The rest were under lock and key in the armory and would take two minutes to retrieve, minutes his team didn't have before the Beast reached the main building with its built-in weapons.

The center feed on the wall switched to the primary camera at the front door Benjamin had darted through earlier. The limo swung into the circular driveway coming to a skidding halt in front of the center building. The locust cloud attacking it from all sides suddenly withdrew, leaving behind hundreds of their comrades inoperable. A second and third security team popped out from both garages and opened fire on the Beast, pelting the outer shell but only making dents. The exterior layers of glass shattered with each bullet impact but clung together as designed, clouding every inch of surface.

The locusts lying on the ground perplexed Benjamin since Shangri-La's signal jammer was inoperable. The only explanation was that the Beast had employed a mobile system, severing the locusts' connection to their operator. If this was the case, their defensive measures might be their only hope of stopping the locusts until Kyle Sands regained control.

He dashed to the desk with the radio and pressed the microphone. "Cease fire! Cease fire! I'm coming out."

"Are you sure, sir?" Matthew asked. The crease at the bridge of his nose deepened with worry. "The capsule is impenetrable. You'll be vulnerable topside."

"The locusts can find a way in. How do you think we breathe down here? They will find a way through the ventilation system. If we close it off, we'll suffocate within hours. I have to go up to buy us time."

Benjamin rode the elevator to the main floor, grabbed the Walther PPK pistol hidden in the corner bar, and stuffed it in his waistband at the small of his back. He unlocked the front door from the biometrics reader, overriding the defensive security posture, and opened it. He stepped out with his hands raised head high and descended the stairs. His security teams moved into position to protect him.

The presidential limo was riddled with bullets, and every window was shattered, making it impossible to see through. Benjamin's only hope was negotiating. He shouted, "We need to talk."

35

The last support vehicle in the president's motorcade sacrificed itself, taking direct hits from two RPGs. The SUV flipped in the air, rolling to the trees in a giant fireball. Lexi's heart pumped wildly, and sweat beads had her bangs sticking to her forehead. The atmosphere in the cabin had become thick and humid from the collective heavy breathing. Six lives were lost moments ago, and the remaining seven had little chance of survival.

The driver skidded the limo to a stop at the portico leading to Foreman's front door. Gunmen appeared from both sides of the building, encircled the Beast, and opened fire. The bullets ripped through the air at an unforgiving pace, creating an earsplitting echo chamber inside the cabin. The brutal assault turned every five-inch-thick transparent armor window into an opaque web of pulverized glass and polycarbonate that weakened with each passing second.

The standoff had become a race to see which would give out first: the car's armor, signal jammer, or the attacking force's supply of ammo. Lexi checked the power level on the one thing saving them from the drones. It had dropped below twenty percent. Defending against the locusts was quickly becoming a lost cause, and the Beast protecting them couldn't last much longer either. With no bomb to diffuse or booby trap to disarm, Lexi had to accept the inevitability—die from gunfire or the locusts. She should have felt like a trapped animal, ready to pounce at any glimmer of freedom or been frozen with fear, but the inescapable circumstance was oddly calming. Death hung overhead patiently like a vulture circling over a pack of injured prey until the remaining fight in them drained to the ground.

She focused on the woman in front of her. The president displayed the same sense of sereneness, accepting their fate with poise. "It's been an honor, Madam President," Lexi said.

"Have faith, Agent Mills. I doubt God wants me to die on my wedding anniversary."

Lexi grinned while the bullets continued their blitz. "How long have you two been married?"

"Thirty-four years." The president squeezed her husband's hand and gave him a loving look, which he returned. "We've had our ups and downs, but love has always been there." She gestured toward Lexi's left ring finger. "How about you? How long?"

"Three months."

The president's smile stretched to her eyes. "Ahh, newlyweds. A magical time of love and unbridled passion. I heard you say Nita before. Is that her name?"

"Yes. She's a wonderful woman. After losing my leg, I'd lost hope, but she showed me no obstacle is insurmountable."

The shooting suddenly stopped, bringing the cabin to an unnerving quiet. They had driven into the hurricane's eye, and this felt much like the calm before the storm. But a slow smile grew on the president's lips. "Like this one, it would seem."

Lexi didn't share the president's optimism until a muffled voice came from outside the limo. "We need to talk."

It was impossible to see through the riddled glass, but Lexi thought she'd recognized Benjamin Foreman's voice. She peered through a section of the window with less clouding but could only make out the silhouette of a man. "I think it's Foreman," she said.

"We can help each other," Foreman shouted. "We have something the other needs."

"We're losing power quickly, Agent Cole," Lexi said, pivoting toward the front of the car. "We need to do something."

"Then we negotiate." Dante picked up the wired microphone and pressed a button on the dashboard control console, activating the public address system. "What do you want?"

"I no longer control the locusts," Foreman said, emotion uncharacteristically lacing his voice. "We're working on the fix to stop them, but it will take time. You have the signal jammer to keep them at bay to let us do our work. I propose a truce so we can work together."

Lexi had no reason to trust Foreman. Everything she'd unearthed about him made her believe he would go to any length to get his program approved. He was not innocent, but the tension in his voice when he mentioned the signal jammer suggested he might be telling the truth.

"Reinforcements are on the way," Dante said.

"The swarm will only destroy them. The only way to stop them is to work together. If you refuse, I'll have no choice but to finish the job the Raven started and take you out with RPGs."

"I think you should listen to him, Agent Cole," Lexi said. "I've talked to him several times. He's the poster child for calm and collected, but he sounds desperate."

Dante rubbed the back of his head again, clearly weighing the circumstances facing him. He shifted in his seat, craning his head toward the rear cabin. "We're out of options, Madam President."

"Living is better than dying, Dante," the president said. "We need to take our chances with this man."

Dante gripped the mic tighter, cracking the plastic casing. His frustration was palpable, but he pressed the button. "All right. Lower your weapons. I'm coming out." He turned toward the back again. "I'll go out first, assess the situation, and knock three times if I think you should come out." He focused on Lexi. "I'll need your team to shield the president."

"We'll do our best," Lexi said, knowing that forming a human shield was futile. They were outnumbered and outgunned, but Agent Cole was much like his protectee. He would go down fighting.

With his pistol pointing toward the sky, Cole exited the Beast and closed their door quickly, locking the rest inside. Lexi heard muffled voices but couldn't decipher what was being decided. She checked the power level on the signal jammer. It was dead, but it was also their one shred of leverage if she found another power source, so she stuffed it into her cargo pocket.

Three knocks on the window.

The driver exited.

"I'll go first," Lexi said. "Then Jan. Nathan, you take the rear."

Moments later, the rear passenger door opened, letting in light and a new sense of danger—they would live as long as Foreman believed they had leverage. Lexi held her weapon in her right hand, keeping it close to her chest to not present an immediate threat, and stepped out, squinting to better see her surroundings.

Dante and the driver were close by, standing shoulder to shoulder and forming the tip of the president's shield. Six men with automatic rifles were fanned out near the front of the house with their weapons in the low-ready position. No RPG launchers were in sight, leading Lexi to believe the threat of using them was merely a ruse to entice them out of the limo. In other words, both sides were bluffing about their leverage.

Benjamin Foreman stood at the end of the portico, appearing like the general in command of his troops. He kept his stare on Dante. Both seemed untrusting at what was about to unfold.

Lexi moved to the left, two steps behind Dante as the next link in the shield. Jan followed, stepping to the right. She looked back at the limo to glimpse the president but was mesmerized by the riddled Beast. A thousand bullet holes covered every inch of metal and glass, a testament to the incredible defensive engineering that kept them safe inside. The president stepped out and slid into the pocket of the human shield, standing proud and unafraid. Her husband was next, and Nathan followed, completing the circle around the Brindles.

Everyone stood silent like gunslingers facing off for a duel at high noon, waiting for the town clock to strike twelve before firing. Moments later, a loud buzz came from the tree line to her right. It sounded like a swarm of angry bees after a predator had disturbed their hive. Foreman snapped his head toward his left. Lexi followed his stare to the tops of the pines. The locusts had regrouped and were moving in. Fast.

"They're back," Foreman said, waving the group forward. He turned on his heel and ran for the door. His security did too.

"Hurry!" Lexi yelled.

She grabbed the president by the upper arm, urging her forward. The formation hustled toward the portico and up the stairs with guns at the ready. The buzzing got louder and louder with each step closer to the house. Dante and the driver made it inside. The doorway was wide enough for only two, so Lexi and Jan fell back, making way for the president and her husband.

The rest stumbled inside. The door automatically slammed shut behind them, and seconds later, the banging started. Like they had attacked the presidential limo, the locusts pecked away at Shangri-La. The agents reformed the protective cocoon around the president in the great room and everyone stood silent. Lexi realized the constant hammering was coming from all directions.

With sweaty bodies and heavy breathing, the standoff inside was as tense as it was outside. Trust was nonexistent, as was power to the signal jammer. Lexi scanned the room, noting the windows were covered with steel panels that weren't there before, making the room resemble a fortress. If nothing could get in, nothing could get out. Translation: even if she managed to power the jammer, the metal plates over the windows would limit its range, making it ineffective until the drones were inside.

The president broke the tension. "Explain how we got here, Mr. Foreman. How did you get in bed with the Raven?"

"There's no time to explain." Foreman turned to his guards. "Close every vent and door. Cover them with towels or something. It will buy us time." After five guards took off, leaving one behind, Foreman pulled out a cell phone and dialed. "Status report...Where is Sands on this?...Wipe the chip and reboot. Tell him to hurry. We only have minutes." He ended the call and returned his attention to the president. "We're working on a fix. Until then, we need your signal jammer."

"First, you drop your weapons." The president stood her ground without as much as a twitch. Precious seconds were ticking away while the pounding on the exterior walls grew louder.

Foreman's nostrils flared. Everyone in the room could see he wasn't accustomed to being the one without leverage. "Fine." He snapped his fingers, and the guard laid down his weapon, which the driver snatched up.

"You too, Mr. Foreman," President Brindle said. "I saw your pistol at the small of your back when you ran tail."

Foreman turned over his weapon reluctantly. There was still the matter of the other guards running about the house clogging up access points, but at least Lexi's side had the upper hand in the room when she revealed her bluff. "Now, your turn. Activate the jammer," Foreman ordered.

The president turned to Lexi. "Agent Mills, show him."

Lexi pulled the jammer slowly from her cargo pocket. "It's dead. We lost power when you shot up the limo."

"It appears we were both bluffing." Foreman's face reddened.

"I can rig it." Lexi reached into another cargo pocket, pulled out her Leatherman tool with a folding knife, and jutted her chin toward an end table. "All I need is the lamp cord over there."

Screams could be heard from the other end of the building, where the second guard had gone to secure things. Lexi surmised the locusts were coming through the vents or chimneys.

"I suggest you get what you need and rig it on the fly." Foreman typically measured every word, but agitation was in his voice, indicating he was on edge. "We can make a stand in my command center below ground. Follow me."

While the others trailed Foreman, Nathan remained while Lexi rushed to the lamp and used her knife to sever the cord from the base. His staying by her side proved that despite their rocky beginnings, they had learned to trust and have each other's back without hesitation.

"Are you sure you can power this thing up?" Worry cut through Nathan's voice.

"I did this once with a cell phone. It should work. Let's go."

Lexi folded her knife on the run and darted toward the hallway with Nathan. The group was thirty feet ahead. A waiting elevator with its door open was at the end of the corridor.

They were twenty feet away.

A loud explosion rocked the building. Everyone in the hallway instinctively slowed and covered their heads. Foreman kept moving toward the elevator. Lexi suspected a cluster of locusts with explosive charges had converged and broken through a weak spot in another part of the building.

She sensed two objects buzz past her head and head down the hallway. The others caught their bearings quickly and continued toward safety.

The guard was in front, only steps behind his boss.

Foreman was ten feet ahead, five from the elevator.

Two feet.

He boarded the waiting car and reached out for his guard, pulling him inside. The door began to shut. "You're too late, Madam President. Take solace in knowing your death will have meaning."

36

The elevator door closed, trapping the rest with the locusts in the hallway. The buzzing sound returned, warning them the swarm was coming for them. Their only hope rested in Lexi's ability to hot-wire the signal jammer.

Dante Cole searched frantically for shelter, checking three doors in the hallway, but they were locked. With nowhere left to go, he ushered his group into the game room they'd passed while heading to the elevator. Lexi and her team followed, closing the double doors behind them. While she laid the power jammer on the table to unscrew the back housing the battery, Dante circled around the pool table and shoved the president and her husband into a small half-bathroom on the far side.

"Put towels under the door," Dante shouted before closing the door. Nathan, the driver, and Jan removed their jackets and stuffed them under the game room doors to slow the locusts' attack.

Meanwhile, as the buzzing got louder and the first drone scouts tapped at the doors, Lexi retrieved her Leatherman tool again and stripped the lamp cord, exposing two inches of positive and negative wires.

The coats below the doors smoldered. The drones had set them ablaze. Dante removed his jacket and thrashed it against the door to extinguish the fire. It worked, but his efforts dislodged the coats from the gaps. Drones seeped in. Their guns were useless against the small devices, but Dante improvised and snatched a tennis racket from the wall display and began swatting at them like he was at Wimbledon's center court while guarding the one door between the president and her sure death.

The others grabbed rackets. Jan had one in each hand. They formed a protective circle around Lexi and swatted away, allowing her to work. After removing the last screw from the jammer's backside, she popped out the battery pack and carefully placed the exposed lamp cord wires against the jammer's battery contact connectors—the red going to the positive and the black to the negative.

A locust sneaked past Lexi's defenders and landed on her left hand. There was no telling what armament it was outfitted with—explosive, fire, electrical, poison—so she swatted it away in a fraction of a second.

Lexi was almost done. She held the wires in position while carefully replacing the battery to support the proper electrical connection. Now came the tricky part while hundreds of attackers fought to get to her—plug the cord into the wall socket without knocking the connections loose.

Dante screamed in pain. Lexi glanced toward him. Most of the drones had focused on him, the only person in a position to defend the president. Several had landed on him, and flames rose from his shirt sleeve. "Hurry, Lexi! Hurry!" he yelled.

Lexi fought the instinct to dash over and come to his aid. She could best help him by disabling every one of those damn locusts. Instead, she swung her head around and spotted an electrical outlet on the wall six feet away in front of Nathan. He was thrashing his racket nonstop like a machine. They were overrun and out of options. The jammer was their only hope.

Lexi held a section of lamp cord firmly against the jammer in her left hand to prevent the wires from slipping and the end with the plug in her right. With the image of Nita standing at the altar in her wedding gown, slipping a ring onto Lexi's finger, Lexi dove for the wall and landed on her belly. The stiff lip from the shell of her prosthetic dug into her skin despite three layers of cotton socks and a polyurethane liner. Her ill-advised maneuver would leave a bruise if she lived long enough.

Locusts landed on her back, arms, and legs. A number stung her as she struggled to low crawl the last foot to the wall socket. Several hot spots formed on her back, likely from fires being set. She continued to crawl. Six more inches, and her arm could reach the wall.

The pain of a dozen electrical charges flowing through her body was excruciating, bordering on debilitating, but she advanced the last inch. She struggled to line up the plug with the socket, but nothing happened once she pushed it in. Panic surged through her until she remembered the device had gone dead and needed turning on. She hoped the jammer memory stored the previous custom settings, blocking the broadest spectrum of signals. If it didn't, she might not be able to focus long enough to reset the device.

More locusts jumped on, and the stinging became unbearable. She summoned every ounce of strength to turn the jammer in her hand, revealing the power button on the other side. Letting go with her left hand was too risky. The wire connections would come loose with one false move. She had to use her right hand.

Every sting sapped more of her energy. The heat on her back had begun to burn, making it impossible to concentrate. She grunted like a bear having stepped into a trap that threatened to cut off its ankle. Lexi forced back the pain and pressed the power button. A glorious green light appeared.

The locusts fell like flies.

The electrical shocks stopped, but the fire on her back continued its assault. Lexi couldn't hold back any longer and let out an agonizing scream.

Something soft enveloped her back, and someone patted the spot where the heat had been the worst. She heard Nathan's voice. "I got you, Lexi. You're going to be fine. We all are. It worked."

Lexi turned her head and craned her neck toward the bathroom where the president was secure. Agent Cole lay on the floor covered with a rug runner. He wasn't moving. "How's Dante? Is he okay?"

"He's burned badly. We need to get him to a hospital." The concern in Nathan's voice was troublesome. With the signal jammer on, they couldn't get a call out for help. The device had a limited range, so leaving the house to make a call while the Raven had control of the locusts was out of the question. Plus, charging the battery fully could take an hour before they could think of leaving. They were stuck in Shangri-La but safe until they lost power.

Lexi shifted to her bottom, and Nathan helped her remove her light jacket. It was partially charred but had saved her from more severe burns. The driver tended to Dante and removed the carpet from his back.

The bathroom door was open. The president stepped out with wet towels in her hands, knelt, and placed them gently over Dante's arms. She raised her stare, locking eyes with Lexi. Her tears expressed gratitude for Lexi saving them and worry for her guard, who may have made the ultimate sacrifice protecting her. The president returned her attention to him. "The cavalry will be here soon, Dante. Just hold on."

"The locusts will eat them alive unless Foreman gets control of them." Lexi extended a cupped hand toward Nathan, asking for help from the floor. Once on her feet, she continued. "The jammer should reach the end of the hallway. Nathan and I will find him. The rest of you stay with the president."

The driver picked up the automatic rifle he'd collected from Foreman's guard and tossed it to Nathan. "Take this. You might have to fight your way in."

"We don't even know your name," Lexi said. She'd spent the last hour with the man who had driven them safely out of harm's way and fiercely kept the locusts at bay long enough for her to employ the jammer and, shamefully, she hadn't asked before now.

"Grayson. Grayson Cabot."

"Thank you, Grayson. We'll be back." Lexi drew her service Glock and slowly opened the door leading to the hallway. The floor was littered with dead locusts resembling the infestations of cicadas found in eastern states. It was impossible to walk to the elevator without crunching several. Otherwise, the corridor was clear.

Lexi stepped out with her weapon close to her chest, ready for an indoor firefight. Nathan was right on her heels. Twenty feet down, she stopped at the elevator and pressed the call button. She expected to hear mechanical rumblings from inside the shaft while the elevator rose to the ground level, but the doors opened instantly. Inside, two men lay motionless—the nameless guard and Benjamin Foreman.

Lexi bent and pressed two fingers against Foreman's neck, but she knew he was dead. The small metal fragments on the floor and trauma at his temple suggested a locust with an explosive charge had found its target. The same damage was present on the guard. Lexi now faced a new dilemma. With Foreman dead, who could regain control of the locusts?

Fishing through his pockets, she found his cell phone, but it would be useless with the signal jammer running. She had one last thing to try. Lexi straightened and pressed the service button on the elevator control panel.

A male voice answered. "Yes, Agent Mills."

"I assume you know Foreman is dead," Lexi said.

"I do. We couldn't risk opening the elevator and letting in the locust, so I sent the car up."

"I've employed a signal jammer that is keeping the locusts at bay. Foreman said someone was working on regaining control of the drones. What's the status of that?"

"The virus has been removed, and the system is rebooting. We should have operational control within minutes."

"Which means you'll have a decision to make. We got off a message at the onset of the attack. Military forces and more Secret Service agents are en route. We can either continue this standoff, or you can give yourselves up. So far, you have done nothing wrong that we know of. The Raven was controlling the locusts during the attack. However, if you resist, the world's largest and most well-equipped military will bear down on you. What will it be?"

37

The EMT applied the bandage gently to Lexi's back between her shoulder blades. Meanwhile, the siren from the ambulance carrying Dante Cole chirped, clearing the two local deputies and Secret Service agents milling about Shangri-La's circular driveway. Her burn wound was trivial compared to Dante's. Only one or two fire drones had attacked Lexi, but over a dozen had set their sights on him. He'd bravely stood in their way, sacrificing his body to protect the president and her husband. That made him a hero in her book.

Nathan Croft stood at the bumper of the open paramedic rig, watching with concern etched on his face. It was hard to believe that two hours ago, they were in Napa, awaiting the president's arrival, and her father was marveling at the prospect of catching a glimpse of her and Tiger Woods. Nathan hadn't left her side since.

"The morphine will last only a few hours," the EMT said while Lexi put her shirt on gingerly. "You should stop by urgent care as soon as possible and have a doctor examine that burn."

"That should be long enough. I'll stop somewhere after this mess is cleaned up." Lexi returned her paddle holster to her waistband and slung the chain with her ATF badge around her neck. "Thanks for patching me up."

"What the hell happened here?" he asked.

"You'll have to talk to one of the agents outside before you leave. The less you know, the better."

Nathan offered Lexi a hand, helping her down the rig's metal stairs. His extra care and gentleness bordered on doting—a sweet, welcome gesture. The pain medication had kicked in and had made her a little woozy. "Willie Lange would like a call when you can. I told her you'd call when we get back to Napa."

"What did you tell her?"

"Only that things were moving fast here."

"Being vague is probably for the best at this point. Where is she?" Lexi asked, referring to the president. She was careful to not let on that the POTUS was on site once the first arriving Secret Service team had ushered her into an armored SUV before the ambulance arrived.

"Waiting for you in the car. She refuses to leave until she sees you," Nathan said.

Lexi chuckled. "She's stubborn." They started toward the president's SUV.

"Kinda like someone I know." Nathan used a playful tone.

Detective Jan Hopkins was several yards away, talking with Agent Grayson Cabot. They joined Lexi and Nathan as they continued toward the makeshift motorcade. Three other black Secret Service SUVs had surrounded the president's vehicle, creating a protective buffer.

"How are you feeling, Lexi?" Jan asked.

"Like I've been tased and barbequed." Lexi's cell vibrated in her pocket, bringing her to a stop. "Hold on, fellas." She retrieved her phone and was relieved the call wasn't from Nita. Talking to her now would only pop the cork holding back the tsunami of emotion fighting to escape. However, speaking to Kaplan was a much safer choice until she could fall into her wife's arms.

"Hope this isn't a bad time," Kaplan said, not knowing what Lexi had been through in the last hour.

"No. It's fine. What do you have?" Lexi tried to sound more collected than she was.

"It took some time, but I finally tracked down the source of the five million dollars. You won't believe who it came from."

"Who?"

"Senator Ed Gotkin."

"Interesting," Lexi said. The Raven had his talons into Foreman and the senate leader, her home state senator. This opened the possibility of more senators or members of Congress being behind the president's attempted assassination.

"I'd call it more than interesting," Kaplan said. "But a transfer for another five million this morning has me worried. It was too easy to trace back to Foreman. Either he's getting sloppy, or it's a setup."

"Thank you, Kaplan. This is a big help. I need you to keep a lid on this. Tell no one what you've found."

"Of course. I saw the video of you during the president's opening remarks at the golf tournament. How are you holding up?"

"I'm fine," Lexi said.

Without media cameras at Shangri-La for the country to see, Kaplan had no way of knowing her assumptions of the locusts and the assassination attempt were spot on. Lexi wasn't the least bit worried about the fallout.

She finished the call, understanding what Foreman had said outside of Shangri-La. He'd said he no longer controlled the locusts, not that he didn't know why the locusts were attacking. The tension in his voice wasn't desperation but anger. He knew exactly what was happening. Gotkin had double-crossed him and had turned the Raven on him.

Lexi continued toward the vehicles. Two Secret Service agents standing shoulder to shoulder, blocking the gap between cars protecting the president, parted, giving her the side-eye while making way for Lexi and her group to pass. They were part of an eight-person team securing the Jackson family home that had arrived within minutes of Foreman's command center regaining control of the locusts and surrendering to Lexi. Those two weren't happy to learn she'd called 911 for Dante, complicating their hope of concealing the catastrophe that had transpired.

After circling the back of the SUV, Lexi discovered another agent guarding the rear passenger door. "The president asked to see us," she said. The agent opened the door and stepped back.

The president emerged from the backseat and gave Lexi a warm hug. "I heard you were a real-life MacGyver. I'm sorry I missed it, hiding in the bathroom."

"The important thing is that you and your husband are safe." Lexi bobbed her head to peer inside the SUV cabin, discovering an empty backseat. "Where is he?"

"In the front seat, calling our children. None of this had made the news, but he wanted to hear their voices." Her expression turned long. "I do too, but we have things to discuss."

"I figured as much," Lexi said. "No one can know about the technology that almost killed the most protected person in the world."

"No, they can't. As you learned firsthand, the locusts open the door to a new level of warfare. My chief of staff emailed information while the EMTs worked on you. I read that the devices modulate their remote connection along the entire spectrum. The only way to defend against it is what you discovered on the fly—a complete communications blackout. If our enemies got hold of this technology, our short-range defenses would be blind defending against it, opening ourselves up to untold dangers. Tell me, Lexi. How did you figure it out so quickly?"

"It's a technique I use while defusing a bomb with a remote detonator when I'm not sure of the frequency being used to control it. I block everything. It cuts me off from my team but is better than guessing wrong."

"Your experience saved our lives. I'm in your debt."

"Like you told Agent Cole, living is better than dying, Madam President." Lexi shifted on her feet to pivot the discussion. "You should know my intel team tracked the money to the Raven. It came from Senator Ed Gotkin."

President Brindle had a decent poker face, but her piercing, silent stare said she wasn't surprised Gotkin was involved. "I see. Who have you told this to?"

"No one else," Lexi said.

"Then you understand why we need to keep this close to the vest until we've built a strong case against him."

"I do."

"In fact, we're putting a lid on everything that happened today. Security Forces troops from Beale Air Force Base are towing and cleaning up the remnants of my motorcade as we speak. Beale will also put out a press release, blaming the helicopter crash on a mechanical failure. An alphabet soup of federal law enforcement agencies will descend on this place to control the narrative. The EMTs and police officers will all be briefed on the need for secrecy. We want Gotkin to think nothing happened today and that the Raven double-crossed him."

"Funny you say that. The money trail makes me think Gotkin double-crossed Foreman."

"Good. He won't think it out of the realm of possibilities and will confront the Raven."

"The Raven won't take it lightly," Lexi said. "He doesn't like loose ends."

"I'm counting on it."

Lexi nodded her understanding. President Brindle didn't want a trial for Gotkin but a bullet in the head. A prosecution of this magnitude would tear the country apart, further dividing the people among party lines.

"Now, for us to continue this ruse," the president said, "I need to be on my way to visit Senator Jackson's family. Someone will take you and your team anywhere you want to go."

"Thank you, Madam President, but I think you might have trouble keeping this quiet. Someone will talk."

"Let's hope it's not before Ed Gotkin gets his due," the president said, leaving no doubt about her intentions. Lexi extended her hand to part ways, but the president hugged her again. "If there's anything I can do for you, Lexi Mills, ask."

Thinking about the past week and her ruined honeymoon, Lexi said, "There is something."

38

Washington, DC, later that evening

Pins and needles, needles and pins. Ed Gotkin swore he'd been sitting on every pointy thing in his DC home since getting off the phone, sealing the president's and Benjamin Foreman's fates. *"Today,"* the Raven had said after Ed had transferred another five million into his account. *"A minor change of venue should get you the desired results while pointing the blame at the thorn in your side, not the Venezuelans."* That was hours ago. Too many hours without a news report of the president's death made him think something was drastically wrong.

The three television screens in his study were tuned to national and local news stations, but neither outlet had picked up the devastating story Ed had hoped would have dominated the airways by now. He was beginning to think he'd been had by Foreman and the Raven, depleting his life savings for nothing.

A knock on the door grated on his nerves. He'd muted his phone to block out the inevitable calls from his aides and told his wife not to bother him the rest of the evening. That woman never could follow directions. And don't get him started on her inability to follow a recipe. He swore she was trying to kill him by indigestion.

"I said I didn't want to be disturbed," he shouted.

The door slowly opened, and his wife stuck her head through the opening. "Are you hungry? Dinner is getting cold."

"If I wanted dinner, I would have called for delivery. Don't wait up."

"I'll put a plate in the fridge so you can heat it in the microwave if you get hungry." His wife's dejected expression before closing the door was classic Marge. She was needy, like an only child vying for attention at every turn.

He pushed back from his desk chair and poured another scotch from the decanter behind him on the built-in bookshelf. After downing the two-finger pour, he fixed another and returned his attention to the television screens. He took a small sip to savor this round but sprayed his desk with twelve-year-old Johnnie Walker while reading the news crawl at the bottom of two screens. *Helicopter crash near president's motorcade. News conference at 7 p.m.*

Another news flash scrolled, bringing a smile to Ed's lips. *Benjamin Foreman, Falcon Industries CEO, dead at 56 from apparent heart attack.* He didn't expect Foreman to die, but dead or alive, it didn't matter. *This was it*, he thought. In a few short minutes, the nation would mourn the loss of a sitting president and blame for it would trace back to Foreman.

Ed freshened his drink and settled deeper into his chair for what should be the most earth-shattering news since Kennedy's assassination. The screens changed to the James S. Brady Press Briefing Room with the empty podium in the center, the American flag on the left, and the official White House emblem in the background. Reporters had filled the seats, and staffers were lined up against the wall near the entrance.

The anticipation was so delicious Ed could taste it. Benjamin was dead and if everything went right today, so was the president. Her vice president wasn't ideal, but he had a much better vision of the United States' role in the world. The country was meant to lead and protect its interests, not bend to the will of the Chinese, Russians, or crime syndicates.

The White House Press Secretary stepped up to the podium, placing her notebook on top. "The Associated Press picked up an official news release from Beale Air Force Base in northern California about the crash of an HH-60G Pave Hawk helicopter fifty-five miles east of the base. I can confirm the craft was scouting a route in advance of the presidential motorcade earlier today and encountered mechanical difficulty. It crashed in an empty field, killing the two pilots. At no time was the president in danger, nor did the incident impact her travel plans."

Heat rose in Ed's neck. His pulse doubled its pace, making his ears pound with rage. The Raven had double-crossed him, and if his instincts were right, Benjamin Foreman was behind it. He considered tossing his glass at the screen, but the resulting racket would bring his nagging wife back for another welfare check.

Needing answers to calm down, he fished out the burner from his top desk drawer and dialed the only stored number. The call connected on the third ring.

"Yes, Senator."

"I trusted you for the last time, Raven. Our history together should have meant something. Why didn't you go after the president today?"

"I assure you we did. We took out every one of the support vehicles, but the technology Foreman developed failed to break through the president's defenses."

Ed snapped to his feet. "You lie, Raven. I saw a White House news conference, and they didn't mention the attack. They said a scouting helicopter crashed before the motorcade rolled through."

"Watch your tongue, Senator. I never lie about my work."

"It's not enough. I want proof of your attempt." The silence on the line was intimidating. Ed checked the connection, finding the line was still open. "If I don't receive it tomorrow, I expect a full refund Monday when the banks open."

"You'll get my answer soon, Senator."

Sundays during Ed Gotkin's childhood meant church, followed by bible studies and mucking out the horse stalls when he got home. In his college years, Sunday was the one day a week he allowed himself to do nothing but watch sports and hang out with his buddies. But since becoming Leader of the Senate, Sundays became prep day for the coming week's political battle royale.

If he had a choice these days, Ed would have preferred to have been knee-deep in horse manure this evening than spend one more minute in his home study listening to Jack Sutton, his loyal chief of staff, drone on about one more backroom deal to get legislation passed. He had a more pressing matter pending. But listen he would until the pretty little staffer next to him left for the night.

"If we put the funding for the I-70 bridge over the Kansas River back into the transportation bill," Jack said, "Senator Rowlings telegraphed he would not block anything coming from the Senate Armed Services Committee."

"I hate having a razor-thin majority. It's open season for every Republican to hold a bill hostage until they get their fill of pork."

"I can't disagree, but the tide will be with us next week," Jack said.

The blonde staffer narrowed her brow. "What happens next week?" Jack's optimism, while correct, may have revealed too much.

"Change of the seasons, Mindy." Ed's quick lie wasn't too far from the truth. The country would soon rise from its winter of impotence and march into a summer of courage and liberation. He stood, grabbing the young lady's coat. "We can take it from here. Go home and have Sunday dinner with your family."

She flinched back slightly. "Are you sure?"

"Absolutely." Ed picked up her satchel. "There's not much more to go over. Go. Enjoy."

Mindy slipped on her jacket. "Thank you, sir. I'll have your briefing packet ready for you in the morning."

Once she left, Ed closed the door behind her and headed to his bottle of scotch. "Want one?" he asked Jack.

"Make it a double." Jack dropped into his traditional leather easy chair. "Still nothing from the Raven?"

"Nothing, and I'm beginning to expect I'll never hear from him."

Ed respected bravado in all forms but not if it meant being ripped off to the tune of ten million dollars. Last night's video of President Brindle stepping off Marine One at the White House South Lawn was the aggravating reminder that his money had bought him nothing. And twenty-four hours after their phone call, Ed still had no proof of the Raven's supposed failed attack on the president the media was still silent on. The only remotely connected mention in the news was Benjamin Foreman's death. A heart attack was a convenient cover story but not proof the Raven had kept his word.

His wife knocked twice on the door and poked her head in without waiting for an invitation. She held up a delivery bag from Ed's favorite eatery. "Your dinners arrived."

"Thanks." He took the bag and placed it on his desk. Before she exited, he looked over his shoulder and called out, "Marge, wait. Mindy left. Would you like her meal? She ordered the chicken piccata."

"I would, actually."

Ed pulled out the three orders. He wished the restaurant would go back to using foil containers with clear tops instead of the folding Styrofoam ones. They were flimsy, and it was impossible to figure out whose meal it was without opening them up. The first container had Mindy's order. It was pure luck he'd opened it first.

"Here, Marge." Ed handed it to her. "We'll be another hour."

Once she left, Ed opened the next container, releasing a swarm of a dozen flies. "What the—"

A bright flash.

39

Lexi drove her Shelby to the outermost section of the lot where the more senior agents parked their midlife crisis cars, straddling the line between two slots. If spaces weren't so plentiful, she would have considered their prudent choice to protect their expensive paint job to be an asshole move. After pulling into a spot—only one spot—Lexi locked up and walked into the ATF building.

Passing through the security checkpoint, she spotted Kaplan standing near the stairs. Kaplan's expression lit up when their eyes met. They hugged. "I bet you never envisioned your honeymoon going to pot like that."

"You have no idea." Not telling Kaplan about her, Nathan, and the president barely surviving the locust attack was killing Lexi. Kaplan was the one person in the ATF she could trust with the information, and she was a friend. But the president's instructions were explicit. She and Nathan were to tell no one. Too much was at risk if word of the locust technology got out.

They ascended the stairs, chatting about Lexi's plan to take another trip with only Nita in another month or two. Stopping at Lexi's floor, Kaplan asked, "Any movement on the thing I found?"

"Nothing I can speak of." Lexi looked up and down the stairs, ensuring no one else was around. "Keep an eye on those accounts but keep it quiet. Report only to Nathan or me."

"You know more than you're letting on, don't you?"

"I can't talk about it. You'll be the first I tell when I can, okay?"

Kaplan's pouty lips said she understood but wasn't happy about it.

Lexi entered the third-floor maze of cubicles and checked her watch. It was almost nine o'clock, two minutes before her morning meeting with her boss, so she walked directly to Agent Willie Lange's office.

Nathan was outside her door. "Get any sleep last night?"

"Not much." Lexi left out the part about the nightmares of locusts haunting her all night. "How was your first night not sharing a room with my dad?"

"Blissfully quiet." He laughed before leading her inside.

Lange stood from her chair and circled her desk, greeting both with a handshake. "It's good to see you two back. You were vague on the phone Saturday night. Where are you at with the Raven?"

"We'd had a long day, Agent Lange, and things were changing fast on the ground," Lexi said. "We still believe the Raven was involved in the death of Senator Jackson and his aide, but we ran into a dead end."

"What about the Falcon Industries weapons program stuck in committee?"

"That, too, is a dead end. We're tracking down money transfers we hope will get us back on the trail."

"So after your little stunt at the golf course, Napa wasn't a complete bust," Lange said with an edge to her voice.

Lexi and Nathan glanced at one another, smirking. "Not completely."

"I'll expect your report by the end of the week."

Lexi and Nathan left her office and retreated to their shared double cubical. Nathan slumped in his chair. "I hate keeping things from her, and I hate the entire country thinking you're the agent who cried wolf."

"It really doesn't matter to me." Lexi didn't care about her reputation, but she did care about losing the respect of Lange and Maxwell Keene. As far as they knew, she'd embarrassed the agency by causing unnecessary panic. Somehow, she would have to earn their trust again. Her phone buzzed with an incoming text message. She read it, smiled, and showed it to Nathan. "Can you cover for me?"

"Go." The joy in his eyes was palpable. After everything they went through, having each other's back, every bit of tension between them had melted away. "Tell me tomorrow how it went."

Lexi parked her Shelby in the open garage bay at the house in Ponder. Her father looked up from the engine compartment of the 1969 Chevy Camaro she'd dinged up in Harrington a few months ago. When she got out, he wiped his hand with a fresh rag and asked, "What are you doing home so early, Peanut?"

"After I met with my boss, I felt tired, so I left."

"Are you coming down with something? You did a lot of running around last week." His brow narrowed in concern.

"Nah, I needed one more day at home." She gestured her chin toward their current pet project. "Have you finished your assessment?"

He placed both hands on his hips. "Mechanically, she's a beauty. Cosmetically, not so much. And you certainly did a number on the fenders."

"You should have seen the pit maneuver I used to stop the Challenger." Lexi recalled the night in Harrington when she drove Deputy Perez's classic Camaro to chase down a killer. She felt at home in that muscle car, and all her NASCAR and FBI defensive driving training had kicked in. She didn't think that night. Instead, she'd acted on instinct. "It was near perfect."

"I'm sure it was. You're a natural behind the wheel. If NASCAR didn't make it so hard for women to drive, and if I wasn't such a bonehead back then for pushing you away, you could have filled up a trophy case."

The back of Lexi's throat grew thick with emotion. Her dad had expressed his pride in her as an ATF agent countless times since their reconciliation, but this was the first time he'd singled out their shared skill. This was a moment to remember. "Thanks, Dad."

His eyes glistened with moisture before he cleared his throat and returned to the Camaro's engine compartment.

The sound of several cars crunching the gravel on the property's access road sounded and grew louder with each passing second. Lexi checked her watch. The timing was right. "I'll be right back, Dad."

Lexi waited for the cars to stop and for her special guest to exit the center vehicle. "Good morning, Agent Mills. I apologize for the short notice, but this was the only break in my schedule this week, and I wanted to tell you something in person."

"No need to apologize, Madam President," Lexi said. "I'm so glad you came. What did you want to tell me?"

"Two small explosions killed Senator Gotkin and his aide at his Washington, DC, home last night. Their injuries were similar to those of Senator Jackson's aide."

"So the Raven tied up his loose ends."

"Better this way than the locust technology coming up during a trial," the president said.

Lexi nodded her concurrence. "Why hasn't it been in the news?"

"We had to get his widow on board first. We'll leak it to the press after five o'clock eastern today, saying both died from a gas leak."

"Thanks for letting me know."

"You understand this can never come to light." The president's expression was stern, reminding Lexi the future of warfare depended on secrecy. Lexi nodded again. "I can only stay for an hour, Lexi."

"Then we better get started." While the others remained by the cars, Lexi guided her guest inside the garage. "Hey, Dad. There's someone here who would like to see you."

"What?" He rose too quickly, banging his head on the edge of the hood. "Dang nabbit. Son of a gun." Lexi and her guest chuckled before her dad turned around. His shocked expression was priceless. "Well, don't I feel like the fool, cussing in front of the President of the United States."

The president shook his hand. "I spent twenty years in the Navy, Mr. Mills. That in no way qualifies as cussing."

"Not to look a gift horse in the mouth, Madam President, but what in the heck are you doing in Ponder?"

"I understand your vacation with Lexi and Nita was interrupted because we called her into action. I wanted to apologize personally for the inconvenience and say that you have one heck of a daughter. She did something very important for which I'll never be able to repay her."

Her father shifted his stare to Lexi, his face beaming with pride. Their eyes met, and he had the same expression he'd worn when Lexi rode her bike without training wheels for the first time. The same look when she walked across the stage for her high school graduation. The same smile when he walked her down the aisle to marry the love of her life.

"I couldn't be more proud of her, President Brindle." He shifted his stare back to her. "Have you met her lovely bride? Nita is something else."

"She's next on the agenda." The president extended a hand toward the garage opening. "Shall we?"

Lexi led the way and entered the house through the porch screen door. A similar scene played out between the president and Nita in the kitchen, and they sat around the table, chatting about how Lexi and Nita had met, their wedding, and their ill-fated honeymoon over pie. After the president left and Nita and Lexi were upstairs getting ready for bed, Nita sat on the edge of the mattress next to Lexi, inspecting the burn on her back between the shoulder blades. She gently traced the edges of the wound.

"I'm guessing the president's visit has something to do with how this happened."

"Yes, it does." Lexi turned on her bottom to face Nita. Keeping a secret of this importance from her wife might strain their marriage, but considering what was at stake, it was a sacrifice Lexi had to make.

"Are you ever going to tell me how it happened?"

"Hopefully, I can someday." Lexi guided Nita gently flat on the mattress and pressed their lips together in a passionate kiss. Having her wife in her arms, safe in their bed, was a luxury Lexi would never take for granted. If the day ever came that Lexi could tell Nita about the day she'd had with the president, it would mean the locust technology was no longer a threat. Until that day, she would keep the secret the world wasn't ready to hear.

EPILOGUE

Robert followed Starshiy up the stairs of his private plane, fearing his old friend for the first time. After sitting across from the brooding man, he buckled in and studied him for hours. For more than thirty years, they had been more than friends, more than orphanage brothers. They were blood brothers forged inside the walls of the roughest home for boys in Brighton Beach. And when Robert was old enough, after graduating from MIT, their bond was refined on the streets of Brooklyn, where the Russian syndicate had a strong foothold. And it had grown stronger when Starshiy branched out on his own.

Their connection was now strained, perhaps irrevocably, because of Robert's adoration for the man who had saved his life. Only five days ago, Starshiy had said his word might not be good enough. He now understood going after Lexi Mills at the bank with the locust was premature and not well planned, but his misguided decision paled in comparison to adding a piece of raven feather into every product he produced. He had left a trail to follow, precisely the one rule the Raven had warned his clients against breaking.

Somewhere over Texas, Robert said, "Can you forgive me?"

Starshiy looked up, locking eyes without the red Raven contact lenses in them. The warmth they usually held for him was gone, replaced by indifference. After several beats, he finally said, "Forgive? Perhaps. Forget? Never. Your foolishness has forced my hand. It is time to take care of Lexi Mills once and for all."

Flashpoint
Lexi Mills Book 6

The stage is set for an explosive showdown.
The stakes have never been higher.
How far will Lexi Mills go to bring a terrorist's reign to an end?

When a top Federal Prosecutor dies in a mysterious car accident right on the heels of a landmark case against the infamous crime boss Anton Boyko, seasoned ATF Agent Lexi Mills is convinced that Boyko is linked to the Raven—the ruthless criminal mastermind she's been hunting for months.

But the Raven is always one step ahead of her. Lexi and her partner Nathan Croft target the shadowy engineer behind the Raven's deadly high-tech weapons system, and the pair quickly find themselves embroiled in a complex plan with the FBI to kill two birds with one stone. When the situation goes critical, Lexi must tread a fine line between getting her man and exposing hidden truths with grave consequences.

The situation is about to boil over, and national security teeters on the brink. Lexi's skills have made her a legend—but who will be left standing when the dust settles?

ABOUT BRIAN SHEA

Brian Shea has spent most of his adult life in service to his country and local community. He honorably served as an officer in the U.S. Navy. In his civilian life, he reached the rank of Detective and accrued over eleven years of law enforcement experience between Texas and Connecticut. Somewhere in the mix he spent five years as a fifth-grade school teacher. Brian's myriad of life experience is woven into the tapestry of each character's design. He resides in New England and is blessed with an amazing wife and three beautiful daughters.

Sign up for the reader list at
severnriverbooks.com/series/lexi-mills

ABOUT STACY LYNN MILLER

A late bloomer, award-winning author Stacy Lynn Miller took up writing after retiring from the Air Force. Her twenty years of toting a gun and police badge, tinkering with computers, and sleuthing for clues as an investigator form the foundation of her Lexi Mills thriller series, as well as her Manhattan Sloane novels. She is visually impaired, a proud stroke survivor, mother of two, tech nerd, chocolate lover, and terrible golfer with a hole-in-one. When you can't find her writing, she'll be golfing or drinking wine (sometimes both) with friends and family in Northern California.

Sign up for the reader list at
severnriverbooks.com/series/lexi-mills

Printed in the United States
by Baker & Taylor Publisher Services